ASHES TO ASHES

Also by Mary Monica Pulver

The Unforgiving Minutes
Murder at the War

Ashes
to
Ashes

Mary Monica Pulver

St. Martin's Press
New York

Design by Holly Block

Library of Congress Cataloging-in-Publication Data

Pulver, Mary Monica.
    Ashes to ashes / Mary Monica Pulver.
       p.   cm.
    ISBN 0–312–02164–X
    I. Title.
PS3566.U47A9   1988
813'.54—dc19   88–12025

First Edition
10 9 8 7 6 5 4 3 2 1

To Captain Arthur F. Caple, Minneapolis Fire Department,
who made my fires more than just smoke.

How can I answer which is best
Of all the fires that burn?
I have been too often host or guest
At every fire in turn.
—Rudyard Kipling

1

THE phone burred softly, just as the cattle stampede was really getting out of hand. It burred again and Zak reached for it without taking his eyes off the TV screen. John Wayne was galloping frantically after the lead animals, trying to turn the herd. "Yeah," Zak said into the receiver.

"We've got a request for a ten-fifty at 901 East Baron," said a woman's brisk voice.

Zak straightened and glanced at his watch. Quarter to midnight; another fifteen minutes and they'd've called Ron. "Okay," he said. "I'm on my way."

His wife looked up from her needlepoint as he hung up the phone. "Where is it?" she asked, knowing what.

"Over on East Baron. Warehouse district."

She nodded, relaxing a little. No bodies piled up in a hallway this time. "Better put on a sweater; it's cool out tonight."

He went upstairs, a short, broad man in his late fifties with graying brown hair, a droopy mustache, and dark, tame eyes behind gold-rimmed spectacles. He changed his house shoes for steel-toed lace-ups, then pulled a thick gray sweater over his flannel shirt. He took a metal box out of the back of a dresser drawer, unlocked it, lifted out a clip-on holster and an aluminum-frame Colt Agent revolver. He fitted the holster to the back of his belt and tucked the gun into it. He was zipping up a hip-length jacket as he came back down the stairs.

She waited at the bottom with his big Thermos. "Be careful, dear," she said.

"I will," he said, offering his cheek for a kiss before going out the door to his little Datsun.

Zak skirted the small downtown area, turned onto Baron and east toward a cluster of warehouses. As he approached, he noted a haze of smoke in the air and then the characteristic stink of burning building. He slowed, pulled to the curb to look. Ahead was a single-story building with smoke boiling up and outward from the roof, window openings glowing at one end. The building was old, half a block long, divided into four stores. The biggest store, Crazy Dave's TV and Appliance, on the end, was well alight. It looked as if two alarms had been called, and the place was busy with pumper and ladder companies: red lights flickering, spots illuminating the building's face, pumper engines roaring. There was virtually no wind, but the fire appeared to have gotten a running start on the fire fighters.

Zak leaned over sideways to punch the glove box open. He reached in for a pad of graph paper and a soft pencil. When he straightened he saw a pair of firemen smashing the window of the Tell the World T-Shirts store next to the appliance store. As the window broke, a large gout of brown smoke was released. A team swinging axes was on the roof of the Bear Foot sporting shoe store. As Zak watched, orange flames leapt up between them. So probably Say It Again Used Books on the end only appeared untouched. Zak grunted, tucked the pencil away in a pocket. He got out of his car, went around to the back and put the tablet on the roof. He opened the rear hatch and fumbled out the big boots and yellow rubber coat of a fireman.

Zak buckled himself into the coat and reached back into the trunk for his red fireman's helmet. A multi-layered scream of approaching sirens told him a third alarm had been called in. He rolled the tablet and put it into his coat pocket as he walked slowly toward the burning building, noting that the windows in the appliance store had broken outward. The smoke roiling out and up was dark in color; pale hoses tumescent with water led into it. He pulled the strap of his helmet under his chin, looked for and found the white hat that marked the Battalion Chief, counted the number of citizens—nine—who had braved the hour and November chill to stand and watch. A police officer was standing in front of them, and they were all watching a ladder-pipe being cranked up. The firemen on the roof were climbing down.

Zak angled across Baron Avenue and continued up Ninth. There was a pumper near the alley, and another behind it; fat five-inch hoses linked them to a hydrant at the curb and pale snakes of smaller hoses wound up the block and into the alley. He'd heard four-alarm trucks arriving, not three.

A squad car blocked the street near the corner, lights blinking—not that there was any traffic to divert. A fierce dance of reflected flame lit the windows of a big old warehouse across the alley from the burning building; the fire was leaping through a double doorway and a small window in the burning building, scattering light up the face of the warehouse.

He retraced his steps to Baron, angled across again, and stopped on the corner to watch. The ladder-pipe spat once, hugely, then began pouring its thick master stream of five

5

hundred gallons per minute onto the roof. The spectators made appreciative noises.

The policeman turned, saw Zak and gestured at him to cross, but Zak shook his head. One of a pair of women in bowling jackets said, "This is a serious fire, isn't it?" The fire engines' roar enveloped her voice, making it flat.

"Yes, ma'm; I'm afraid it is. Was it already burning when you got here?"

"Yeah, but not as bad as it is now."

"Were you the first spectators to arrive?"

"Uh-uh, but we were next. We were on our way home from the League Night banquet, but decided to stop awhile. I didn't know you went right into a place that's on fire. I thought you stood outside to spray water."

"And they broke the door down to get into that shoe store," said the other woman. "Is that legal?"

"Yes, ma'm. Who was already here when you arrived?"

The second woman pointed at the trio of businessmen next to her. "They were."

The trio glanced up and came around the bowlers. They stood in the gutter facing Zak, engulfing him in an aura of alcohol. One said, "Yah, we seen the whole thing, right, guys?" and they all agreed they'd seen the whole thing.

"Were you the first to arrive?"

"You bet," said the man proudly. "We followed the fire trucks. Saw them barrelin' along an' followed. Very interesting to see how fast they set up."

"Would you mind telling me your name?" asked Zak.

"Me? Why?" asked the nodder, abruptly suspicious.

"Because I'll be investigating this fire, and you may be able to tell me something of value. But I won't know until I can go in for a look; so rather than ask you to wait around, perhaps for hours, I'll take your names and phone numbers and call you if I need to talk to you."

"Oh. Sure, why not?"

Zak reached for his paper and pencil. The men gave their names and said they were computer-marketing reps, in town for a regional seminar. They all agreed Zak could call and leave a message at their motel if he had any questions.

Zak also took the names of the lady bowlers and four college sophomores, one of whom was finding the scene totally awesome.

Zak put the notepad back in his pocket and crossed the street, bound for a pair of firemen in white helmets. Here the engine noise was louder, and the two were leaning in turn toward one another's shoulder, shouting an exchange of information. As Zak stepped up on the sidewalk near them, one nodded in comprehension, clapped the other on the shoulder and climbed into the back of a big van, a mobile command post that was the department's newest acquisition.

The other, preferring to supervise out in the open, stepped back into the street for a look at the master stream drenching the roof.

Zak followed. "You sent for me, sir?" he shouted politely.

The man, much bigger and taller than Zak, started. "Oh, hi, Zak! When did you get here?"

"A couple of minutes ago! Is it as bad as it looks?"

"Worse!" Battalion Chief Tellerman said gloomily. "I think we're going to lose the whole building! Here, let's get back where we can talk!" He led the way up the street, away from the burning building, then turned to listen.

"Where was the fire when you arrived?" asked Zak.

"Just in the appliance store. Two fires, back and front, much bigger in the back."

"Completely separate?"

"I guess not, but linked by a thin line. It was the smoke made me call you. It was dark enough to be from a refinery

7

fire. And when the first team broke in, they reported a smell of gasoline.''

"Damn. Are you close to knocking it down?''

"In the appliance store, maybe. In another twenty minutes.'' Tellerman smiled down at Zak. "How about you lend a hand while you're waiting? I've got a spare air bottle.''

Zak grinned back up, his droopy mustache lifting to display small square teeth. Tellerman was teasing, of course. Years of eating smoke had damaged Zak's lungs. When his heart had begun complaining of the extra work, they'd offered him the job of arson investigator to hold him until he could retire, which would be next year. But it was kindly teasing, a way of saying, I know you're still a fireman, that you remember how. "No, thanks. I'll check in with the Deputy Chief. Then can I come back and talk to you some more?''

"Sure. I'll wait in my car.''

Zak found the Deputy Chief busy and distracted in the command post, so he merely announced his presence on the scene. The man waved over his shoulder in acknowledgment; Zak closed the door and climbed back down.

Tellerman's official red sedan was parked kitty-corner from the burning building, engine running, heater on. Zak climbed into the passenger side of the front seat and produced his pad of graph paper. "You must have put in a call for me as soon as you arrived,'' he said.

Tellerman had removed his white helmet and unbuckled his coat, but was still a massive presence in the car. He consulted his watch. "Yep, I'd make that about forty minutes ago.''

Zak noted the estimation of time. "How did you get into the building?'' he asked.

"Front and back doors of the appliance store,'' said Tellerman. "Both locked.''

"Any sign of forced entry?''

"One small windowpane broken in back. Snap lock, you

8

can reach it from the window. Talk to Breck; he led the hand-line in back there and reported the window.''

"But it's a double door, isn't it?"

"Double width, but just the one door. I went back for a look myself."

"Other windows intact when you arrived?"

"The front windows blew outward just as we arrived. Apart from the window in back, that's all there is."

"What about the other stores?"

"You'll ask, of course, but I didn't see any sign of a break-in, and no one else has said anything. They broke into the appliance store, Zak, must have. You can't get from one store to the other from inside, and the fire started in the appliance store. But once the fire got up into the cockloft, it just ran along and fell into the other stores through the ceiling. Not a thing anyone could do to stop it. There's not a wall in the place that'd slow a fire down for more than fifteen minutes. No firewalls, no sprinklers, and a common cockloft—my favorite recipe for losing a building."

"Anyone inside?"

"No, thank God."

"Was there anyone around outside when you arrived?"

"Uh-uh. There was a carload that must've followed us. But nobody already here having multiple orgasms over the flames, if that's what you're hoping. And no guilty-looking car speeding off, either. No traffic at all, in fact."

"Who cut the utilities?"

"Breck, I think. He found the boxes."

"Who turned in the alarm?"

"It came in on the 911 number. We got a report of flames in the warehouse, but it turned out it was the store. Reflection of flames in the windows.'' Zak nodded, remembering how real the reflected flames had looked when he'd walked down Ninth.

"You're sure the fire started in the appliance store?"

"It was going very well in there with no sign of it anywhere else when we arrived."

"You said black smoke?"

"And your characteristic dark-red flames. Also, this fire was a real boomer."

The big walkie-talkie on top of the dash said, "Tellerman?"

Tellerman picked it up. "Yes, Chief?"

"The owner of the building, one David Wagner, has arrived. He's asking to speak to someone in charge."

"Ten-four," said Tellerman with a sigh. He turned to Zak. "You've heard of him, no doubt."

Zak frowned. "Have I?"

"He's Crazy Dave, remember? The guy who did those crazy radio commercials a few years ago. He sold stereo equipment for weird prices, like ninety-seven dollars and twenty-two cents for a turntable."

Zak nodded. "That's right, I remember now." His son and daughter had listened to the rock station playing those commercials, which, for a while, were almost as popular as the terrible music they sponsored. Funny how something as pervasive as that could almost vanish from the memory once the repetitions of it stopped. "I'll come with you and talk to him."

"Be my guest."

Dave Wagner was a handsome man with a strident voice, so well proportioned that they had come quite close before Zak realized how small he was. Wagner stood in the street in front of the spectators, arguing loudly with the policeman that he should be allowed to cross. His dark sweatshirt had a white motto on it, and his pale jeans ended in clean white sneakers. "That's my place! All my stuff is in there!" he was yelling. "Get outta my way, dammit!"

"Mr. Wagner?" said Tellerman when they were close enough to be heard.

10

"Yeah! Can you tell this turkey to get outta my way?" The motto on his sweatshirt said "Hell I'm Better."

"I don't think that's a good idea, sir. I'm Battalion Chief Tellerman. I understand you wanted to talk to me?"

"I got a lot of money tied up in this building, you know! You gonna let me try to rescue some of my stuff, or would you prefer we stand around and watch it burn up?"

"It's like this, Mr Wagner. I can stand here and argue with you over the merits of going into a building full of superheated air without so much as a hat for protection—or you can promise to behave like an intelligent person, and I can go back to my job." Tellerman's voice was perforce loud, but his tone was gentle.

"So how about in the meantime some of you firemen try saving some of the merchandise? That building's gone, right? I mean, look at it! But I got some big-screen TV sets in there, VCRs, and high-quality microwave ovens. We got plenty of sidewalk over there; can't you bring some of my stuff out before it all burns up?"

"No, sir. Our task is to get the fire out before it spreads to the rest of the block." He raised a forestalling hand. "Wait, just wait, and think a minute. The kind of fire we've got going here won't leave anything to rescue even if we started now."

"Are you telling me just to stand here and watch my whole life go up in smoke?" yelled Wagner.

"Surely you carry insurance," offered Zak mildly.

Wagner scowled at him. "Who the hell are you?"

"Captain Isaac Kader."

"Well, that's terrific! Now there's two of you not doing your job! Shouldn't you be squirting water or something?"

"No, sir, I'm from the Arson Squad."

". . . Arson?" It was as if someone had unscrewed a leg and drained all the fury out of Wagner. Suddenly he was hard to hear. "You think someone set this fire?"

11

"I'm here to determine the cause, that's all."

"Oh."

"Can I assume from what you just said that you own the entire building, not just the appliance store?"

". . . So what?"

"Nothing, except that the owner should be notified of the fire."

Belligerence crept back into Wagner's voice. "So I'm notified, okay?" He turned his shoulder to Zak to ask Tellerman, "You think it's gonna burn out all the stores?"

"I take it you are refusing to answer any more of my questions, Mr. Wagner?" said Zak.

Wagner glanced at Zak. "What are you, a cop?"

"No, sir; I'm a fireman."

"So what does that mean? You don't have to tell me I've got a right to remain silent?"

"Do you think you need to be warned? I was thinking I ought to find out what happened before I arrest anyone."

Wagner shifted to confront Zak, frowning. Tellerman stepped back out of range, and when no one objected, he turned and hurried away. The uniformed patrolman, still recovering from Wagner's fury of two minutes ago, remained watchful. Wagner asked, "If you're only a fireman, how can you arrest anyone?"

"I get a warrant from the county prosecutor," said Zak, with an air of stating the obvious. "But first I have to find out if anyone needs to be arrested, and I do that by finding out what happened. Do you have any objection to that?"

Wagner glanced at the burning building. Smoke was still choking the broken windows, despite the broad stream of water pouring across the threshold of the appliance store. He grimaced, disgusted. "Hell, there's probably nothing worth saving in there anyhow. What do you want to know?"

"How about we get out of the way of the fire fighters here? My car's parked just up the way, and there's a Thermos of coffee in it. We might as well get comfortable while we wait.''

"Sure, okay.''

. . .

Zak's glove box held a bag with half a dozen Styrofoam cups in it. He removed two, filled one and handed it to Wagner. "It's decaffeinated, I'm afraid," he said. "And there's no sugar or creamer.''

"I like it black," said Wagner, taking the cup. "Thanks.'' He sipped gingerly; the coffee was very hot.

Zak filled the other cup for himself and leaned back in the seat to look at the fire. The entire building was now involved, despite the aerial ladder's efforts. "Do you have a list somewhere of just what was in your store?''

"Sure, only it's in a hanging file in a drawer of my desk in my office, in my store.''

"Does that file come before or after the one with your insurance policies in it?''

Wagner laughed. "Just after.'' He sipped again. "My policies are at home, actually. My insurance agent has an appointment with me Monday evening to discuss increasing my coverage. How's that for locking the barn door after the horse has been cremated?''

"Do you know if there are any code violations in the building? Wiring or heating, like that?''

"No, the building inspector was in early this summer. We had to replace a light bulb in an exit light, and a couple other little things, as I recall. All taken care of months ago.'' Wagner snorted. "A freakin' light bulb, as if that makes any difference now!''

"You were very prompt on the scene, if I may say so. How did you find out the building was on fire?''

"Hell, we were the ones who called you!'' Wagner grinned at Zak. "Sounds crazy, right? Just like the old Crazy Davey —but it's the truth! I was engaged in a friendly game of cards

13

with four buddies and we saw it out a window. Counted the streets over and —by God, it's right behind me—we thought it was the warehouse, y'see. We called 911 and then I got to thinking how narrow that alley is between the warehouse and my place, so I figured I better come on over, and son of a bitch, it's my place all the time!''

"You saw it out a window?"

"Yeah." Wagner looked over his right shoulder and pointed. "See those three high rises over there? Summerside Condos. I was in the middle one, twelfth floor, place belongs to Ron Tollefson." He looked back, saw Zak writing, and added, "The other three were Toby Modreski, Murray Jones, and Dennis Baer.'' He spelled the names. He didn't know Dennis' street number, but gave his phone number and the addresses of the two others.

"You'd all been there some while before you noticed the fire?'' asked Zak.

"Oh, hell, yes. Been there all evening. Toby and I had supper there with Ron, then Dennis and Mur came over and we started playing.'' He looked out the window at his building and sighed. "Should I call my tenants tonight or try to catch them in the morning?"

"That's up to you, Mr. Wagner.''

"Is there going to be anything worth saving when this is over?''

"Not much, I'd guess.''

"Then what the hell, let them get some sleep. It's the least I can do.''

. . .

The fire was still burning in the bookstore when Zak sent Wagner home. He consulted with Tellerman, who agreed he could begin looking around.

Burdened with his heavy metal kit, prepared to drop it and run at a shouted warning of collapsing roof or flashback, he

14

picked his way around puddles and over water hoses to the entrance of the appliance store.

There, he stood and let his nose confirm what Tellerman had reported. Sure enough, there was, faintly, a raw stink of gasoline under the greasy stench of burned building. He put the heavy steel box down, pulled the graph-paper tablet from his pocket, twisting it between his hands to remove its curve, and fished for his pencil.

The ceiling was partly intact, though firemen from the ladder companies were using long pikes to pull down what was left of it. Above the ceiling Kader could see giant holes in the roof, acting as chimneys for the smoke still in the air. Several large, heavy floor lights had been brought in. Their beams cast eerie shadows, piercing the gloom like lighthouse beacons on a smoggy night.

The wrecks of appliances were everywhere—except the center of the floor, which had a hole about nine feet in diameter in it.

Partially burned console TV sets formed an uneven row along the front wall under the broken windows, their imploded screens like eyeless sockets. A ruin of refrigerators lay on their backs near the rear of the store, doors open; beside them, a sextet of stoves looked—in the smoky light and at this distance—as if nothing more than a good scrubbing would restore them. Filthy water stood in pools over what had once been carpeting.

A half dozen fire fighters were sifting debris in a search for remaining crumbs of fire, walking gingerly on the weakened floor and staying well away from the hole.

The face masks fire fighters wear distort vision, and the air tanks are cumbersome, so they are removed as soon as possible. A man working near Zak was snuffling loudly, his blackened face was tear-streaked, but his face mask hung loose around his neck.

Zak began a swift sketch of the store's layout, confirming what Wagner had told him. Television sets in front; VCRs, stereo tape decks, record turntables in what remained of the middle; stoves, microwave ovens, refrigerators toward the back. Small appliances over there, floor and table lamps on this side—he bent and picked up a flap of metal, rubbing it with a gloved thumb to disclose a tarnished, partly melted brass leaf. The floor lamp it had come from was leaning against what had been a big window fan, and Zak noted its location on his diagram before going back to the kit for a small, empty, unused paint can and a Sharpie pen. He put the fragment into the can, marked the can with the pen.

The appliance store had once been two stores, and the wall between them had not been completely removed; a ruined partition thrust out from the back. Zak went cautiously to the front of the partition, squatted to note the depth of the charring at its base and looked up to trace the burn pattern where the flames had climbed to eat into the ceiling. He marked the place on his sketch, then squatted to press his fingers into the guck on the floor. He sniffed at the sample thus gathered; then went back for another, larger, paint can and a spatula and collected a few ounces of the guck.

Paint cans are relatively cheap, chemically inert, and airtight. They're harder to break than glass bottles, and they don't tear like plastic bags. Zak marked and initialed the can, then looked for other significant evidence. He wasn't being thorough at this point; he was merely gathering sights and samples that might evaporate or get moved out of place.

Shelves on the partition had held telephones. Wilted metal parts stood up around the plastic puddles that had been their shells. Beyond them more melted plastic—radios? tape recorders?—made surrealistic shapes on the shelves. This had been a quick, very hot fire.

A line of char formed a narrow border along the base of the partition. He followed it to the rear wall and through a set of doors to a room where appliances were delivered or sent out.

At one end of the room was a big old freight elevator, its interior blackened, and beside it a stairway to the basement. The shattered door hung open, and the steps were badly spalled. Zak went down.

Appliances from the first floor had fallen through the hole into a jumbled heap in the middle of the basement, and water pattered from a dozen places around the edge of the opening, forming an unholy fountain. Otherwise the basement was mostly empty. Three refrigerators loomed blackly above and beyond the shattered jumble in the center, and near the back two stoves huddled together like frightened orphans.

Keeping an ear cocked for warning shouts or the creak of disengaging timbers, Zak moved slowly away from the foot of the stairs. A fireman was on the other side of the basement, pulling crumbling boards from the brick wall.

Nearby was a waist-high heap of mushy stuff that might once have been flattened refrigerator boxes. Zak stooped and used his pencil to probe the mush, measuring its depth. It became solid a few inches down, and he used his gloved left hand to lift the mush aside. It was cardboard, all right, and in the middle intact, barely even wet. He lifted an edge; farther down it became charred again. He looked around. The boxes had probably been leaning against that wall, falling over after the fire had reached them, to burn again on top, sandwiching the unburned section.

The heaped shape of the cardboard made it appear to be draped over something. Zak lifted it further to look—and dropped it, backing off, swallowing. The fireman pulling down the plaster saw his hasty move and called, "Whatcha got? More fire?" Without waiting for a reply, he came at a trot and used his pike to lift aside the burned cardboard—then backed off himself, sucking air through his teeth. A new smell wafted into the room, a sweet smell mixed with the stench of burned meat. "Oh, Jeez!" whispered the fireman. "Oh, Jeez!"

17

2

IT was not yet time to close up shop, but Brichter was alone in the squad room. McHugh was running another of his endless sting operations; Captain Ryder was at a lengthy department-head meeting upstairs; Johnson was taking a sick day.

Not that Brichter was lonely. He enjoyed solitude, particularly when engaged in paperwork. He could mutter esoteric curses, drink too much coffee, whistle difficult fragments of some Bach fugue over and over without anyone complaining.

The door opened—it would—and he looked up to see Eddie Dahl, a Homicide investigator. "Hiya, Obie; how the hell are ya?" asked Dahl. Dahl was a narrow-bodied man with a hatchet face and big hands at the ends of his skinny wrists.

"Busy," Brichter said curtly, and resumed whistling. He was checking one column of figures against another.

"Say, listen, I got a little problem maybe you can help me

with." Dahl came into the room, closing the door behind him. "Won't take you ten minutes, probably."

"Ask someone else, okay?" Brichter did not like Dahl.

"No, listen a second." Dahl reached for a straight-backed metal chair beside McHugh's desk, flipped it around with a practiced hand, and sat down. "Remember that fire Thursday night in Crazy Dave's TV and Appliance?"

Dahl's dark eyes dropped and lifted, and Brichter, aware that his tailor-made suit had just been noted and priced, waited for the grimace of envy before replying. "Remember I said I was busy?"

"No, listen a minute," insisted Dahl. "The place was torched; Arson says there's no doubt about it. And more, that body in the basement, which is how I got called; be dipped if the ME don't decide someone hit him on the back of the head. What I figured, it was a burglar trying to cover his trail. But Zak Kader says he may have been a burglar, but he was also someone who knew how to set a fire."

"Kader?"

"Captain, from Arson. A torch job, he says, though you gotta remember, Zak's a fireman, not a cop. But he's damn sure it was a set fire, not an accidental one. And Zak says Wagner's got a bad case of the shorts, which brings us to motive, right? Now I talked to Wagner Friday and asked him where the burglar's vehicle was, if that was a burglar in his basement, and he says maybe it was two burglars, and one came back to set the fire to cover their tracks. But there hasn't been any big surge in the local hot-appliance pipeline the last couple days, which you'd expect from the size of the list he gave me of stuff he thinks might be missing from his store. And who's gonna come in from out of town to hit just his place? I mean, the guy was selling schlock and rebuilts. So I haul him in again today and after he finishes blowing into his

19

hanky, he lets on as how, okay, if it's straight arson, it was ordered set by a certain Mr. Vigotti. He says the man's a loan shark, and he's sucked Wagner good and dry. Says he's in so deep, Vigotti's been threatening—get this—to burn him down."

Brichter, who had been listening despite himself, looked at Dahl with cool gray eyes long enough to make Dahl aware of the pause, then said, "So?"

Dahl gestured impatiently. "Well, hell, Obie, Vigotti's connected, ain't he? And this is the Organized Crime Unit here, right? So tell me, is Wagner in that kind of trouble with a loan shark named Vigotti?"

"Dunno."

"I thought you guys kept track of things like that!"

"When loan sharks allow cops to audit their books, maybe we can quote names and numbers. All I can do is agree that Tony Vigotti is a member of our local criminal organization, and is rumored to loan money at illegal rates of interest to people who will put up their bodies as collateral."

"Has he ever burned anyone down before?"

"McHugh would know more about him than I do."

"Yeah, but you're here, and I'm asking now."

"Well, I recall about two years ago Vigotti supposedly hired a kid to throw a Molotov cocktail through a pizza-store window; but the kid later said it was his own idea."

"What do you think?"

"I think the kid probably made a wise decision in changing his story."

"So this story Wagner is telling could be for real."

"Sure."

Dahl stood. "Could you come and talk to him?"

"Who?"

"Wagner."

"Now?"

"Yeah. He's upstairs."

"Why?"

"Because you can tell better than me if he's lying. I mean, so okay, you're not the expert, you still know more about loan sharks and Tony Vigotti than me, so maybe you can tell if Wagner's tears are fresh from a crocodile. I don't want to turn him loose and have him do a flit. Like I said, won't take you ten minutes, probably."

Brichter looked at his watch. Another two minutes and he'd have been gone. And never in the fourteen years he'd been a cop had a request for ten minutes of his time ever taken less than an hour. "Let me call home and say I'll be late first."

.　　.　　.

Homicide was on the second floor of the Safety Building. Dahl led Brichter through the deserted squad room to a narrow corridor, down it to a steel door with wire glass in its small window. He glanced in, pulling a ring of keys from a pocket.

Brichter put a hand on Dahl's arm to stop him. "I thought you said he wasn't under arrest."

"He isn't. But he's really spooked, says talking about Vigotti can get you killed. So I locked him in here."

Brichter shrugged and Dahl opened the door.

Wagner was a handsome man, but small, and so scared he seemed even smaller, hunched on a gray metal chair placed crossways to the end of the metal table. His skin had gone sallow and was pulled taut across the bony structures of his face, and his mouth was stretched into a meaningless smile. He was wearing filthy jeans and a white sweatshirt streaked and smudged with soot. "Goat Ropers Need Love Too" the shirt said in red letters. "I was down at my building when Sergeant Dahl came for me," Wagner said. He put a casual elbow on the table, but his sinewy fingers immediately began beating a tattoo on its surface, and he yanked it off again.

Dahl threw Brichter a see-what-I-mean? look and went to sit at the other end of the little table.

21

There was a third chair; Brichter took it and hauled out a fat notebook from an inside pocket. "Sergeant Dahl says you've been telling him about a loan shark operating here in Charter."

"Yes, he says I owe him a hundred and twenty-two thousand, five hundred dollars until tomorrow, when it will go up thirty-seven hundred dollars; and it will keep right on going up three percent of the new total every week, until my insurance check comes and I can pay him off."

Writing, "Did you borrow money from him?"

"Yes."

"What's his name?"

"Mr. Vigotti."

"His first name is . . . ?"

"I don't know, he never said."

"He's been making threats because of your inability to pay?"

"Yes."

"To your face or on the phone?"

"Both. It started on the phone. He said he'd make a bad example of me, break my arm. But a couple of weeks ago he sent these two big clowns to my store to get me. They brought me to him, and he said if I didn't pay him everything I owed him in two weeks, he'd torch my store."

"Did you believe him?"

"Sure!"

"So why didn't you pay him?"

"I *couldn't!*" Wagner was getting strident. "This's been going on over a year, and the bastard's bled me white!" Wagner stood and leaned on one hand toward Brichter, the other open toward the ceiling. "I tried to explain how things were, but he just kept *yellin'* at me!"

"Settle down, settle down," said Dahl. "Just take it easy." Wagner looked over his shoulder at Dahl, then slowly sat down again.

"This Mr. Vigotti," said Brichter. "What does he look like?"

Wagner sniffed, wiped his nose on his forearm. "Big guy, close to six foot, built real solid. Wears white shirts and a tie, always, like a salesman, and slicks his hair back like with motor oil or something." He watched Brichter write this down and added, "His hair is black, with a little gray in the sideburns. I figure he's maybe fifty, fifty-five. Got brown eyes, squinched up narrow, and he smokes big cigars."

"Tell me how you got into debt to him."

The little man shifted uneasily and nodded sideways at Dahl. "I already told him."

"So tell me."

"Well, business has been bad off and on for the last three-four years. And someone told me that if he liked me, I could get hold of operating cash from Mr. Vigotti."

"Who told you this?"

"Do I have to say?"

"It may help me to believe your story."

Wagner thought about that for almost a minute. "Okay, his name is Dench LeBrett. I met him at a party or something. I don't know exactly how he found out I needed money, but you know how it is, you talk with this guy and that guy about how shitty business is, how it's short-term, of course, but how banks don't like to loan money to people who really need it, except maybe farmers, which is okay, I guess, because we all got to eat, and—" Wagner stopped, having wandered from his point, then recalled it and set off after it again. "So word gets to him, I suppose, and this LeBrett calls me on the phone. And he says he can put me in touch with someone named Vigotti who can make loans with no collateral, except his interest rates are a little higher than normal and you better be sure you make your payments on time. I laugh and say that sounds like a loan shark, and LeBrett says maybe he is. So I throw the piece of paper I wrote the phone number on in my drawer and try to forget it. But a month later I'm hurting for just a quick couple hundred and my bank don't allow overdrafts anymore, so I call him. And he loans me three hundred just like that, I don't even sign an IOU, and I pay him back a hundred a week for four weeks, and he's like a pussycat every time we meet.''

"Where did you meet?''

"Chauncey's, on Milford, every Wednesday. So pretty soon I'm into him for nine grand, making payments on the dot, and I'm wondering why I was scared to call him in the first place. Then he tells me how, since I'm such a good customer, he can loan me more at a lower rate, like three percent a week, and all I absolutely gotta pay is what he calls the vig, by which he means the interest, the three percent. The principal I pay off whenever I can, he says.''

"And you borrowed more from him at this special low rate?''

"Yeah, twenty-four grand. I mean, I borrowed fifteen new grand, but I added the nine grand I already owed him onto the new loan at the lower rate. I pay the vig and some on the principal and get it down to twenty-two grand. I was setting up for my red-tag sale and I thought I could pay off a real big chunk from that and then the rest no problem, but my sale was a flop and then one of my tenants has a heart attack and I couldn't get someone new in there for three months and— well, I was wrong. But he's not mean about it, even when I miss a payment; he just adds it on to the principal. I'm thirty grand in the hole, when I borrowed another twelve grand a couple months later. He was pretty good about it, just hauls out this wad of hundred-dollar bills and peels them off, and says, 'You still pay the vig on Wednesdays, okay?' The vig on forty-one thousand is twelve hundred bucks a week, you know? I lose another tenant and there's other bills to pay, and there's weeks my store don't gross enough to keep me even, and pretty soon I'm hardly paying anyone else trying to pay him. But even that don't work, and I get behind. At first he don't care, he just adds it on, but every time he does, the vig goes up, and I can't pay it. Then he starts getting impatient, and I'm nervous, but I still can't get caught up, and pretty soon I don't want to hear him yelling at me anymore so I don't call him to say I don't have the money, because I figure if I don't turn up at the bar with it, he knows it's because I don't have it. Finally I'm only turning up about every other week, or every third week, bringing two, three, five hundred at a time. When I got it, I bring it. When I don't, I don't. Well, that's not good enough. He starts calling me, madder and madder, every day; first at home, then at work. And I'm so upset, I can't take care of business and there's a month I don't pay him at all. And now I don't need to call him, he's calling me—it seems like every couple hours. The vig is up to over thirty-five hundred; the principal's like, I don't know, more than a hundred eighteen grand. There's no way I can handle that. Finally he sends these two creeps around, it's right in the middle of the day, and they walk me out of the store and put me in a car and take me to him. He's almost crazy he's so pissed, but I'm so relieved those two weren't taking me someplace to shoot me, I can hardly hear what he's saying. What it turns out is, he says by the terms of the loan he can call the whole thing in with two weeks' notice, and this is it. If I don't pay up, he'll burn me down and take it out of the insurance." Wagner glanced at Brichter. "That was two weeks and five days ago. My store burned down one day after the deadline."

"Has he called you since?"

"One time, to ask if my insurance was paid up. I said yes and he said he'd be in touch."

"We'll be putting a tap on his phone," said Dahl.

"How long ago did you borrow the twenty-four thousand?" asked Brichter.

"July of last year. And twenty-four weeks later the twelve." He cocked his head sideways to watch Brichter write this down in his notebook. "I kept thinking that things would look up, that I could make it and go pay him off and things would be fine again. Only it just kept not working out."

"When did you first borrow money from him?"

"Around Christmas time year before last."

"Were you aware when you borrowed the money that you were engaging in an illegal transaction?"

Wagner hesitated. "Both you and the shy gotta know it's illegal, or we can't prove it's a case of loan-sharking," prompted Dahl, earning a glancing blow from fifty-below gray eyes.

Wagner sniffed and scratched his cheek with a sooty forefinger. "Ah, well, yes, I guess so."

Brichter nodded, writing. "And Mr. Vigotti told you in clear English that he would physically harm you if you failed to keep up your payments."

"He said he'd break my arm."

"Those were his exact words?"

Wagner thought. "On the phone he goes—he says, 'Skinny people like you got arms snap like kindling. You just put the wrist on the curb and the elbow in the gutter and you stomp one time. How'd you like to go around with your arm in a cast, huh?' And he laughed. And he said, 'That's an old building your store is in, I bet it would burn real good. You better make sure your fire insurance is paid up, 'cause I don't wanna burn you down and still not get paid.' And finally he said, 'I should make you my bad example. We can't let people start thinking they can welch on me.' I wondered if he meant he would kill me." Wagner looked down into his lap. "I tried, you know? He scared me, and I really tried. I set up this

26

special sale to raise the money, unbelievable prices, and he called me Wednesday night and I said I needed more time. I begged with tears in my eyes, but he hung up on me."

"Why didn't you come to us then?" asked Brichter.

"Because he said he'd kill me if I went to the cops. He didn't laugh when he said that." Wagner sighed. "I sat down and figured it out last night: I paid that bastard twenty-five thousand, six hundred dollars, and I still owe him the whole thirty-five grand, plus a hundred and twenty-five grand in back interest."

Dahl shot Brichter a fast look of inquiry, and Brichter returned a brief nod. "Not anymore you don't, Mr. Wagner," said Dahl, grinning. "Not anymore."

. . .

It was dark when Brichter got home. There were lights on in the barn, so he went in there. Kori was standing in the arena with her standard poodle Michael D'Archangelo by her side. She was wearing old riding pants, a pale-yellow shirt, and tan knit vest. Her incorrigible hair, at this end of her working day, had managed to escape its braids in enough quantity to create a dark mist around her lovely head.

Michael glanced at him and grinned, but stayed where he was. Danny, Kori's young groom, was talking to her, one hand holding the lead rein, the other on the neck of a bright bay yearling filly.

There is virtually nothing as pretty as a purebred Arabian yearling filly, so Brichter leaned on the fence to watch.

Danny was saying, "I noticed there were streaks of damp down the wall when I went in there yesterday, so I went up a ladder this afternoon. Looks like some shingles came loose during that windstorm last month."

The filly reached forward with a narrow muzzle and blew in Danny's ear. He pushed her away. Kori said, "I can't remember the last time we reshingled the maternity shed, so

27

I suppose we're due for that kind of problem. Okay, trot her off; let's have a look."

Danny turned and trotted off with the filly. The filly was a burnt-orange color with black legs, nose, mane, and tail; slim and very leggy. She was carrying her head and tail high, aware she was—and pleased to be—the center of attention.

"Okay, bring her back!" called Kori.

Danny slowed to a walk and came around. "Hi, Sergeant!" he called, waving at Brichter at the fence, and Kori turned, too.

"Hello, *fy'n galon*," he said.

"Peter, when did you get here?" she asked, smiling, starting for him.

"Just now. Who is that, Chinook?"

"No, Solar Wind." She leaned across the fence to kiss him. "Ron's coming by tomorrow to look at her again. It's going to cost him double for not buying her as a weanling." She turned and called, "Put her away, Danny!"

"Yes'm." The young man led the filly off toward a box stall.

"Nice, isn't she?" asked Kori.

"Very."

Michael came to lean against her leg and she put her hand down to stroke the dog's topknot of curls. She smiled at her husband. "But not nearly as nice as Chinook. I despair of ever giving you an eye for a really fine horse."

"I can tell which is better when they're side by side," he said. "Supper ready? I'm starved."

"The chicken's baked all to pieces, just the way you like it."

She opened the gate to the arena and came through, maneuvering so as not to brush up against him. "I'm all over horse."

"My hand washes," he replied, taking hers, and they walked

together out of the barn, across the wide gravel and up the grassy lawn to the big old house, the dog following.

He really did like his chicken overdone, and they ate in silence until the edge was off his appetite.

"How was your day?" she asked at last.

"Routine." He chose not to bring his work home with him, and rarely offered more than this single-word comment on his day. He asked, "How was yours?"

"I got a card reminding me Michael's refresher lesson is next month. They're really proud of him, and they say they'd like to take him to a show."

"Will you agree?"

"No, his picture might turn up in a newspaper, and I'm not anxious to advertise Michael's special talents—that's why I got him in the first place, remember?" Like other wealthy people, their house had a good alarm system; but she was out of the house most of the day, and her husband was in a profession that bred enemies. She refused to carry a gun, and after looking at several decided not to buy a German shepherd or Doberman pinscher. But Brichter insisted she do something, and so she bought Michael, a fuzzy black puppy who grew up into—and a little beyond—the size his breed was meant to be when they were first used as hunting dogs: twenty-eight inches high at the shoulder and two ounces less than sixty-five pounds. He had done exceptionally well in obedience and then guard-dog training, but his amiable grin and the cap of curls he wore tilted rakishly forward were excellent camouflage for his skills.

"Anyway, I haven't spent the time it would take to make him competitive in a national event," said Kori. "Hal's just impressed because he's a poodle. Are you ready for dessert? It's your favorite, cherry pie."

"And the chicken is another favorite. Are you buttering me up for something?"

To his surprise, she blushed. "I'll get the pie."

He frowned after her as she vanished into the kitchen. There was a minimum of manipulation and plea-bargaining, as she called it, in their marriage. He was twelve years older than she was, the senior partner in most other respects, too; but the ranch—and the money that supported their comfortable life-style—were hers. She tried never to use the money as a weapon; nor did she use her looks—but then she never had to. After nearly four years of marriage he was still shaky-handed at times around her. The clear gray eyes, a shade darker than his own, the incredible purity of her complexion, her dark, electric hair, which clasped her shoulders and his hands when he released it from its customary braids, her deliciously tiny waist and long, strong legs—he took a hasty pull at his coffee, reminding himself that bedtime was at least three hours away yet.

She came back with the pie and waited until he had tasted his before saying, "You're too perceptive sometimes, you know that?"

"You do want something, then?"

"Yes."

"What?"

"A baby."

"*What?*" He could not have been more dismayed if she had said she wanted him to turn in his badge and take up selling aluminum siding.

"I know we agreed when we married that because we'd both come from such—odd backgrounds that we probably ought not to have children."

"Not probably, *fy'n galon*. Wouldn't."

"All right, wouldn't. But I've changed my mind."

"Why?"

"Because I want one, a piece of each of us put together into a new life."

30

"You sound as if you've been reading *True Romance*."

"No, I've been helping Anne teach Benjamin to walk and, oh, Peter, when he comes chortling all proud toward me, my heart just breaks. I want us to reconsider our decision."

He pushed his plate away. "I might have known my dear cousin was behind this."

"No, she isn't, Peter! She has never suggested I have a baby! And it's been my idea for her to bring Benjamin over! After all, I am his godmother, and I adore watching him turn from that ugly red mite into a real person. Admit it, Peter: he's a pet, and you love him, too."

Brichter shrugged. "He's a whole lot like every other baby I've seen, loud at one end and no sense of responsibility at the other." He grinned, and got a faint smile in return. Encouraged, he continued, "They're far more trouble than they're worth, babies. And you'd be an unhappy mother, you know. You like order and cleanliness, both impossible to maintain with a baby around. And they're not like horses, ready to leave home at six months; you're talking about an eighteen-year job raising one to some sort of maturity. And there's me to contend with. I don't like babies; they make me itch."

"Not if you keep them clean," she said.

That was a last attempt to lighten the discussion, which thereafter deteriorated into a real argument.

The next morning they were cool and distant over breakfast, but she called after him as he went out the front door, and came to throw her arms around him. "Don't go away angry," she murmured in his ear. "I love you, I love you, I love you."

He hugged her back, happy the quarrel was over, and went out to start the big engine of his car and roar off to the office in good humor.

3

BRICHTER walked into the basement squad room whistling the trill that goes on and on in the Little Fugue, and which can be tiresome to listen to unless the mind's ear is supplying the other parts, which in Brichter's case it was. He walked across the room straight to the coffee urn, still trilling, and lifted his mug from the metal tree. He had nearly filled it before he got to the part where the trill ends in a little run down the scale. He stopped for air and to say, "Hi, Cris."

Sergeant Crispin McHugh said, "I take it we are in a good mood this morning." He was a large man with a deep, rich voice.

"Sure." The melody continued in Brichter's head. "Why, shouldn't I be?"

"Eddie Dahl's in talking to Frank."

"Okay, so he is." Brichter walked to his desk. *Bum, bum, bum; bum-bum bum-bum bum-bum-bum-bum.* "Remember that memo Interim Chief Cunningham sent out last week? 'All requests for information or assistance between detective divisions will be made through the division heads.' Fast Eddie came by about quitting time last night and asked me to interview Dave Wagner about that arson fire last week.''

Cris brightened. "Will you go?''

"Already did. Now he remembers the memo, and ergo, he's in covering his ass this morning." *Bah deeda bum, bah deeda bum.*

Cris relaxed into a grin. "Uh-uh, he's in asking that you be assigned to work with him on the case.''

The music stopped. "How do you know that?''

"Because he came in and said, 'Mornin', Captain, may I talk to you for a minute? It's about a case I'm working on. I've got reason to believe an organized crime figure may be involved.' '' Cris had a talent for mimicry, and he got just right the beggar's whine that appeared in Dahl's voice when he needed a favor. "Since Frank knows how I yearn to place Vigotti's ass in the state pen, I thought it would be me, but since you already talked to Mr. Wagner, guess who Frank'll assign to work with him?''

"Shit," muttered Brichter.

"I told you to quit when you married all that money.''

The door to Ryder's office opened and he came out, Eddie Dahl close behind with a complacent air. Ryder, a comfortably padded man approaching his middle sixties, said, "Pete, glad you're here. I'm assigning you to work with Sergeant Dahl on the Wagner arson case.''

．　　．　　．

A few minutes later Dahl followed Brichter out of the squad room. "So first thing we do is haul Vigotti in and talk to him,'' Dahl was saying. Brichter opened his mouth, then closed it again. He didn't agree that this was their first move, but neither did he wish to start off the partnership with an argument.

Brichter did not work well in harness with anyone, much less someone like Dahl; this was going to be particularly hard since the case was Homicide's and Dahl was therefore the leader.

"Let's take your car," said Dahl, and Brichter bit his tongue again, harder.

They went out the steel door from the basement corridor into the underground parking ramp. Brichter started for the distant corner where he parked his car.

"I know someone who can get you reassigned to a spot closer to the door," offered Dahl.

"Yeah?" But Brichter preferred his car out of the way of careless door openers and envious hearts.

Dahl chuckled, set his short legs dancing in a boxer's movement. "Yeah, I'll talk to him tomorrow. There's other favors I can do for my partners. Wait and see, we'll be great as a team."

"I'll write that down so I don't forget it."

Dahl laughed, then leaned, ducked and threw a light punch. Brichter ignored it, so Dahl danced and poked again, more aggressively. The punch was blocked, Dahl felt a light blow on his face, another to his ribs, and Brichter was ten yards away, walking.

"Hey!" said Dahl. "Damn! Where'd you learn that?"

"You wouldn't believe me if I told you. Come on, let's get this done." Brichter was still walking.

Dahl hurried after him, frowning. But by the time they reached the distant corner, he had recovered his good humor. "Oh, yeah; there she is!" he said. Brichter's car was a broad, squat, fish-eyed sports car, the model *Motor Trend* calls Big Mutha: a rich, arrest-me red Porsche 928S.

Brichter went to unlock the door on the passenger side for Dahl. "Coming?"

"Sure, sure." Dahl came to bend his narrow frame into the tan bucket seat, and Brichter went around to unlock his side.

"I guess you're used to it by now. But, holy cow, Obie, this is one machine. I mean, I never even rode in a Porsh before. Look, the whole inside is leather, even the goddamn ceiling!"

Brichter got into the driver's seat. "Porsche."

"Yeah, I saw your vanity plates. Cute, Portia the Porsh."

Brichter started the engine.

"How fast will Portia go?" asked Dahl.

"Faster than I can legally drive her." Brichter rolled up to the exit door, where the car broke a light beam and called someone's attention to the fact that he wanted out. The door rose to the loud ringing of a bell.

"Have you ever opened her all the way up?" asked Dahl as they climbed the steep ramp to street level and turned right.

"Yes."

"How fast did she go?"

"I was too scared to notice."

Dahl laughed. "You don't deserve a car like this, you know that? Any time you want to try it again, let me know. I'll come along and read the speedometer for you."

"I'll write that down, too."

The Porsche had been waiting in the drive when they came home from their honeymoon, and he had been shocked to discover it wasn't a visitor's but his, a gift from his bride. And he'd been ashamed at first to bring it to work—not wanting to appear to be rubbing his new wealth in the faces of his fellow cops. Worse, the machine was so powerful, so different from anything he'd ever handled, he had to drive it as cautiously as a little old lady. But then Kori, bless her, signed him up for Skip Barber's famous course, and by graduation he was beginning to grin at what he'd once found spooky. He'd decided to hell with it and requested he be allowed to use it on duty too, even though the city wouldn't pay him mileage or help with the extra insurance burden. Dahl was wrong; he'd never gotten used to owning it, but neither would

35

he ever again find driving an ordinary car a satisfying experience. There are some things money *can* buy.

In less than six minutes they were into one of the better suburbs of Charter. Turning onto a quiet circle road, they found Vigotti in his driveway, just about to get into his car. He stood behind his Buick in the driveway, waiting for them to get out and come to him. He raised both eyebrows when he saw Dahl, and his glance shifted back and forth between Brichter and Dahl.

"Morning, Tony," said Brichter.

"Brichter, isn't it? I recognized your car."

"Sergeant Brichter, yes. Charter Police. You're out early."

"Am I?" Vigotti looked at his watch, a thin gold wafer on his hairy wrist. He was a broad, strong-looking man with shining black hair combed straight back. "Not so early; I have a business meeting in twenty minutes." He looked dressed for it, in conservative dark suit, dark-red tie, and glittering black shoes.

"Who you meeting with?" demanded Dahl.

The dark eyes again shifted. "Why do you ask, Sergeant . . . Dahl, I believe?"

"We want to talk to you. Downtown." Dahl moved his weasel shoulders and lifted his narrow chin, a tiny reprise of his boxer's dance, daring Vigotti to make something of it.

The eyebrows went up again. "Am I under arrest?"

"No," said Brichter, wishing he dared kick Dahl. "Just some questions."

"About what?" Vigotti reached into an inside pocket and Dahl immediately took two steps backward. Vigotti laughed and produced a leather cigar case. "Nervous, ain'tcha?" he said, pulling the top off and taking out a fat black cigar. "Care for one?" He held the case out to them.

"Knock it off, Tony," said Brichter. "Look, you want us to give you a ride, or will you meet us at the Safety Building?"

36

Vigotti grinned and reached into a side pocket for a lighter. "It would almost be worth missing my meeting for a ride in that car. No, I'll meet you there, but in an hour, okay? I really have to go to this meeting."

"All right," said Brichter before Dahl could object.

"What room do I ask for?"

"Room 212," said Dahl. "Homicide."

The lighter halted in mid-rise, then continued. "Okay, Safety Building, room 212, in an hour."

As they drove away, Dahl said, "I bet he brings his lawyer with him."

"I think maybe we alarmed him back there," agreed Brichter, biting hard.

"Meanwhile," continued Dahl, "we got an hour to kill. How about we go to that shop that gives free doughnuts and coffee to cops? Nobody's rich enough he can pass up an offer like that, right?"

Brichter said, even more sharply than he meant to, "How about we go back to the Safety Building instead?"

Dahl, surprised, said, "Sure, okay. I mean, I've got a couple of things I could do till Vigotti shows."

"I should talk to Captain Kader; I'll try to be down before Vigotti comes in, but you can reach me there if I'm not."

.   .   .

Charter's Safety Building looked like a step pyramid in four decreasing layers. The third floor was where the Chief of Police's suite and other administrative offices were. The Arson investigators had been tucked in near the Fire Chief's office. It was a single-desk office, but with evidence of two personalities: parchments showing graduation from two schools of fire science, two spindles for phone messages, framed portraits of two different wives. Zak Kader and his partner worked alternate twenty-four-hour shifts, including Saturday and Sunday.

Zak was on again today, sitting behind the desk filling out a report form, referring to graph-paper notes, humming softly to himself behind his mustache.

"Captain Kader?"

He looked up, surprised; he hadn't heard the door open. The man standing there was about five ten or eleven, fashionably lean in his expensive black suit, his thinning no-color hair cut in an unobtrusive style that probably cost thirty dollars a hit. But there was about him an air that said "cop." Maybe it was the very cool light-gray eyes.

"Yes?" said Zak.

"I'm Detective Sergeant Brichter."

"Yes?"

The thin mouth quirked sideways. "I'd like to talk to you about the fire last Thursday night at Crazy Dave's TV and Appliance Store."

"I thought Sergeant Dahl was assigned to that."

"I take it Sergeant Dahl didn't mention me to you."

"Should he have? Come in, Sergeant." Zak opened the middle drawer of his desk and slid his notes and report form into it. "How is it you took over from Sergeant Dahl?"

Brichter closed the door. "I haven't taken over. Sergeant Dahl asked me to assist with the investigation. I'm with the Organized Crime Unit."

"What has Organized Crime got to do with the Dahl fire?"

"It appears that the fire may have been ordered up by someone associated with organized crime in Charter."

"I see. What is it you want to know?"

Brichter came to stand across from Zak. Zak fancied he was being weighed in some cop balance and, as usual, found wanting. Brichter really did have the coldest eyes he'd ever seen.

"Could you tell me what you found that made you decide it was arson?"

Irked, Zak said, "You mean, what makes me think I know the rules of evidence?"

"No, I want to know why you think this is a case of deliberate burning of property with malicious intent. Which is, I believe, the legal definition of arson, unless the lawmakers have moved things out from under us again."

"Sit down, Sergeant," said Zak, a little ashamed of himself. He bent and opened a deep drawer in his desk, came up with a bulky file folder and opened it.

Brichter sat on a metal chair with a blue plastic seat. "I got the call at quarter to twelve last Thursday night," Zak said, looking at the photocopy of the incident report on top. "Battalion Chief Tellerman put in the request." Consulting his notes to ensure accuracy, he went on to describe his arrival, his encounter with Wagner, his preliminary findings, and the discovery of the body. "At that point, of course, all things came to a halt until a detective from Homicide could arrive, and that's when I got to meet Eddie Dahl."

Brichter looked up from his note taking. "I take it you consider him typical of our detectives?"

Zak yearned to say yes, because Dahl, like every other police detective he'd met so far, treated him as if he were incompetent. But Dahl had been worse. He'd more than not listened; he'd interrupted Zak's narrative to ask questions Zak had already supplied the answers to, and interrupted the answers to complain about the muck in the building, as if Zak should have cleaned up after himself. Zak opened his mouth and despite himself the truth came out. "Not typical in all respects."

Again the half-smile pulled Brichter's thin mouth sideways. "Apart from a stink of gasoline, what makes you think it was arson?"

Zak turned over a page in the file and looked at a dark and

smeary photograph taken inside the burned-out building. "There was a char pattern consistent with use of accelerant," he said, tracing a shape with a stubby finger. "See here, several sources of fire linked by abnormal char lines." His finger moved along the photograph, following the indication. He looked up and saw baffled interest. "It's here, believe me. And the fire was too hot for the length of time it burned, considering the fireload."

"Fireload?"

"Caloric value in Btu's per pound times the estimated weight of the contents divided by the area in square feet. That store had a wooden interior, and it was filled with particleboard, plastic, artificial fibers, and a lot of enameled metal. So the fireload in the appliance store should have averaged two hundred fifty thousand—more by the console TVs, less back by the refrigerators. It takes a well-ventilated, unattended fire about an hour to reach seventeen hundred degrees, the melting point of brass. This fire was only half an hour old when the first trucks arrived, and at that point only one pane of a small four-pane window in back was broken. The fire was out less than forty minutes later, for all practical purposes. Yet I picked up a piece of partly melted brass in the store."

"I suppose that's why they call it accelerant," suggested Brichter.

Zak smiled. "Yes. As for negative indicators, there was no evidence of electrical short, no space heater in the area where the fire started, no thunderstorm reported in the city that evening, and none of the employees was a smoker, nor were customers allowed in the basement, where the fire started. Even without the stink of gasoline, that was a suspicious fire."

Brichter nodded and wrote in his fat notebook. "Does that type of building burn easily?"

"Oh, absolutely. It was an old building, single-story, brick exterior but wooden interior, common cockloft. It was divided into four shops, without a firewall or a sprinkler system. It had an inverted roof of wood under tar paper. Have you ever heard the term 'taxpayer'?''

Again the half-smile. "Frequently."

"No, I mean as a type of building. Put up cheap and fast as a way to make the land on which it stands pay its own taxes until something better can be built. Wagner's building has been paying the taxes on that lot since 1904. Its loft was tinder-dry; once the fire spread up there from the appliance store, there was no stopping its movement to the other stores."

"Would you say it was a professional torch job?"

"I'd say it was set by someone who had a good idea of what he was about."

"Do you think the body belongs to the person who set the fire?"

"That's the easiest explanation, isn't it? No one's come forward to identify it, everyone connected with the store has been accounted for, and Mr. Wagner has stated that there was no one authorized to be in the building after hours. I suppose it's possible that our arsonist stumbled across a burglar who happened to be in the place at the same time and sapped him, but that calls for a nearly unbelievable coincidence. I don't buy the burglar angle at all. If he was a burglar trying to cover his tracks with a fire, where's the car or pickup or whatever he was going to use to carry away his loot?"

"You said the body was badly burned. How certain are we the victim died of a blow to the head?"

"Have you seen the autopsy report?"

"No, Eddie has it. But I'll talk to our ME later today. I suppose she knows a skull can fracture from the heat of a fire."

"The report says definitely a blow to the back of the head, not caused by a fall—something about coup?"

41

"*Coup contra coup*. Okay, I understand. Any description of the victim?"

"About five nine, muscular build, not a teenager, not an old man. He had a healing case of ulcers. There was a piece of intact skin in the left armpit; from that she concludes black hair, dark complexion, and probably brown eyes."

"Is she sure he was dead before the flames reached him?"

"Yes. Most people are, you know."

"Yes, I remember from my paramedic schooling. It's smoke inhalation that gets, what, eighty percent of them?"

"Unless they die from poisons released by the flames."

"Really?" The tone was not doubting, but that of a bright man presented with an interesting bit of new information. "Oh, of course. Artificial fibers, right? Strange new compounds forming in the heat to turn your blood into a poison, melt your liver, and eat holes in your kidneys."

Zak shook his head. "No, I mean old-fashioned hydrogen cyanide, the stuff they use in gas chambers. The worst are synthetics treated to burn slowly. Polyurethane, for example. When it burns at a high temperature, it gives off carbon dioxide, water vapor, and nitrogen. When it smolders, it releases hydrocyanic, formic, and hydrochloric acids, formaldehyde, acetone, methanol, and God knows what else.

"You sound like a chemist."

"A fire fighter today can use a degree in chemistry. It used to be all he needed were leather lungs and a fire hose. Now he wears a space suit and still is more likely to die in the line of duty than a police officer." Zak winced; this man hadn't asked for that.

But Brichter only nodded and said, "It's called progress; entropy doesn't seem to apply to civilizations."

Zak nodded back, thinking of his laboring heart. "Like people, they die of complications."

42

"I assume there was enough body left to get a carbon-dioxide reading?"

monoxide

Zak had to look for that. "Hm, yes. CO blood level reading two point seven percent."

"And a heavy smoker has a higher reading than that. So all right; he was dead before the fire got underway, presumably from the cranial injury. Could something have fallen on him?"

"It doesn't look that way. Everything that fell seems to have fallen as a result of the fire."

"Maybe the fire started with an explosion."

"I thought of that," said Zak. "An explosion can throw a man against a wall or stairway hard enough to fracture his skull—but one that powerful would leave traces that survive even a fire. In this case there was no sign of an explosion. Though this fellow was asking for one. There was sufficient candle wax to cast doubt on any second-beer alibi."

"Second beer?"

"You lay your trailers, light a candle, and you're working on your second beer in a distant tavern before the fire starts."

"Ah." Brichter wrote again. "You're sure about the candle?"

Zak turned to another photograph, equally dark and smeary, of a small area of the basement floor. "Here, near the center of where the fire started: traces of candle wax." He glanced up at Brichter, who had stood to look at the photo, saw a frown indicating Brichter saw nothing of the sort. "It's there, believe me. I have a sample of it."

"Very nice detective work."

Zak smiled. "No, the fire started here, it was a suspicious fire, so I knew where to look and what to look for."

"I am nevertheless impressed. Was the body found near the source of the fire?"

Zak went to the back of the file, where his diagrams were.

43

"No, it was over here, about six yards from the stairs. I was surprised by it; usually you can smell them. I noticed there was something under a pile of cardboard, took a look, and there he was." The drawing indicated a figure on its right side, one arm and foot pulled up.

Brichter sat down again. "How did he get in?"

"A rear windowpane was broken inward, which is not the direction they go when stressed by heat. And the phone line, which would have carried the alarm if Wagner hadn't been disconnected for lack of payment, was cut outside the building, and not by one of us."

Brichter, writing, asked, "You're sure the fire started in the basement of the appliance store?"

"Oh, yes. The arsonist laid trailers—in this case, toilet paper soaked in gasoline—across the floor from the candle, up the stairs, and between two, possibly three, concentrations of accelerant on the first floor. But it started in the center of the basement."

"What made you decide Mr. Wagner might be involved?"

Zak shrugged. "You always look at the owner first. His bank says he's behind on his first and second mortgage payments and has recently been turned down for a loan. His life-insurance company says he hasn't made a payment in eighteen months. He is behind on his car payments and personal loans at a couple of finance companies. He owes two months' phone bills at both the store and his apartment, two months' rent, four months' utilities, and has a history of erratic payment to all of them going back more than a year. Wagner was adequately insured and he had taken the insurance policies home, which may mean he knew they were in danger of being destroyed in a fire—though he says he had them at home because he had an appointment with his agent to look at ways of getting the same coverage for less money. I haven't been able to get hold of his agent yet to see if that's true. I find it significant

44

that the only payment he was up-to-date on was his property insurance."

"He says he was bled white by a loan shark who was threatening to burn him down."

Zak considered this, and nodded. "All right, that might explain both his arrears and why he was careful to keep fire coverage current. How was this discovered?"

"Eddie brought Wagner in for interrogation, and when he realized he might be charged with arson and murder, he started talking about a loan shark. That's when Eddie came to get me, since it appears the loan shark is an organized-crime figure in Charter."

"I see. I'm not familiar with that kind of indebtedness. This is only the fourth suspicious fire I've investigated officially, and the first where the evidence has been so solid."

"Against Wagner?"

"No, that it was arson. The problem with arson, of course, is that a fire destroys evidence. This fire was spotted and reported earlier than it might have been, considering its location in the warehouse district, but the building is still a total loss. It's only because I was called to the scene while it was still burning that I was able to accumulate most of that evidence."

The door opened and Dahl stuck his head around. "Obie, Vigotti's here."

"Thanks, be right with you." Brichter stood. "That's Mr. Wagner's alleged loan shark, here to be interviewed. May I come back with more questions, Captain?"

"Of course." Zak stood and put out his hand. "It was a pleasure to meet you, Sergeant Brichter."

. . .

On their way down the corridor, Dahl asked, "Ain't he cute? Just like a real de-tec-uh-tive. Provided he keeps his Geritol dosage way up there, of course."

45

"He seems to know what he's doing."

"Sure, he talks a great game. But can you see him in a shoot-out? Watch him scramble back and call for help. And it won't be the fire department he calls."

"Last time I was in a shoot-out, Eddie, it wasn't the fire department I called for backup, either."

Dahl laughed and hurried ahead of Brichter to open the door to the stairway for him.

.   .   .

Vigotti was waiting in the same windowless little interrogation room Wagner had sat in. It was painted a soothing blue and furnished only with the small table and three chairs. Vigotti was sitting in the one bolted-down crossways to the end of the table. A tiny foil ashtray had been provided for his cigar, but he was playing the cigar smoker's game of allowing the longest possible ash to form.

"Sergeant Dahl said he was surprised I don't have my lawyer with me," said Vigotti without preamble when they entered the room.

"I don't see why," said Brichter. "You're a long way from needing a lawyer, Tony. Sorry to take you away from your business like this, but it shouldn't be for long." He sat down and pulled out his notebook. "Eddie, would it be possible for you to call Captain Ryder and tell him where we are? Take your time, okay? Ten minutes."

He let Dahl catch the merest flicker of his left eye, and Dahl grinned and said, "Sure."

As soon as Dahl had closed the door behind him, Vigotti said, "So, you think I know something about a fire, right?"

"What fire?"

Vigotti grinned. "Come on, Sergeant, you think I didn't ask around before I came down here? You think maybe I was born yesterday?"

"No, you've been around some while, Tony."

46

"So you want to talk to me about the fire last Thursday in that building where they found a body afterward, right?"

"I want to talk to you about the owner of that building."

"Who's that?"

"Dave Wagner."

Vigotti sat back in the chair and drew lightly on his cigar while he thought. "I don't think I know the guy."

"That's not what he says. He says you loaned him some money."

"He says that? He show you his copy of the IOU? I don't loan money to people I don't know without getting an IOU."

"He says this was a special loan, the kind you don't sign papers over. He says you demanded an illegally high rate of interest on the loan, and that when he fell behind on his payments you threatened him first with physical harm and then to burn down his building."

Vigotti snorted. "He must've been smoking some of those funny cigarettes you can buy on the schoolgrounds any afternoon. Which I wish you cops would do something about; I don't want my kid buying any of that shit."

"You say Wagner's mistaken?"

"I say he's a goddamn liar."

"Well, you see, Tony, it's like this. I believe you do make clandestine loans to people, and that people who fail to pay what they owe become very accident-prone. They fall out of windows, and wander into dark alleys and get mugged, and pick fights with people twice their size. I sometimes wonder if there's a connection."

"Why don't you ask them if there's a connection?"

"None of them seem to want to talk about it. Until now."

"No, this is different. This guy didn't have an accident; according to you, someone set fire to his store on purpose."

"I assume you have an alibi for last Thursday evening?"

Vigotti leaned sideways to break the long ash into the little

47

ashtray. "Absolutely. I was home watching television with my wife and son."

"Any visitors?"

"No, but I had a couple of phone calls, last one about ten-thirty. What time did the fire start?"

"Sometime after eleven."

"Hell, I was in bed by eleven! What do you think, I sneaked out of bed with Constancia right there beside me so interested in her book she never noticed, and went driving off in my pajamas to throw a bomb through a store window?"

"Last time you wanted a firebomb thrown, you hired someone to do it for you, Tony."

"You are speaking, I think, of an incident where the kid changed that fairy tale for the truth, that he thought that up himself, for a prank. But if you're going to start with the accusations, I want to call my lawyer."

"I'm not accusing you of anything—yet. Has anyone you know gone on a sudden trip he maybe won't be back from?"

"I don't think so. Why?" Vigotti seemed genuinely puzzled, then his brow cleared. "Oh, the body, right? No, it's nobody I know."

"You sure?"

Vigotti glanced sideways at Brichter. "You aren't going to ask me to look at it, are you? 'Cause I ain't looking at no piece of burned meat that used to be someone. Ask around if you want, but you think I wouldn't notice if someone who hangs around isn't hanging around anymore?"

"No, I guess not."

"Sure." Vigotti sat back again and puffed on his cigar. "So what else do you want to know?"

"That's all for now."

"Good, I can go, then?"

"We'd better wait for Sergeant Dahl to get back. He may

48

have some questions for you. Thank you, by the way, for agreeing to come in like this and answer a few questions."

"Any time. How come you're working for him nowadays?"

"What makes you ask?"

Vigotti shrugged. "No reason. He just doesn't seem your type."

4

I HOPE I made a good decision here, thought Dahl, ducking hastily into an opening in traffic on the belt line. Obie's a subtle bastard, and sharp as hell. I hope he don't find out I picked him up on purpose and get to wondering why.

But it wasn't as if Dahl had a choice. His expenses alone made action imperative. He'd cut way back on the graft when the new Chief took over, like everyone else. But now, with Internal Affairs breathing down his neck, he'd had to cease activities altogether. Too bad the bills didn't slow down: car payments, house payments, child support, the riverfront property up in Wisconsin he'd stupidly agreed to buy on a contract for deed, the new suits, the good shoes, the vacation in the Bahamas already contracted for.

Used to be, Internal Affairs was a joke. Now, a pair of hot dogs worked there, and they were like smoke alarms once they got a whiff of something. And Eddie was hot as a pistol, he knew that. So he needed a friend, someone who could protect him.

Brichter was perfect: bright, hard, so clean it hurt to look at him in sunlight. And he was married to lots and lots of very clean money. Even better, his wife was hanging out with the Chief's wife. So make friends with Brichter, and, if you can, get next to the wife and impress the hell out of her. The smell of clout and money would drive out the smell of smoke.

It wasn't as if Eddie were a bad cop. He was a fast, aggressive investigator, and made a lot of arrests. He knew his city well, had plenty of contacts and informants. He knew where the really bad guys lived, where the bawdy houses were, the gambling establishments, the shooting galleries. He firmly believed most of what went on in these places were crimes only because self-righteous legislators said they were—often the morning after visiting them.

Victimless crimes, the kind where buyer and seller were equally willing, should be removed from the books, according to Eddie. Even drugs. Any airhead who allowed himself to get sucked into addiction deserved to be eaten alive. It was evolution in action.

And Eddie's role in this continuing evolution had been to allow the public to have what it wanted, within limits. It couldn't be stopped, but it should be controlled.

Eddie's opinion notwithstanding, some things remained illegal. And Eddie had expenses. So in return for his protection certain people had contributed to the Eddie Dahl Welfare Fund. Which contributions had dried up since the city got religion and put Malcolm Cunningham in charge of the police department. Malcolm wouldn't last, human nature being what it was, but meantime Eddie would have to go with the flow, and cross himself piously whenever Malcolm looked his way, just like everyone else.

Dahl was so busy with his thoughts he nearly went by his exit and had to cut across a honking lane of traffic to make it.

A few minutes later he was pulling up to a garage in the middle of a row of town houses. Toby Modreski's place.

Modreski had been one of the poker players last Thursday night. He worked at County General Hospital and kept very screwy hours; Dahl was therefore able to arrange this meeting during his own normal working day. He found Modreski in bathrobe and slippers, drinking coffee and watching a soap opera. His wife, he explained, was at work.

Modreski went to snap off the TV. He was tall, with a long, bony face and a great beak of a nose between deep-set blue eyes. "Always glad to cooperate, of course. Can I get you something? A drink? No, that's wrong, isn't it? Have a seat. Would you like a cup of coffee?"

"No, thanks," said Dahl, sitting on the near end of the couch, his cop antennae extending. Modreski was just a little more nervous than the ordinary citizen being interviewed by a cop should be. Dahl went through the usual preliminaries of getting the name spelled right and the several phone numbers at which Modreski could be reached, taking care not to further alarm his subject. "You're not a doctor, right?"

"That's right. My degrees are in business and hospital administration. My title at County General is Assistant Administrator."

"How long have you known Dave Wagner?"

Modreski said "Ahem," and thought. "Four years? Maybe longer." He sat down on the very front edge of the recliner and leaned forward, elbows on knees, hands loosely clasped. "I went to grad school with Mur—who is Murray Jones—and he knew Dave from somewhere way back. When my wife and I bought this town house, Mur said he had a friend who could get me a good buy on a TV set and VCR. And that was Crazy Dave Wagner. Mur was right, Dave gave me a real deal. But he's probably won back four or five times what he saved me on the stuff I bought."

Surprisingly, Modreski blushed. "I mean—" He reached forward and picked up his cup from a butcher's-block coffee table. "We just play for fun." The cup was empty, but he seemed unsure whether to put it back down or not. "Poker," he added.

"But you do play poker for money, right?"

"Ha. I mean—yes. Just friendly games, and the stakes are pretty low. And not very often. Well, not that not very often." He stopped, boggling a little at the tangle he'd made of his sentence, and glanced at Dahl, who was tactfully not writing any of this down. "Twice a month," he conceded.

"You always play at Ron Tollefson's place?"

"No, it moves around. It's supposed to be everyone taking turns, but it's most often my place or Ron's. Mur's wife doesn't like him gambling, Dennis lives even further out than I do, and Dave moved into this closet-size apartment last year and there's not room for five people in it. I mean, it's not a slum, but the bed comes down out of the wall."

"Did you take that as evidence his business was failing?"

"No, he seemed to have money otherwise. He did at least his share of calling the bets, and bought the snacks and beer when it was his turn. I took it as evidence he was spending most of his nights at his girlfriend's place and only rented this apartment so he'd have a place to pick up his mail."

"What's his girlfriend's name?"

"I haven't got any idea. In fact, I don't know that he's got a girlfriend. I only assumed he did, as an explanation for the dinky apartment. Ron, Denny, Mur, and I were laughing about it the night of the fire, making up descriptions about her and her job—you know, making her a cow and saying she cleaned cages at the zoo. Because he never talked about her."

"What did he say to the teasing?"

53

"Who?"

"Wagner."

Modreski leaned forward and put his cup on the table. "He wasn't there."

"I thought he was there the whole time."

Without looking at Dahl, Modreski said, "No, he'd forgot the beer, and it was his turn, so out he goes."

"What time was this?"

Modreski sat back in his chair. "He wasn't gone very long, you know. Hopped in his car and was back in no time at all."

"You're sure he took his car?"

"Yes, I'm sure. Because he always goes to this one liquor store, because the store always has his brand of beer, y'know? Shell's or Snell's, from would-you-believe Minnesota. I've never seen it sold anyplace else in town. And that's the kind he came back with."

"What time did he go out?"

Modreski blew until his hollow cheeks filled. "He said he bet he'd be back in less than twenty minutes, so I remember looking at my watch. We played four-handed while he was gone. He came back and said, 'See? Twenty minutes,' and I said 'No, twenty-two and a half minutes.' He said I had to deduct a minute going down in the elevator and a minute coming up." He glanced at Dahl and blew again. "It was eleven twenty-three by my watch when he got back."

"So he left at eleven-oh-one?"

"Yeah. He came back with the beer and a big bag of cheese curls, and Ron got a bowl out for the curls, and we popped open the beer and took a break from the cards."

"Was it during that break you saw the fire?"

"Yes. But there wasn't remotely enough time for him to go to the liquor store, buy the beer, then drive all that way to his place, which is not on the way—the opposite, in fact— dump kerosene on everything and set it on fire, and get back

54

to us. He was gone twenty-two minutes, just long enough to get to the liquor store and back."

"What's the name of the liquor store?"

"Ogden's. It's on Fourth and Washington. West Washington."

"Funny one of you didn't mention this before."

Modreski picked up his coffee cup and peered into it again. "Dave asked us not to," he said. "We met Saturday night and talked about it, and he showed us how there couldn't've been time for him to get to Ogden's and his place both and back in the time he was gone—but, he said, cops like to mark their cases solved—" He stopped. "Anyhow, we agreed not to mention it."

"So why are you telling me about it now?"

Modreski continued looking into his cup, as if finding the answer there. "Because I don't like lying to the police. Dave wouldn't burn his own place down, I know that. That store was his life. And like he said, there just wasn't time for him to do it in the time he was gone. So the truth can't hurt him."

· · ·

Dahl drove back into town, heading for the warehouse district; then rethought his strategy and stopped by a phone booth. He dropped a quarter into the slot and dialed a number from his notebook.

"Murray Jones, please," he said when someone answered, and waited.

"Mr. Jones? This is Sergeant Dahl, Homicide. I know what you told me when I talked to you before, but I just want to check: Did Mr. Wagner by any chance leave your poker game last Thursday evening for a time, returning with beer and a snack to share with you and the other players?"

"Uh," said Mr. Jones, "well . . ." And it transpired that Jones's amended story was virtually identical to Toby Modreski's. Wagner had gone out at eleven and returned about twenty minutes later with two six-packs of that Minnesota beer he liked and a big bag of cheese do-jiggies; and yes, a few minutes after opening a can of that same beer, he, Murray Jones, had spotted distant flames out the big living-room window. Jones hadn't meant to lie, but Dave was a good guy, and why distract the investigators by sending them on a wild-goose chase? There was no way Dave could've gone for beer and to his appliance store both, not in the time he'd been gone.

Dahl went from the phone booth to Wagner's building. As he hoped, the little jerk was there, watching a bulldozer with a big toothed scoop shove down blackened brick walls and push the rubble into the basement. Four battered dump trucks blocked half the street, waiting to haul away the leftovers. Wagner, looking tired and depressed, was sitting on a front fender of his black LeBaron. He was not aware of Dahl's arrival until the detective clapped a hand on his shoulder.

Wagner jumped. "What—! Oh, it's you, Sergeant. See them over there? Do you know what it's costing me to have them do that?"

"No, but I—"

"Twenty grand! Can you imagine it? It cost six thousand alone to get the sewer disconnected! I just lost my livelihood, and they're charging me to get rid of the remains! Don't ever buy a building. 'Buy land,' my gran'dad used to tell me; 'they ain't making any more of it'; and he was right. But he forgot to warn me: 'Don't buy land within city limits that's got a house or a store or even so much as a pigsty on it.' "

"Gee, I guess things are tough for you right now, Mr. Wagner. I bet you could use a drink. Maybe you should stop by your friend Mr. Tollefson's place on your way home and see if there's any of that Minnesota beer left over from your poker game."

Wagner didn't move for just a second, then he hopped off the fender and walked away, hands stuffed into the back pockets of his jeans. His black sweatshirt said in cream letters: "Life Is a Bitch and Then You Die." Dahl let him go, and in less than a minute Wagner turned and came back. "Who told you?"

"Does it matter? But it wasn't just one of them."

"Are you going to arrest me again?"

"You haven't been arrested once, yet. But it's not smart to lie, and even dumber to try to get witnesses to lie for you; now I'm going to have to double-check every item that's gone by you on its way to me. It annoys me having to do that, Mr. Wagner, and I get real hard to get along with when I'm annoyed."

"All right, I can appreciate that. And I'm sorry. I wish I'd stayed there the whole time. If I'd known, I would have. But it was my turn to buy the beer, so I just went out and got it. Got it and came straight back. It was my usual place, they may remember me. Ogden's, in the Charter LeGrande."

·   ·   ·

Ogden's Liquors was a small, shaggy establishment occupying an outside corner in the lesser of Charter's two downtown hotels. It was fourteen minutes from Wagner's building; Dahl had clocked it. The store reflected the in-progress gentrification of its neighborhood by featuring both cheap and expensive spirits and wines. A small chill box in the back was one-quarter soft drinks, three-quarters beer, including Schell's Deer brand from exotic Minnesota. Dahl lifted a six-pack out of the box, then continued looking around. There were dusty bottles of mixer and, down one side of a short aisle, flavored popcorn, potato chips, corn chips, cheese curls, and several kinds of peanuts.

The man behind the counter asked, "Can I help you find something?"

Dahl came over to the counter and displayed his gold badge and ID card.

"Can I help you with something, sir," said the man. It was

not a question. He was bald, with a beer belly that sagged into his white apron.

"Maybe. What's your name?"

"Ogden Koch. I own this place."

"You know a guy named Dave Wagner? Owns Crazy Dave's TV and Appliance."

Koch said warily, "Not away from here."

"He a regular?"

"Yeah."

"Did he come in last week?"

"Twice, I think."

"What days?"

The man scratched his belly. "Monday and Wednesday?"

"Are you sure it was Wednesday?"

Koch shrugged. "No."

"Could it have been Thursday?"

"Sure."

"What time Thursday?"

Koch sighed and thought. "Okay, late. He was my last customer. I remember because he usually comes in earlier, on his way home from work. Like he did on Monday." Koch frowned. "Or maybe it was Tuesday."

"Never mind Monday or Tuesday. How late on Thursday?"

"After eleven. Ten, maybe quarter past. He bought that same brand you got there, Schell's Deer brand, which is what he always buys, except he bought two six-packs instead of his usual one, and a jumbo-size bag of something—popcorn, I think. And a *Racing Form*."

"Did he seem in a hurry?"

The man shrugged. "He said, 'Who do you like for the Exacta on Saturday?' And I said, 'I heard Lamplighter's ankles were sore,' And he said, Thanks for the tip' and 'I got to get back to my poker game,' and he left. He's a sporting man, I guess."

58

"You're sure about the time?"

"Yeah, because late-night business has been lousy, and I've been closing up early. He was my last customer, the only one I'd had for an hour, and I locked the door not too long after he left, at eleven-thirty." He looked at the beer. "You want that?"

"Yeah."

Koch's fingers punched stiff keys on the old-fashioned cash register. "That'll be two-fifty."

"No, pal; this is evidence, see?"

"Of what?"

"Of whether or not someone's lying to me."

"You gonna give me a receipt?"

"For a lousy two and a half bucks?"

"If I owed it to them, they'd come after me."

.   .   .

Dahl went back to his squad room. That shithead Koch had spoiled his plans for beer with his supper with his insistence on a receipt—but on reflection, maybe it was just as well. Brichter was big on details, and Dahl was out to keep him happy. He shoved the bag into a desk drawer. Thinking of Brichter made him reach for the phone. He punched a four-digit number and told Brichter, "Wagner's alibi fell apart, then pretty much put itself back together." He explained, concluding, "Modreski's right; it wouldn't't've been possible for him to get to the liquor store, go to his appliance store and get back to Tollefson's place in twenty-two minutes. It took me fourteen minutes to drive from Wagner's store to the liquor store, nine and a half to get from Ogden's to Tollefson's condo, and eleven to get from Tollefson's to Wagner's again. Even running it at night won't change things much; it's not the traffic so much as it's all one-way streets and the lights being set at twenty-eight miles an hour through that whole district. So that's thirty-four and a half minutes travel time right there, plus he must've spent four or five minutes in the liquor store,

59

and he had to go clear down into the basement of his place to knock that guy in the head. Jones says he was gone twenty minutes, and Modreski, who claims he looked at his watch when Wagner left and again when he got back, for the purpose of timing him, says it was twenty-two and a half minutes, including the ride in the elevator, to make the trip. I got hold of some of that beer; it's a brand I never heard of before. The liquor-store owner says he's the only place in town that carries it."

"So the alibi hasn't completely fallen apart, then."

"No, it's just a little bit more real, even, don't you think? I mean, like you said, one reason guys hire torches is so they can set up solid alibis, right? And here he's setting himself up a beauty, and then he spoils it by leaving at a critical time. And another thing: Dennis Baer says Eddie was wearing new white sneakers that night, and he figures they'd've noticed if he came back with blood on them, or if he smelled of smoke or gasoline. Anyhow, why would Wagner want to kill someone he'd hired to do the job? You got anything on Vigotti?"

"Not much. I asked Philadelphia PD for a report and they said they'd get back to me. New York has nothing on him, he beat an extortion rap in Trenton back in the fifties, and he did a little jail time in Atlantic City. But he's from Philadelphia; he moved here nine years ago from there."

"Good work. I think we're close to breaking this one, so what do you say to a little celebration? I'll buy, you choose the place."

"My wife is expecting me home for dinner."

"Yeah, and with that sweet thing waiting, who wants to go out with a homely guy like me? See you tomorrow."

5

"**B**UY you a refill, Cris?" asked Dahl.
McHugh looked up. He had been sitting alone in a small booth in his favorite watering place. His wife was working late and he preferred coming home to a house she already had lit up for him. "What do you want, Eddie?"

"To buy you another of whatever you're drinking, okay?"

McHugh was about to say no, then sighed. "Oh, what the hell. Scotch and water, no ice."

Dahl hurried off, placed the order and came back. "Here y'go!" he said cheerily, sitting down across from McHugh and pushing the heavy glass toward him. McHugh was a larger-than-life type, with a lived-in face quick to show whatever emotion he cared to convey. It was currently looking wary, but nevertheless a thick hand reached for and took possession of the glass.

Dahl was drinking beer himself. He took a sip and asked, "So, how's tricks with you?"

"Fine."

"Yeah, with me, too." Dahl took a deeper pull at his beer, licked suds away with a fast, narrow tongue. "Obie and me are doing pretty good with that arson case we're working together."

"Uh-huh." McHugh stirred himself enough to take a sip of his drink, then stirred himself further to look interested. Dahl smiled; he'd ordered Chivas instead of the house brand, and McHugh was one of those who could taste the difference. "Making any progress?" asked McHugh.

"Oh, sure. Obie's one sharp guy, y'know? Right in there with the right questions, never misses a thing. I'm learning technique from him all the time. Only, y'know, he's kind of hard to get to know." Dahl's narrow face twisted sideways in an effort to abstract. "Like he's got a wall up around him. I keep trying to let him know I'm his friend, but I don't know, he doesn't respond somehow. He's hard to talk to on a personal level."

McHugh nodded. "He's hardly ever anxious to make friends."

"Yeah, but you're a friend of his, right? How'd you do it?"

"Helped him out when he asked me to."

"Yeah, well, he isn't asking me for any help at this time."

"So maybe you should wait until he does."

Dahl hunched forward, hands overlapping around the glass of beer. "No, you don't understand. I think being friends will help us work together better. This is a complicated case we're working on, and I want it to end in a good bust, so someone goes to jail. I get this feeling he don't trust me all the way, and I need to kind of push him over that."

"There's no way anyone can push Brichter over anything, Eddie. If he's made up his mind about you, you're not gonna change it in a hurry, I don't care what you do."

"So give me something that will work over a long time, okay? This is one of those cases, y'know? Could go on for months."

"You're asking an awful lot for the price of a Scotch and water."

"Can I buy you another?"

McHugh's mouth twitched and he wiped it with the edge of his hand. "No, I've got to head for home in a couple of minutes." But Dahl kept looking earnest, and McHugh sighed. "All right. He seems to be a real hard case, but he isn't. It's all front; like you say, a wall, built around a sensitive, super-bright softy. Now the wall is real, and he defends it; on the other hand, he does let people in. About one person a year gets to stay, and it's almost never the one who comes yelling and banging on the door. You got to be subtle. Be friendly, but don't keep pointing out how much you'd like to be his friend. And watch for signs. I mean, maybe he already likes you. He's not gonna take out an ad in the paper to let you know."

"What will he do?"

McHugh thought. "He'll start talking about his car. Or, if he really likes you, his wife."

"He gave me a ride in his Porsh the other day, told me he scared himself the first time he wound it all the way up. Is that like what you mean?"

McHugh nodded. "On the other hand, he doesn't like people who pronounce it 'Porsh.' "

"Huh?"

"It's pronounced POR-shuh. Like his vanity plates say."

"Oh." Dahl blinked, then laughed. "Oh, I get it: Portia! Kind of a reminder how to say it. Okay, so I pronounce it Porsche and just go on being nice to him, right?"

McHugh took another sip of his drink. "The only people he lets be nice to him are people he doesn't like."

63

Dahl frowned, baffled, then decided this was one of McHugh's more subtle jokes and grinned. "Not even his wife?"

"You want to be his friend? Be very careful to him about his wife. She's his soft spot."

"Because of the money?"

"That, too. But haven't you noticed he's not as likely as he used to be to open you up, scoop out your intestines and hand them to you?"

Dahl wasn't prepared to say he thought it was Brichter's sudden wealth that made others find him more amiable. "Well . . ."

"Sure you have. He saw her one time and turned from Mr. Razor-Lips into Cupid's Favorite Plaything. Once I stopped laughing, I felt sorry for the poor bastard. Fortunately, she decided she liked him, too; and after they got the honeymoon out of their systems, he settled down into someone almost nice to have around. Oh, he's still got a mouth on him, but his heart isn't in it like it used to be."

"What's she like?"

"About as good and gentle a person as you'd ever hope to meet."

Dahl was surprised. "I only seen her a few times, but it seems to me she's always looking like she smells a dead fish."

"That's because she's shy. She grew up all alone out on that ranch, never met people her own age, had exactly one friend, that Professor Ramsey who teaches history at the college. It's a good thing he was also a friend of Pete's, because Pete about scared her to death, coming on so hard and fast after he got her away from that piece of filth who was her uncle. It was Ramsey who explained to him why he should back off, and to her that Pete meant no harm. She's not as bad as she used to be, but she still likes people to approach her gently, give her time to get to know them. In that respect she's very much like him. After that she's a pushover, especially if they're kind to animals, carry a badge, or know something about medieval history. And if she really likes someone, sooner or later Pete will, too."

"Pete?"

"The one way you'll know he's decided you're his friend is that he'll ask you to call him Peter."

•   •   •

They were sitting in the living room after dinner. He was reading *Motor Trend* and she was reading an extra-thick edition of *Arabian Horse World*. Michael lay on a strip of carpeting in front of the fireplace, and all was quiet and domestic. Brichter felt her eyes on him and looked up from his magazine.

"Don't forget," she said, "fighting practice in the barn on Sunday. By the way, Rose says St. James wants us to put on a demo on the church lawn for their Mayfair this spring. You'll be there, I hope. They want a tourney, and we need another fighter."

The local branch of the Society for Creative Anachronism kept its educational attribute honor bright by putting on public demonstrations of medieval foot jousting, crafts, music, and dance. Brichter preferred the closed-door, just-us type of event for several reasons. "I suppose Mrs. Cunningham has already told her husband that one of his detectives is also Lord Stefan von Helle, Esquire to Baron Sir Geoffrey."

She smiled. "He's coming to the Mayfair just to get a look at your eccentric self."

"You're kidding."

She laughed at the expression on his face. "Of course I am! He's agreed to shill for the ring-toss booth."

"How did he get talked into that?" Chief Cunningham was very insistent on maintaining the dignity of his office, to compensate for the shame that had been brought on it by his predecessor.

"When Rose wants something, she generally gets it. She

65

even got our sexton, who is at least as huffy as Malcolm, to agree to sit on the bench in the ducking booth."

Chief Cunningham's wife was chairing the Mayfair Committee, Kori was her most committed volunteer co-worker, and they were becoming fast friends. Kori continued, "But I think the best part will be watching Malcolm calling, 'Roll up, roll up! Three rings for a quarter!' "

"Malcolm?"

"She calls me Kori and I call her Rose. We talk about our respective Peter and Malcolm—he sounds a perfect lamb when he gets home and puts his gun away. Rather like you. Interim Police Chief Malcolm Cunningham is such a mouthful; what do you call him?"

"Sir."

She giggled. "Actually, Peter, it's a very good cause. Half the money we raise goes to the Food Shelf and the other half to start a battered women's shelter. And the committee is all excited about having us joust on the church lawn."

"Oh, all right, count me in. But for a group of High Church Episcopalian ladies, you have some strange ideas about suitable religious entertainment. Fighting in armor, ducking the sexton. What next, the stake?"

"We're church-militant, remember. Anyway, it's not all violence; they want us to do a maypole dance as well."

"I hope you didn't explain the meaning behind the maypole—phallus and fertility rites and all that."

"I didn't need to; when was the last time you saw me dress in homespun and bonnet for church? Episcopalians are not exactly Puritans; we know where babies come from, and most of us approve of the method of starting them. We gave up churching women after childbirth a long time ago." She put her magazine down. "Speaking of which—"

"Sweet Jesus," he groaned, "yet more trouble. Will you lay off about a baby? No, that's wrong. Think about that baby,

66

all right? What kind of life would he have? Abused children become abusive parents, remember? And we were both abused children.''

"Not always, they don't. And I'm not so sure I was an abused child.''

"A criminal uncle got custody of you after murdering your parents and kept you prisoner on this ranch for fourteen years. Somehow I interpret that as abuse.''

"It wasn't like being in prison. I went here and there—horse shows, museums. He loved me, Peter.''

"He was scared you'd tell on him.''

"No, he wasn't. How could I, when I didn't remember anything about it? Only at the end, when I started having nightmares that turned out to be memory, then he got scared. But you rescued me, and took me out into the wide world, and held my hand so I wouldn't be afraid, and I fell in love with you and married you. Somehow that isn't such a sad story. And it's only scary in one little place.''

"So you think it's okay to lock a kid up close to home: no pajama parties, no summer camp, no secret experiments with lipstick in the school rest rooms.''

"I wouldn't dream of locking up a child. Nor would you.''

"No, I wasn't locked up; my father beat me.''

"Yes, when he was drunk. Have you ever been drunk?''

"Twice.''

"And you're what? Thirty-six? That must be some sort of record.''

"Thirty-six is too old to start a family.''

"It can be worrisome if the woman is thirty-six. But I'm only twenty-four.''

"*Fy'n galon*—''

"Don't call me that when we're quarreling, unless you're ready to quit.''

"I've been ready to quit since this morning.''

67

"To yield, then."

He stood. "Very well. Mrs. Brichter, will you excuse me?" And he put on a jacket and went out to go roaring off in his beautiful car, driving too fast over miles of back roads and thumping the steering wheel between gear changes.

.   .   .

Brichter found McHugh in a booth in the back of a bar not far from the Safety Building.

"Can I give you a ride home?" he asked, easing himself into the seat opposite.

"What are you doin' here?"

"Looking for you. I need to talk to you. Are you sober enough to listen?"

"Sure. Who tol' you where I was? Eddie Dahl?"

"Laura. She figured you stopped for a while and forgot to keep track of time."

"She's a very unnerstanding woman, you know that?"

"Yes."

McHugh squinted at Brichter. "But you and Kori went a round or two this evening."

"What makes you say that?"

"I'm a con man, remember? Even pie-eyed, which I am not, I can tell when a man's got his jaw screwed down tight. What's the problem?"

"Katherine thinks we should have a baby."

McHugh laughed. "Terrific; it's about time!" He caught Brichter's wince and said, "Aren't you glad?"

"No. I'd make a rotten father, and I can't believe she really understands what being a mother is. She's got this romantic dream of the rosy cherub sleeping in a cradle draped with ribbons, and I can't talk any sense into her. She'd never even held a baby until Susan handed Benjamin to her. He's one of those nice, cheerful babies that happens one time in a thousand, and based on just him, she's decided she wants one."

"You're sure it's just that?"

"What else can it be? Hell, we had this all out before we got married. She was an only child, and so was I. She never got to play with kids when she was one, and she's had very little contact with them since. I didn't like being a kid, and I don't like being around them now. But it's not just her ignorance and my dislike. Both of us tend to hide our emotions; we can only just stand to hold hands in public. If we ever had a kid we'd have to hire someone to come around and hug it, or it would never find out what a hug was."

"Bull."

"What?"

"Bull. Anyone who has been around the two of you for more than a day knows there is some kind of primal bond there. The relief I feel because you *don't* explore one another's erogenous zones in public cannot be measured in finite terms, but in no way connerdicts my belief that you have a singe problem with the wallpaper in your bedroom. Go on, Pete, have a kid. He'll make Susan's Benjamin look like the world's smallest curmudgeon."

"Do me a favor, McHugh?"

"Anything."

"Stay away from my wife until I talk her out of this. Now finish your drink. It's time you went home."

McHugh was led outside, where the cold air made him whoop and then break into song, though he shut up again once put into the passenger side of Brichter's car. "I thought we were takin' my car," he said, rolling down the window.

"You think I'm going to leave mine parked outside a bar at this hour of the night? I'd come back and find a few crumbs of glass to glue into my memory book. You can walk over from work and retrieve your car tomorrow."

"You're right, you know that? You're completely right."

Brichter got in his side and started the engine. "What do you know about Tony Vigotti?"

"The man who knows ever'thing is asking *moi?*"

"Who says I know everything?"

"Everyone. We talk about it sometimes. It's my theory your mother was frightened by the Library of Congress."

"Your theory's a load of old codswallop. It took considerable time and effort to become as offensively knowledgeable as I am. Roll up the window, will you? It's cold."

"Sure," said McHugh, obeying. "You actually study up on all that weird stuff?"

"No, I dance naked at midnight around a stack of esoterica, repeating an ancient secret chant, and the data stored in the scrolls is magically transferred to my brain."

McHugh nodded. "I thought it was something like that."

"For example, on my last dance I learned that there is less violence involved in loan-sharking than is commonly thought. That, in sober fact, loan sharks are fairly patient with borrowers who fall behind—after all, the interest just keeps piling up."

McHugh chuckled and asked, "If that's a sober fact, what would a drunk fact be?"

"You in my front seat."

"I ain't drunk, jus' a little tired. So what makes you think Tony Vigotti is any different from the average loan shark?"

"Nothing. I'm asking you: Is he different?"

McHugh shrugged. "He's quicker than the normal shark to play rough."

"Even right now? I hear Joe Januschka's ordered all his people to run quiet for a while, until Chief Cunningham becomes less of a new broom."

McHugh made a waving gesture. "Well, I heard some of Tony's customers thought that meant they could slow down on making payments, and found out Tony's not the type to pay attention to Joe Januschka if it's going to cost him money."

"Can he get away with that?" Brichter slowed for a light, which turned green just as he came to a complete halt.

"Sure. A loan shark is a free agent. Tony's connected, but his loan business is his own. Joe don't own a piece of that; he gets no cut. Tony may feel Joe has no right to order him to lay off." He looked out the window. "Where are we going?"

"I'm taking the long way home, so we can talk some more. Okay?"

"Sure. What was I saying?"

"What about Tony's customers? Some of them are connected, too, aren't they? Won't they complain to Joe if Tony cuts rough with them?"

"He hardly ever has to lean on the wise guys. They know the rules. Besides, the kind of wise guy that uses a shark uses him all the time. Take bookies, for example. Every so often someone's gonna run a winning parlay on you. You can't go to First Federal and ask for a loan, right? So you use a shark. If you welsh, what happens next time a customer hits you for some big money? The shark's gonna tell you to go climb a tree, that's what."

Brichter's sideways smile appeared. "I suppose. Now say I'm a businessman with a money problem. I'm not connected; how do I obtain the services of a loan shark?"

"You talk to everyone about your problems and hope someone who knows a loan shark will make an introduction, which he will if he thinks you're okay. The go-between is usually someone who's a customer of the shark himself. It's not unknown for bookies to offer the services of their favorite loan shark as a perk to their customers."

"You think that's how Dave Wagner met Tony Vigotti?"

"I don' know diddly about Wagner. He may be a good businessman, he may be a bad businessman. But hear this: Most people who go to loan sharks get into and out of the relationship with no problems. The ones who get in serious trouble with loan sharks tend to be gamblers, or embezzlers, people whose problems are ongoing rather than short-term. Tony's not a mind

71

reader; he can't always tell why a person has come to him. And, of course, he's in the business of loaning money to crooks and bad risks. He tries to make up for this by landing hard on people who fail to meet their obligations.''

"So, okay, let's suppose I'm a potential customer: Just how much interest would I be charged?''

"Depends on how much you borrow. I think Vigotti could probably loan you fifty big ones, easy. If you're already a customer, and never gave him any problems, his interest rate on something that size might be five percent, or even as low as two. He likes those vig loans. They can go on forever, as long as the borrower wants to make just the interest payments." McHugh rolled down the window to sniff the air. He had a quick metabolism and was already nearly sober. "Let's turn this around. Say you want to be a loan shark. You loan someone five Gs.'' He rolled the window up again. "You charge three points a week—three percent. That's a hundred and fifty dollars. That's a week, Pete. Week after week, without a nickel of it going to reduce the principal.''

"Not every loan is a vig loan, though.''

"True. The other kind are knockdown loans. You loan someone a thousand dollars and collect a hundred a week for thirteen weeks, then turn around and loan it out again.''

"Less what your muscle charges you for the occasional kneecapping," said Brichter dryly. "Still, maybe I should discuss loan-sharking as an investment possibility next time I meet with my banker. Meanwhile, how likely do you think it is that Vigotti decided he didn't need any more grief from Crazy Dave and had him burned down?''

"Oh, it's something he's capable of, absolutely. But I'd have thought he'd try running a bust-out on him first. You know what a bust-out is?''

Brichter nodded. The owner of a business allows, or is forced to allow, a crook to become a silent—but controlling

72

—partner. The crook uses the owner's credit to buy merchandise, equipment, office supplies, anything he can, and doesn't pay the bills. He sells everything fast and cheap, pockets the money and walks out, leaving the owner bankrupt. "But in Dave Wagner's case," said Brichter, "Wagner was already busted. Vigotti couldn't have ordered a gross of pencils in Wagner's name except for cash on delivery."

McHugh shook his head. "Then I'd say a smart investigator like yourself should be looking for a previous pattern of arson you can legally introduce in a courtroom during Tony's trial."

• • •

Vigotti stayed in the dark-windowed car until it had pulled into the big garage and stopped, then used the door that went directly from the garage into Januschka's house. He was shown to the den by Januschka's bodyguard.

The room had recently been remodeled and now resembled a wealthy lawyer's office. Vigotti stood still a moment, waiting for his eyes to adapt. Dark paneling and green-shaded lamps made a dim cavern of the room. One wall was all books in matching sets, the lettering on their spines making tiny golden gleams in the murk.

"How ya doin', Tony?" came a rough voice. Januschka, a large shape in a tufted-leather club chair, was the speaker.

"Fine, Joe. What are you, trying to save on electricity or something?"

"Hey, don't you know class when you see it? This room cost me twenty-eight thousand dollars!"

"Sure I know class—when I can see it."

Januschka laughed. "Come over and sit. Want a bourbon?"

"Thanks." Vigotti crossed the lush carpet, which was deep brown or rich wine, he couldn't say for sure which, and took the other club chair. Over here the light was better and he could see that under the banter and behind the smiling coarse features, Januschka was seriously angry. Vigotti licked his lips and wished for a cigar. Joe had quit smoking and wouldn't let anyone smoke in his house.

There was a little table beside Januschka's chair. On it were a silver tray, an insulated ice bucket, a decanter, and two thick-bottomed glasses. Januschka put a single cube into each glass with a pair of tongs and sloshed a generous dollop of liquor over them.

"Thanks," Vigotti said again, taking his and tasting it. "Why do you want to see me? And why did I have to sneak in like that?"

"I don't want anyone to see you visiting me. You're very hot right now, you know. I hear Brichter's on to you."

Vigotti snorted. "Shit, he's got nothing."

"He always starts out with nothing. Then he gets plenty. If it was just Eddie Dahl, I wouldn't worry. But that goddamn Brichter—"

"Brichter won't find anything because there's nothing to find."

"Have you quit being a shy?"

"Hell, no!" Vigotti frowned, wondering what Januschka was getting at. "You aren't going to ask for a look at my books, are you? Because I'm not—"

"I asked you over to find out why you haven't laid off the rough stuff," interrupted Januschka. "You know they're running a reform movement in town, you know all of our operations are supposed to be running real quiet until things cool off, you know the cops would like nothing better than to make a case against your operation, and through you get to me. But I'm repeating myself; I told you all this a month ago."

"I did lay off," Vigotti said sullenly.

"No, you didn't. What's his name, Grenelski, he's been in the hospital a week now."

Vigotti took a big swallow of his drink. "He fell in his bathtub. He told everyone that."

"He told everyone that because you told him that if he told the truth, you'd send Nish over to talk to him again. That's also why Harry Geil says a hammer fell off a shelf and busted his kneecap. He's one of us, you know."

"All the more reason he should know better than to try to walk on me. What the hell am I supposed to do; let them think you've tied my hands? You know what that would mean!"

"You got so much money stashed away, you could afford to lose every nickel you got out on the street right now and hardly feel the pinch." Januschka took a swallow and continued, "But that's not the point; the point is, if I tell you to lay off, even if it means you eat crackers and milk the rest of your life, you lay off."

"You got no right—"

"I got every right. I got a duty even. What you're doing can screw all of us. You been operating on your own so long, you maybe forgot you're still signed up, that you got to answer to me. So tell me: Who did you hire to torch that building?"

Vigotti's eyebrows rose. "Torch what building? I didn't hire anyone!"

"Are you telling me you didn't burn Crazy Dave down?"

"That's right."

"You goddamn liar."

"It's the truth!" Vigotti leaned forward and put his glass on the tray.

"Then who the hell did?" asked Januschka.

"How should I know?"

There was a brief silence, then Januschka said softly, "You *fucking* liar."

"All right then, the little turd burned his own self down, for the insurance, so he could pay me off!"

"The cops say he's got an alibi."

"Sure he does! That's what they do, you know. They hire somebody, then make sure they got an alibi."

75

"Yeah, you know all about that, don't you?"

"You goddamn right I do! And if I hired someone to set that fire, how come my alibi is that I was home in bed, instead of out playing poker with four witnesses? Is this why you asked me over, so you could play prosecuting attorney with me?"

"You may need the practice. A month or two from now it could be State of Illinois versus Anthony Vigotti, on a charge of arson and murder."

"Murder? Like hell, murder! Crazy Dave hired some amateur who got caught in the fire he tried to set."

"The man in the fire was dead before the fire got to him."

"Where'd you hear that?"

"It was on the evening news. He died of a fractured skull. They got an autopsy report and everything."

Vigotti gave a brief, sharp nod. "So that's why Eddie Dahl's in charge of the investigation. Murder outranks everything. Otherwise, I wondered if someone finally got to Brichter. I mean, why else would he be taking orders from Eddie?"

"Stick to the point, Tony. The point is, we got Arson, Homicide, and Organized Crime dicks all looking right at you. We got to stop it now. Time was, we could buy and sell cops, evidence, a judge, whatever. It's harder now, but maybe I can still do something. But I need to know what they can find out before I can fix things. I need for you to quit lying to me."

"There's nothing for them to find, goddammit! Nothing! I didn't do it!"

"Next you'll be telling me you never loaned Dave Wagner a dime."

"Sure I did! I loaned that bastard thirty-six big ones! Three points a week I was charging him, and he couldn't even keep up with the juice. I finally told him he had two weeks to pay up the whole thing, including the back vig. The day after the deadline his place goes up in smoke. I call him, and he says he's insured, so everything's jake, not to worry. Then next

76

thing I hear, he's crying on the cops' shoulders, saying I burned him down, the shithead!''

"Well, someone did. The cops say there was 'evidence of accelerant.' ''

"Yeah, surprise. That's why I decided to stay out of the arson business. One sniff, and they call the fire marshal. And that murder thing's a crock; I remember hearing about a guy trying to have himself a successful fire, and he pours the gasoline here, and some more over there, and by the time he's got it like he wants it, the place is full of fumes. He lights a match and bam! the insurance goes to his widow. I bet you anything you want the same thing happened here.''

Januschka took another swallow. "Okay, okay. I suppose you been staying away from Wagner since he went to the cops?''

Sometimes Januschka asked a question like that, putting it casually, showing the answer he wanted, and all the while knowing what the real answer was. Vigotti, knowing this, hesitated.

And Januschka leapt into the hesitation furiously. "You goddamn stupid son of a bitch! What the hell do you use for brains anyhow?''

"What's he gonna do? Tell the cops he saw me in a grocery store? 'Cause that's what happened. Me and Howdy got him in between our grocery carts and smiled at him, then let him go. Never said one word. I bought fifty dollars' worth of groceries and went home. Wagner never saw Howdy before, so he can't even say for sure he was with me. All the scare —and I won't deny Wagner about peed his pants—was in Wagner's own head. That'll teach him to go to the cops about our private business.''

There was a long, angry silence on Januschka's part. "But you still say you didn't burn him down?'' he asked at last.

"Check it out: you'll find I ain't talked to anyone about a

77

torch job. And anyhow, all my people are accounted for, so who was it they found in the basement? It's nobody you or I know, Joe; I swear.''

Januschka swirled the melting ice cube in his glass, then finished his drink, put the glass on the tray beside Vigotti's. "Okay. Maybe we have to look for another angle on this one. I'm glad I had you over so we could straighten this out.''

"Me, too." Vigotti stood. "Anything else bothering you?''

"Plenty, but it's no concern of yours.''

"Look, I'm sorry. I guess I didn't understand how hard things are for you right now. I'll lay off everything, okay? I won't even talk rough at them for a while.''

"Good, but that's what I thought I heard from you a month ago." Januschka stood. "Come on, I'll walk you to the car for your ride home.''

．　　．　　．

When Brichter came into the bedroom that evening, she was already in bed, back to him, her long black hair in its nighttime braid.

He discarded his robe and slid between the crisp, fragrant sheets, put his head on the pillow and felt all desire for sleep vanish in the wake of another pressing need. He held his breath to listen. No, she wasn't asleep. "Tired?" he asked.

"Not especially," she murmured.

"Um, Mrs. Brichter . . .

"Seeing that our acquaintance is of such long standing," she said, rolling over to reach for him, "I think you might take the liberty of calling me Katherine." Which was her real name, the one he used in speaking of her, since he never called her Kori.

Needs are not always logical. Kori and Peter had been quarreling and he, who loved her desperately, needed comforting. So he turned to her. And she, with her need to comfort the one she was distressing, welcomed him.

6

"**P**ETER, will you be home tomorrow?"

"What's tomorrow, Saturday? I think so, why?"

"I'm going to contact the Labor Pool and see if they have any carpenter types looking for a short job, and if I do, I'll want you to supervise." Kori often hired casual laborers. She worked them hard, paid them well, and recommended the best of them to her friends.

"What needs doing?" asked Brichter.

"The maternity-shed roof is leaking; it needs new shingles on one end."

"And you want *me* to supervise? You know I can't tell a hammer from a screwdriver." This was scarcely an exaggeration; under directions amounting to "Hit it here, again; now here, and again," Brichter had managed to hammer out a suit of armor, but on completing this task, which he had undertaken only because of his oath of fealty to Sir Geoffrey, he had

79

allowed his membership in the Armorers' Guild to lapse and had been seen as recently as August hiring someone to replace a buckle on the grip of his shield.

"Yes, but you can tell when someone is working or loafing, can't you? I forgot; Mrs. Gonzales and I are waxing the floors this weekend, so I can't do it myself." Mrs. Morales was the Tretower cook and housekeeper.

"Oh. All right. Since I'm to supervise, how about I find the people for you, too?"

"Thanks, I'd be grateful for that." She resumed buttering her toast in silence. He was not always perceptive about her silences, but this one did not feel companionable.

"Are we still having our quarrel?"

"Yes."

"How long is this going to go on?"

"As long as it takes."

.   .   .

Brichter was writing up an interim report when McHugh came through and stopped to ask, "How's it going with the Wagner case?"

"There's movement. We've got three suspects: Vigotti, Wagner, and the usual Person Unknown. Vigotti's saying nothing, Wagner's scared stiff, and until we identify the body we have no lead on Mr. Person. But it's early days yet."

"Dahl behaving himself?"

Brichter shrugged. "He has the brownest nose in the department, but he seems to be doing his share of the work on this. Oh, hell, that reminds me . . ." He reached for his phone. "Katherine asked me to find two people from the Labor Pool to do some roof repair on the ranch this weekend. Replacing shingles on a shed."

"Do they have to be from the Labor Pool?"

"What do you mean?"

"Well, you haven't invited me out for a while."

80

"If you think I'm going to just hand you a chance to talk to her—"

"Whoa, take it easy. I'm trying to find something to do this weekend that doesn't involve drinking. Laura's company is sending her to Denver for the weekend, some kind of training session for company lawyers. I need something to keep me busy."

"I thought you were working on a sting."

"Not until late Saturday night. I need to be alert and sober, which I won't be if I sit home with the tube. I promise to behave and not hint I want to stay to supper."

"The deal is five-fifty an hour plus supper."

"I accept."

"Can you find a partner? She asked me to hire two people."

"No problem."

* * *

Dahl opened the door to the Organized Crime Unit squad room and stuck his hatchet face in. Brichter wasn't at his desk, and Dahl was about to withdraw when he heard the magic word. McHugh, back to the door, was on his phone.

"Sure," he was saying, "you know Mrs. Brichter could afford the best contractor in the state, even just to nail a few shingles on a roof. But she's got this cockamamy notion about sharing the wealth—weather forecast? No, why?" Pause. "Well, it's close to the end of November; what did you expect? No, okay, if you don't want to, that's fine. I've got a whole list of people I can call, no problem." McHugh hung up, but didn't immediately dial another number. In fact, he sat back with a discouraged air that made Dahl think perhaps that last call had been to a name near the bottom of his list.

Dahl slouched casually into the room. "Hi, Cris," he said.

McHugh turned around. "Obie's out."

"Yeah, but it's you I want to talk to. I hear you're looking for someone to help him out this weekend with a little carpentry."

81

"Where'd you hear that?"

"Well, for one place, right here. I open the door and you're getting a turndown for the job."

"So?"

"So why didn't you call me? You know I've done carpentry in my spare time for years."

"I thought you were an amateur electrician."

Dahl nodded, "That, too. I do a lot of things. So how about it?"

"I dunno."

"Why not? Brichter and me, we're getting along fine. I took your advice about him, and we're working along a lot smoother nowadays. And maybe if I come out there and do a good job, we can get along even better." Dahl put on his best seeking-approval look and McHugh sighed.

"Oh, what the hell. Pick me up at one-thirty. You don't need to bring any tools."

"Thanks, Cris. You won't be sorry—and I'm already grateful."

.   .   .

Saturday dawned gray and cold. Brichter found the twenty-four-hour weather channel and discovered the prediction was for cloudy and cold, followed by rain mixed with snow, probably before nightfall.

"Maybe we should call this off," he said at the breakfast table.

"No, Peter, we can't. I've got three mares who will foal in February, and they'll need a nice, dry, warm place to have their babies. The weather between now and then isn't likely to improve."

"What did horses do before there were people to build them maternity sheds?"

"Lose a lot of good-looking babies. It was survival of the lucky—those who happened to be born when the weather was

82

nice. But that was also before there were people willing to pay thousands of dollars for a good-looking foal, even if it was born on a messy day."

.   .   .

Kori and Brichter were on the porch when they saw a late-model car coming up the drive. They started down the sloping lawn to meet it. It crossed the racetrack and made a U-turn, coming to a stop at the front-lawn side of the barnyard. McHugh, in baggy overalls and frayed gray jacket, got out from the passenger side and waved. Then Dahl got out.

"Uh-oh," said Brichter.

"What's wrong?" asked Kori.

"Nothing," said Brichter. "You go back in the house."

"Why? Who's that man with Cris?"

"His name is Eddie Dahl."

"You're working with him, aren't you?"

"Yes. Go back in the house."

"Why? This is my job; you're only the foreman." And she stepped off the porch and started down the sloping lawn. He gritted his teeth and followed.

McHugh, prepared with an ordinary greeting, saw the expression on Brichter's face as he and Kori came up to them, and said, his voice falsely hearty, "You asked me to get a second man, and this guy says he's done a lot of carpentry work."

Dahl, in old workboots, stained khakis, and hooded gray sweatshirt, came around the car to smile at Kori, grin more broadly at Brichter. "I thought maybe you'd like someone with experience, so I volunteered," he said.

Brichter said, "It's not enough of a job that we need an extra volunteer after all, Eddie. Danny's here, and there's me and Cris, so you go back into town."

Dahl looked almost comically quashed and McHugh said, "Yeah, but then how do I get home?"

"I'll drive you."

Kori said, "Mr. Dahl, you said you know something about carpentry?"

"My uncle was a house builder. I must've shingled a thousand roofs when I worked summers for him."

"If we only need one person to help you and Danny," she said to Peter, "maybe it should be this one."

"But Pete promised me supper," said McHugh, genuinely disappointed. "And anyway, it'll hold things up for an hour if someone has to take me home now."

"Oh, for heaven's sake, then both of you stay," said Kori. "It's cold enough that you'll be glad to make short work of the job. Come on, I'll show you to the shed."

The maternity barn was the size of a double garage, painted cream with green trim. Danny, in patched riding pants and old brown jacket, had put a ladder up. Two knee-high stacks of green shingles were on the ground beside him.

Dahl, who really was a good amateur carpenter, went up first and showed Danny and McHugh how to remove the shingles they were replacing without damaging the good ones. Before long, several square feet of board were exposed.

"Oh, shit, look at this," said Dahl.

"What's the matter?" asked Danny.

Dahl pressed a finger into the wood, which gave like soggy newspaper. "The wood here is rotted real bad." He straightened and shouted for Brichter, who had gone to find another hammer.

"What do we need to do?" asked Brichter a few minutes later.

"Replace the wood," said Dahl. "You can shove a nail into this stuff with your bare hands, and the first windstorm will pull it right out again. We'll have to keep taking up shingles until we uncover all the rot."

"Good thing I bought extra shingles," said Danny.

McHugh said, "Yes, but how about wood? Are there any boards around the place?"

"There's fence boards," said Danny. "Plenty of them. Unpainted. And we've got a big old table saw, too, so we can cut them to size. It's old, but it works fine."

Dahl said, "Can we bring it out here? Then we won't have to keep running back and forth."

"Good idea," said Brichter. "Cris, you go with Danny and get the saw. Eddie and I will keep taking off shingles."

The saw was half-dragged, half-carried out, and then they discovered that there were only two of the heavy-duty orange extension cords available to bring power to it. Their combined length was not enough.

"Hey, I may have a cord in my trunk," said Dahl. He did, and the saw was set up near the ladder.

Nearly two-thirds of the shed roof had to be uncovered before the end of the rot was found. Soon the high-pitched snarl of lumber being sliced filled the barnyard, its pauses filled with the sound of nails being driven. Brichter insisted everything be done carefully despite the darkening sky and quickening wind. Dahl agreed. "Does you no good to do a job like this half-ass. You might as well not do it at all, because sure as gun's iron, you're gonna have to do it again." Danny and McHugh shortened their necks, blew on stiffening fingers, and kept their curses to themselves.

But finally the new boards were covered with new shingles. McHugh drove the last nail home as the first icy drops of rain bounced off the back of his head. The men hustled to put the ladder and saw away. Dahl grabbed an extension cord from Brichter and ran to put it in his trunk; and the men fled up the lawn to the big old house, where they were greeted by the warm smells of chili and cornbread.

The Tretower house had been built shortly after the Civil War, in that cluster of steep roofs and corbeled chimneys called Queen Anne style. It was much too big for just two people, but Kori had been raised in it; and Brichter, who had as much of the Victorian in him as the medieval, had to try hard not to show his extreme pride of shared ownership. Danny went to the half-bath downstairs while Brichter took Dahl and McHugh to the big one upstairs, with its boxed-in tub and dolphin-shaped fixtures. He smirked with satisfaction at Dahl's muttered "Holy shit."

Washed and thawed, they met in the formal dining room. Porcelain soup bowls on plates were covered in two instances with plain white envelopes, with McHugh's and Dahl's names printed on them, but the men sat anywhere and handed the envelopes back and forth. Dahl would have refused his, but saw McHugh tuck his away, so he shrugged and followed suit.

The table was long, with fat carved legs, and was covered with an immaculate linen cloth. The room was high, with ropes of plaster flowers draping the upper walls and dark wainscoting below. There were old paintings of sinewy horses showing the whites of their eyes at storms, at cougars, at being ridden sidesaddle by stoic ladies with improbably tiny waists. Dahl looked around and said, "Shouldn't we be eating in the kitchen? This room makes me feel like a bum."

"You shouldn't need a decent room in a decent house to make you feel like a bum, Eddie," said McHugh.

"Listen to who's talking," said Brichter, starting a swell of immense satisfaction in Dahl's breast—that collapsed when Brichter continued, "the man with a hole in the seat of his pants!"

McHugh said, "I don't have a hole in the seat of my pants!"

"Yes, you do," said Danny.

McHugh stood and twisted around, trying to see. "No, I don't."

When Kori came into the room a minute later carrying a big white tureen with pottery geese marching around it, she stopped in surprise. Danny, Dahl, and her husband were gathered to inspect the seat of McHugh's overalls.

"You can see his long johns through it," Danny was saying.

"Yeah, but there's threads across it, so it's not really a hole," said Dahl.

"If you gentlemen will be seated," said Kori, "I will put this down and you may serve yourselves."

"You be the judge, Mrs. Brichter," said Danny. "Would you say that's a hole in the seat of those pants?"

Kori spared a glance as she put the tureen on the table. "I'd say he could stand at least a patch, if not a new pair." She left the room again.

"I don't think it was nice of you to ask Mrs. Brichter to look at a hole in the seat of McHugh's pants," said Dahl piously, as the men sat down again, laughing.

"Yes, why'd you call her attention to it, Danny?" said Brichter, grinning. "Now he has to keep his back to her the rest of the evening."

"There's a couple of shingles left over," said Danny. "And some nails. Maybe we could work something out for him."

"Aw, come on, guys! They were okay when I put them on! Any hole in them I got sliding up and down that roof."

"Maybe you should sue Obie for damages," suggested Dahl.

McHugh leaned forward and murmured, "An old partner of mine shot a guy in the ass one time. The guy said he was gonna sue, but I asked him how'd he like to bend over and show his scar to a jury and he never said another word about it." He leaned back, smiling. "So I don't think I will, either." The men laughed.

87

Kori brought dishes of sour cream, chopped onion, grated cheese, and hot sauce, and the men began to fill their bowls and flavor them from the dishes. She went out once more and returned with a block of butter and a platter of cornbread. She took an empty place and asked, "What have I missed?"

"Nothing much," said Brichter.

"Just shop talk," said McHugh, winking.

Dahl tasted his chili and said, surprised, "Mrs. Brichter, this is really great stuff." In his experience, rich people's versions of poor people's food tasted terrible.

"Thank you," she said. "I'll pass your compliment on to our cook. Now, do go on; I love to hear shop talk."

There was a mildly embarrassed pause, then McHugh said, "I remember a time, back when I was in uniform, I stopped this pickup out on the edge of town for running a stop sign. The driver jumped out and took off, and I ran after him yelling 'Halt!' but he wasn't stopping. I didn't know what I had, an armed robber, an escaped felon, or what. He ran off the road into this field and I went after him. It was night, the light was bad, it was snowing and slippery as all get out. And, sure enough, I tripped and fell full-length into a puddle of slush. I was so doggone mad, I raised up and threw my flashlight at him—and I hit him smack on the back of his head, knocked him cold. Turned out he was only seventeen. He ran because he was drunk and driving his uncle's pickup without permission."

"Why didn't you shoot him?" asked Danny.

"Funny thing, I didn't even think about pulling my gun."

"In a situation like that you should have," said Dahl. "What do you think, Obie?"

"Maybe on some unconscious level Cris was aware the runner was just a kid," suggested Brichter. "The way he was running, the shape of him, something said he was a juvenile."

McHugh shook his head. "In the dark, and snowing? I think it was just pure dumb luck. But whatever, I'm glad I didn't shoot him. There would have been all kinds of hell to pay."

Dahl said, "Luck probably explains it." He pointed at Brichter with his spoon. "You're another one with luck, you know that?" He turned to the others. "I remember the time Obie and old Billy Bill were sharing a patrol car. They got a call to look for a prowler. Bill was driving, so when they came up this alley and spotted someone hustling around the corner of a garage, it was Obie who went after him."

Brichter tried to catch Dahl's eye without success, so he took a chunk of cornbread off the platter and feigned indifference while Dahl continued. "Obie ran around the corner of the garage and at that exact second there was a shotgun blast. Bill thought he'd just lost a partner. He bailed out, pulling his gun, to go see. He came around the corner and there the prowler was, face-down on the ground, crying like a baby."

"It was Obie who shot first," guessed Danny.

"No, the shotgun was still in the squad," said Dahl. "The prowler had shot Obie point-blank in the face with a twelve-gauge loaded with number-six shot."

Kori, shocked, said, "You're making this up; something like that would have killed him!"

Dahl smiled. "No, ma'm; I saw them the night it happened. I was there when Obie and Bill brought the man in; Obie said the prowler shot at him and missed."

"Come on!" scoffed Danny. "You can't miss with a shotgun at point-blank range!"

"Well, this jerk did," said Dahl. "And he was so surprised that Obie didn't fall down dead that he handed the shotgun over without Obie even asking for it. When Bill arrived, Obie was putting the cuffs on him, and he was crying, saying 'Please, sir, it just went off. I didn't even know it was loaded, it went off just by itself . . .' " Dahl was quoting in a high-pitched weepy voice and everyone laughed but Brichter.

Dahl said, "I remember Obie saying at the jail that he would have believed him, only he was trying to stop himself from coming around that corner because he heard the sound of a shell being pumped into a chamber."

"That's why I don't go hunting," said McHugh. "I hear that sound and I'm on the ground. It sets off *all* my alarms, nice and loud."

"You should have seen our faces when he and Bill walked the kid into the jail," said Dahl. "Obie's hat was a mess; it was hanging in shreds all down his forehead and over his ears. Bill had this big scared grin on his face and the kid was still crying. Obie was white as a ghost, and when we heard what happened we weren't sure he wasn't one!"

"I remember hearing about that!" said McHugh. "Was that you, Pete? They said this uniform brought in a guy who shot him in the face with a twelve-gauge—and missed. How come you never told that one on yourself?"

Brichter shrugged. "Nobody'd believe me."

"You could send them to me; I'd back you up," said Dahl. "I was there and I saw it. You were deaf as a post, but there wasn't a scratch on you." He turned to Kori. "They finally made him go to the hospital and let them look, because nobody could believe it. He said he'd felt the blast of the pellets going by, and his hat spun around on his head a couple of times as it disintegrated, but it didn't even fall off."

"I guess when your number's up, your number's up," said Danny. "And when it isn't, it isn't."

"Maybe this is what God had in mind for you," agreed McHugh, looking around the room and including Kori in a friendly glance. "And He wasn't going to let anything get in the way of this."

Kori reached for a square of cornbread. "I hope this is pure serendipity," she said, "and what God has in mind for Peter isn't due until he's ninety-three." She looked at her husband. "I'll watch out for him after that."

Brichter did not reply. After a glance at him, and her, McHugh said, "You know, people have this notion that cops are heroes or bullies, living a life of danger, but what they really are, most of the time, is overgrown kids. Like football players, or actors. You should see the crazy things they do, the practical jokes they play on each other."

Dahl said, "Obie, remember the tricks they used to pull on you?"

"No." Brichter's reply was like a slammed door.

"Like what?" said Kori, throwing her husband A Look.

Dahl said, "Aw, it's just fun, nothing serious. Like someone put superglue on my combination lock at work. When I find out who, I'll do something back."

Brichter had caught Dahl's eye and silently, earnestly warned him to drop the subject. Dahl glanced at Kori, who was looking amused and interested. So far, none of Dahl's efforts had produced a thaw in Brichter. McHugh had brought the subject up—and what was it McHugh had said? If Kori liked you, sooner or later Pete would, too. Dahl reached for a square of cornbread and said, "Every cop I've ever known plays practical jokes. Some are mean, some are just plain sneaky. I remember last winter someone sprayed tear gas on Cris's heater. He'd gone to—well, he had to leave his car for a minute or two, and while he was gone, someone came by and did it. He was on a long stakeout and he alternated between freezing to death and crying that whole night."

McHugh laughed his richest, and said, "If I ever, ever find out who did that, I'll break his neck!"

Dahl said, "But Obie's had his share, too. Remember, Obie, that time someone hired a woman to dress up like a five-dollar

91

whore and come down to the station two or three times a week asking if her boyfriend Obie Brichter could come out and play? And there was the time someone stole your shoes—'' But Dahl was laughing too hard to continue.

"Not all of that sounds very funny," said Kori.

Dahl, still grinning, said, "Yeah, but Obie found out it was one guy doing most of it, and he got his revenge. Remember, Obie?"

"No." But this time the door didn't slam.

"What did he do?" asked Kori.

"He put live pigeons in the guy's locker. Twelve, fourteen, twenty—I dunno, lots of them. He did it right after the guy went on duty, so they were in there the whole watch. The guy comes in, and he opens his locker and whoosh!'' Dahl gestured outward expansively, wiggling his fingers and cooing like a pigeon. "It was like opening day at the Olympics. Just about surprised the poor jerk into a stroke, and you should have seen the inside of his locker. Took him about four seconds to figure out who did it, and he went roaring right out looking for Obie, but couldn't find him, and by the time he got back, the whole locker room was feathers and pigeon do." The people at the table were looking at Brichter and grinning, but he had assumed a mildly perplexed air. "Everyone," continued Dahl, laughing, "everyone's complaining, and the watch captain says, 'Clean 'em up.' And this poor guy says, 'Hey, I didn't put them in there.' And the watch captain says, 'They come out of your locker, didn't they?' He borrowed a fishing net and a chair, but it still took him the rest of the night to catch those damn pigeons." Everyone was laughing now, including Brichter, but Dahl hardest of all. "Our sides ached for a week after that," he concluded. "Because the old Birdman had it coming. I was glad Obie finally gave it to him."

"That was a cute trick," said Brichter, "but it wasn't me.

Birdman said it was, and the captain called me in about it, but I convinced him I didn't do it."

"Birdman," said Dahl to Kori. "That's been his nickname ever since. He's tamed down a lot since those days, but anytime we want to get a rise out of him, we stick a feather under his windshield wiper."

"Pretty slick, Sarge," said Danny.

Brichter shook his head. "If I'd done something brilliant like that, don't you think I would've been there for the grand opening? I was in bed asleep when he opened that locker." Brichter's mouth tweaked sideways. "But I was sorry I had to miss it."

Dahl, knowing he was on a roll, said, "I was going to do something to a friend one time. I was on patrol, and I stopped at a pet store near the end of my watch and bought a mouse and hid it in my pocket. I was going to string it up by the tail in his locker, which I figured would make it nice and mad, then watch him try to figure out how to get it out without it biting him. But this was right after the pigeon thing and everyone was being very careful to either be there or lock up, so I had to take it home. I kept it in a mayonnaise jar overnight —had to throw out half a pint of mayonnaise to get the jar— but his locker was like a drum the next night, too. Two days later I found myself buying mouse food for it so it wouldn't starve in the meantime, and by the middle of the next week he was sitting on my shoulder watching TV with me and I was calling him Mickey. It started to look like a mean thing to string Mickey up by the tail, so I said the heck with it and bought him a regular cage and a water bottle and when the landlord reminded me there were no pets allowed, it really hurt to give him away to my nephew."

Everyone laughed at this, and Kori gave Dahl a warm look that made him glow all over.

7

S UNDAY the weather continued raw and wet. Danny, who was currently an atheist, paid the price of his nonbelief by doing the Sunday morning chores alone while his employer went to church. After Kori returned and changed, she went to the kitchen and prepared a Sunday brunch for Danny and her husband. Then Peter immersed himself in coffee and the Sunday papers while an icy rain rattled against the windows and Kori and Danny discussed wolf teeth, colic, summer itch, thrush, quittor, canker, bog spavin, thumps, ascarids, brain fever, navel-ill, strangles, screw worm, and other pleasures of horse ownership.

· · ·

Joe Januschka was choosing a pair of slacks to wear when his phone rang. He let it ring four times before he went to answer it. "Yeah?" he said.

"Tony, it's Mrs. Vigotti."

"Good morning, Connie; what can I do for you?"

"Tell me where Tony is."

"Tony? Why should I know where he is?"

"He came to see you."

"No, he didn't."

"Yes, he did; someone picked him up Thursday night and brought him to you."

Januschka let amused disbelief show in his voice as he said, "And you think he's still here?"

"Don't play with me, Joe. I think you sent him somewhere. I want to know when he'll be back."

"Constancia, I didn't send for him. I haven't seen him for over a month. But what's this you're saying, he hasn't been home in how long?"

"Three days."

"You haven't heard from him?"

"Nothing, not a word. Someone picked him up and never brought him back."

"Hmm."

"I'm thinking I should call the police, report him missing, but—"

"Yeah, Tony never thought much of the cops. They always gave him a very hard time." Januschka stopped to listen, frowning; Mrs. Vigotti was making crying noises at him. "Hey, hey, now, take it easy. The very worst, he had an accident or something. You'll get a call in the little while from a hospital asking if you could please bring a box of cigars to this grumpy character before he bites a nurse's head off."

That seemed to help, the snuffling slowed. "Yes, yes; maybe you're right."

"Sure. But if it'll make you feel better, and you haven't heard by this evening, go ahead and report him missing. Meanwhile, I'll ask around. If I hear anything helpful, I'll call you, okay?"

"Yes, please. Thanks, Joe."

•　　•　　•

Lord Stefan von Helle was struck so tremendous a clout on the helm it set his ears ringing.

"Temper your blows, please, my lord, or you'll kill your humble squire," he said.

But Sir Geoffrey wasn't listening; he was explaining the blow to the novice standing beside him. "See? You start with your sword well behind you. Come straight at your opponent's face, and just as your arm reaches its maximum extension, snap your wrist so the sword comes around and connects with his head." He repeated the blow in slow motion, bringing his fist forward as if he were going to punch his target and only at the end of the swing bringing the duct-taped rattan sword around and into contact with the metal helm. "Not only will this give your blows more power, you aren't telegraphing the landing spot you're aiming for."

It was nearly half past two, and nine people wearing armor in various stages of authenticity and repair had gathered in the dirt-floored arena in Kori's barn. The local chapter of the Society for Creative Anachronism was holding fighting practice. The best-looking armor belonged to Baron Sir Geoffrey of Brixham, but his squire, Lord Stefan von Helle, wore forty pounds of cold-hammered steel shaped into something a fourteenth-century knight would have found acceptable for the practice list. Three of the others were wearing something less impressive and/or authentic: combinations of boiled leather, metal, and hockey pads. The worst armor belonged to the novice, a big fellow with streaky blond hair that hung well over his ears and the nape of his neck. His helm was rusty, dented, and borrowed, and was currently sitting on the back of his head like an ungainly hat. The rest of it consisted of pieces of carpet cut to the correct shape and held together with an assortment of straps, string, and duct tape.

Sir Geoffrey said, "All right, now let's do it again; only this time, Steffy, I want you to block."

96

There was an observers' gallery a safe distance away, a dozen folding chairs on which were seated seven ladies, one with a baby, and four gentlemen. They wore the comfortable versions of medieval garb they called "grubbies," mostly faded tunics and simple gowns under hooded cloaks or short capes. One of the men was sitting cross-legged on his chair, playing a lute. His tune was elaborations on "Greensleeves." Kori—presently calling herself Lady Katherine of Tretower—had been whistling variations on his variations that twined in and around what he was doing. But she'd stopped now, to watch Lord Stefan in the list. In Lord Stefan's armor was Peter, and he looked to be collecting bruises that would need attention at bedtime.

Lord Stefan was a more tenacious than coordinated fighter, but tenacity is a virtue, and Geoff was a merciless teacher. Her husband had developed incredibly quick reflexes over the past several years. It had helped him with driving school; she wondered if he also found it useful in his work.

Brichter—Lord Stefan—hoisted his curved wooden shield to a sixty-degree angle, resting it on his shoulder, and looked over it at Sir Geoffrey. His wooden sword raised and resting on his other shoulder, he bent his knees slightly and began stepping sideways to the right. Sir Geoffrey began a similar move to his right, and the novice hustled back out of the way. Lord Stefan used almost the same snapping motion with his shield to block that Sir Geoffrey used to strike. Again and again, with snakelike quickness, Sir Geoffrey struck, and each time Lord Stefan blocked: high, low, low, straight ahead, low, high, high. Finally Sir Geoffrey shouted, "Lay on!" and Lord Stefan began returning the blows. Cut and snap, swing and block, at the head, at the ribs, at the shoulder, at the thigh; block and reply, until the music of the lute was drowned in the noise of combat. Just as it became unendurable, Sir Geoffrey lowered his sword, stepped back, and bowed. Lord Stefan returned the compliment, then dropped his sword and shook

97

his shield until it came free of his grip and removed his heavy steel helm to reveal sweat-soaked hair. He said with a grin, "Pick on someone your own age until I get my breath back —an it please you, my lord."

Sir Geoffrey removed his own helm to reveal dark-auburn hair and beard equally wet about a handsome young face. Dark eyes gleaming with laughter, he replied, "I think we'd both do well to let the others work for a while—an it please you, my lord."

The medieval formula was spoken by each with genuine courtesy. This might be only a practice session, but medieval courtesies needed practice, too.

Among the watchers was Kori's old tutor and friend, Professor Gordon Ramsey. He turned to say something to her and frowned, because she had gone white. "What is it, pet?" he asked.

"Nothing, nothing. I'm just tired from sitting so long. Could you come with me up to the house?"

"Of course. It's time I started the Brie tarts, anyway." He stood and helped her to her feet. He was not quite a head taller than she, and with his fair coloring and stocky build would not have been taken for a near relative. But at one time she had fantasized that he was her father, a comment on their relationship neither ever mentioned but both remembered with amusement and fondness.

Brichter, who was being helped out of his breastplate, glanced over and saw them. "Going so soon?" he called.

"Gordon has to start the tarts now," she called back, and he nodded and twisted around so the novice could unbuckle another strap.

It had become customary that once a month the weekly fighting practice turned into a proper gathering. The numbers varied, and so each brought a contribution to a potluck dinner served in the big house.

Ramsey was not an official member of the group—his tunic was borrowed and too tight around the belly—and anyway he wasn't very interested in the fighting. He'd come because he saw too little of Kori lately, and because he'd heard something in her voice when she'd called to invite him.

She tried not to lean on his arm until they were out of the barn. "What's wrong?" he asked.

"Nothing."

"Rubbish!"

"All right." She stepped away from him and pulled the hood of her cloak up against the rain. "I'm pregnant. People who are pregnant get dizzy sometimes. Come on, let's get up to the house."

"I thought you and Peter agreed—"

"We did." She started across the gravel of the barnyard, and he hurried to catch up with her and take her arm. Her movements were still a little shaky.

"What does Peter say?"

"He doesn't know. He thinks our agreement not to have a family is still in effect."

"When will you tell him? Or do you plan to wait until it becomes obvious?"

"That will take a while. I'm barely a month gone. Meanwhile, I've begun a campaign to change his mind, but so far no luck. I don't want to just tell him because he may think I did it on purpose, when I didn't. And he may try to talk me into an abortion and I won't—" She stopped and her pointed chin became more stubbornly obvious. "I won't!"

They continued up the walk. "Weren't you on the pill? I thought that was a very reliable method."

"So did I. But the pill they prescribe nowadays is so low a dose of hormone that if you miss taking it by as few as eight hours you're at risk."

"And you missed taking it by eight hours?"

99

"More like ten or eleven. It happened at a horse show last month. I was in Louisville, showing Breezy, Chinook, and Copper Wind. Breezy was in the baby class, and you know how they call them first thing. I overslept and everything turned into a mad rush. But we took first, and had to mix celebrating with getting Chinook put together for her yearling class, and when that was over we found that Coppy had spilled a full bucket of water in his box and sat down in it and he had to be washed and dried all over again, and—well, it wasn't until that evening, when we were discussing the problems of show-ing a mare in estrus, that I remembered. I went straight off and took it then, and another in the morning as usual, and by the time we got home I'd forgotten all about it. But when I stopped for the five days, nothing happened. I called Dr. Miller, and he said come in. He has a very sensitive urine test kit, and ten minutes after he took the sample away he came back and said it was positive. He took a blood sample as well, and called day before yesterday to say it was positive, too." Her left hand drifted to her abdomen, and her shapely mouth sud-denly recurved itself into a smile. "I'm going to have a baby."

They climbed the wide wooden steps to the big wraparound porch of the house. Ramsey asked, "Seriously, when do you plan to tell him?"

"As soon as he agrees it would be a good idea."

. . .

Dahl woke late and something warned him to lie perfectly still. After a minute he tried opening his eyes. A cold light stabbed fiercely. He rolled over to bury his face in his pillow, a move-ment that set off huge pain explosions all around his head.

"Oh, shit!" he whispered, and cradled the pillow in his arms until the noise subsided.

What had brought this on?

The word, came a sarcastic reply from inside his aching head, *is hangover*.

He'd gone out to celebrate. Mrs. Brichter had been won over and that meant Obie was as good as bought and paid for. So off with the working clothes and on with the good wool slacks and lemon-yellow sports coat. Down to the bank, slip the cash card into the money machine, and it's party time. A drink or two at Chauncey's, a dance or two with some young chick to warm things up. Then move on, find some cop buddies, joke around awhile, buy a round so they can join him in a toast to his new partner and good friend, Peter Brichter.

He winced at that; a lot of people knew him as a holdout in the general softening toward Brichter, so he had meant to let it be Brichter who told everyone they were now friends. But what the hell; did it matter who did the telling?

His attempts to trace last night's events further blurred. They had gone on to a place with a small dance floor and a loud band. Hallomar's, probably. Or was it the Meet Market? There had been a good-looking woman in there somewhere, a fine dancer, but she disappeared and was replaced by another, less attractive one. And there'd been a second trip to the money machine. Or was it a third? He seemed at some point to have been accused of becoming a bore on the subject of his good friend Peter Brichter. But everyone seemed to know Peter was what his friends called him, so how could he claim to be a friend unless he called him Peter, too? Often and publicly?

That homely gal had been a lot of fun. He remembered the hilarious dichotomy of bending an elbow across his steering wheel and looking over a shot glass through his windshield. And then, abruptly, there had been a naked breast, small and rubbery, and . . . He reached out, very carefully, so as not to jostle anything, and touched the expanse of bed beside him. Empty. The bed must have been hers. How had he gotten home afterward? He couldn't remember. But it appeared she hadn't come with him. He breathed a sigh of relief, carefully, so as not to set off the explosions again.

But just an hour later, he was at his workbench in the basement of his house, fiddling with the orange extension cord he'd retrieved from his car trunk, wiggling the plug end up and down over and over. A mug of coffee was on the bench beside him. He stopped to take a drink, then picked up the probes of a Keithly Model 580 ohmmeter, a beautiful and highly sensitive device, one of his most prized possessions.

The meter was stolen property. He'd acquired it while investigating a homicide by bombing about eight months ago. Two street gangs had been escalating a quarrel into real violence, and a van had blown up, killing two members of the Street Warriors and severely injuring a third. But it turned out the kids had blown themselves up. One—the literate one—had found a recipe for nitroglycerin and they had broken into Midland Lab Supply, looking for the ingredients. Unfortunately, they found them. They stole other equipment and chemicals to mask what they were up to, and used an abandoned farmhouse as their laboratory to mix up the explosive. They were on their way back to town with a pint jar half-full of the stuff when they hit a pothole and blew the van in half.

The surviving kid told Dahl where to find the rest of the stolen items, and Dahl turned everything in but the meter. He'd been looking for a new meter for some while; his old Hewlett Packard wasn't right for the purpose he had in mind.

Dahl clipped the probes to the prongs of the plug, then jumpered the two live contacts of the female end together. He bent over the meter. The needle was indicating higher than normal resistance in the wire, but not yet high enough. He sat back in his chair and began wiggling the cord again. Dahl nursed his hangover by thinking nice things about Sergeant and Mrs. Brichter.

8

KORI was a natural early riser, but she had a hard time rising Monday morning. The rain continued, the wind had come up and was buffeting the house, seeking entry with cold, wet fingers. The urge was to snuggle close to Peter, an inviting sleeper beside her.

But the horses in the distant barn were waiting for a visit from the lady with the pitchfork and the food and the Dandy brushes—and Peter might wonder why she was reluctant to be up and shining as usual, so despite a nagging backache and the urge to nap just a few more minutes, she slipped out and had a quick wash. She got into her working clothes—thick socks, old riding pants, heavy green sweater. She stepped into the Wellington boots standing on the back porch, pulled a rain slicker over all, and ran for the barn.

Horses in the dim morning, like humans, reveal differing personalities. Some are fresh and hungry. Her three mares of this type knocked on the bottom half of their stall doors with impatient hooves as soon as they heard her enter the barn. She had arranged their stalls so they were taken care of first, in order to shorten the uproar.

Copper Wind, her stallion, was at the end of the row. He was his usual morning self—cozy and sleepy, wanting to be petted and coaxed. He nudged her arm and slobbered on her shoulder, grumbling softly when she shoved him away. After cleaning up his loose box, she allowed him two minutes of undivided attention, stroking his nose, picking straw out of his mane, scratching him in his favorite places, then gave him his morning rations.

Across the aisle, the next two mares were nursing mothers. While one wanted to share her baby, the other wanted to be left alone. They moved reluctantly as their night leavings were pitchforked up and fresh straw put down, and nipped halfheartedly at their oats. Kori made sure the foals got a taste of oats.

When she came to the seventh box, there was still no sign of Danny. She had eight mares and two yearling fillies in addition to her stallion, not too many for one person to handle, unless that person was married to a man who liked his wife to join him at the breakfast table unaccompanied by the smell of horse. Kori's growing annoyance was not helped by the seventh horse, Blue Wind, who was in a very frisky mood.

"Settle down, you stupid old horse!" Kori did not swear, nor did she waste any creative talent in rebuking an animal whose language capacity was limited to about twelve words. She would have Danny take Blue for a long, cold, wet ride; it would teach both of them a lesson.

"Hi, you in here?" called a voice. Kori went to look at her groom as he loped across the arena in her direction. "Sorry I'm late!" He added breathlessly, "Late night last night." He was young and leggy, rawboned under the overnight bristles, with a shock of uncombed mud-brown hair and narrow brown eyes.

"I thought you were at home last night," she said. "Or did you leave your lights on when you went out?" Daniel Bannister lived in a cottage on the ranch, a free perk he greatly appreciated, though he did not relish the sharp eye of his boss.

"Uh, no," he said with an uncomfortable shrug, "I didn't go out; I had company in."

The shrug told her all she wanted to know about the number and gender of his company and the probable entertainment featured. Bannister looked over his shoulder. "Cripes, what a day!" he said. "Do you think it will clear off later?"

"I doubt it," she replied, allowing herself to be diverted. Danny was, after all, almost twenty-two, and had yet to be accused of kidnapping any of his late-staying guests. "I'm about done here," she said. "You finish up, have breakfast, then saddle Blue and take her for a good ride. Don't get her overtired, but make her glad to be back home."

Blue Wind had been shipped off to a famous stable to be bred and had come home in a shocking state: head-shy, constipated, footsore, and not pregnant. But she was nearly recovered. "Better work her on the lunge first; she's really fresh."

"Yes, ma'm."

"Oh, and Stormy looks a little lame on her near fore. Turn her into the arena before you take Blue out; if she looks lame to you, call Ben." He was the Tretower veterinarian.

"Yes'm. She's bigged up fast the last month, hasn't she?"

"Yes, and Ben hasn't seen her in a while. I wonder if she's carrying twins. That'll be all we need." Twin foals complicated delivery, and their small size and low birth weights often made raising them difficult. Also, only one Arabian foal per mare per year can be registered; the other twin, no matter how perfect a match for its sibling in beauty, would never command its sibling's price.

Kori glanced at her watch, yipped and ran for the house to prepare her husband's breakfast.

She put his plate of real ham and imitation eggs in front of him and sat down to her own meal in silence. Just because they were engaged in a quarrel was no reason not to feed him. On the other hand, friendly conversation would have been hypocritical.

He responded in kind for a few minutes, then said, "Look, I know one way to end this. I'll call our doctor and make an appointment for a vasectomy."

"Do," she said, "and I'll sic Michael on you when you try to come home from it."

He grinned lopsidedly. "Michael is a friend of mine, too, remember."

"Friend, schmend," she said.

"Come on, *fy'n*—I mean, Katherine. He'd attack a stranger on command, but not a member of his household."

"He is a professionally trained guard dog. He'll attack whomever I tell him to attack."

Brichter looked at Michael, who was dozing on his strip of carpet by the door. There were Michael-size strips of carpeting all over the house; Michael was a famous sleeper. "He's not a real professional, is he? And, anyway, he obeys any command I give him, too."

"Would you bet your coat sleeve on that?"

"Order him up and let's see."

"Sure?"

"Go on."

They both stood. "Michael!" she snapped, pointing at her husband, but looking at the dog. "Watch him!"

And the dog in one motion was on his feet, staring at Brichter.

"Michael, sit!" ordered Brichter.

"Urrrrr," said Michael.

"Down, Michael!"

106

But Michael was judging the distance from where he stood to where Brichter was, gauging the height of the table between them and estimating the amount of haunch-thrust it would take to cross it, and the bite-down pressure he would apply to bring lower canines across upper canines right through the suit, shirt, skin, flesh, and bone of Brichter's right arm. Michael was too busy hoping Kori would give the exciting release command to listen to Brichter. "Urrrrrr," he pleaded.

"Jesus," whispered Brichter. "Call him off."

"Out!" ordered Kori, and the dog relaxed, shook himself, and lay down again.

"Would he have obeyed if I had said 'Out'?"

"No. The only thing the object of his attack can do to help himself is lie perfectly still. Which I admit isn't very easy to do when Michael is trying to pull your arm out by the root. No vasectomy?"

Brichter sat down and muttered to his eggs, "Who needs a vasectomy? Just tell him to aim low."

. . .

It was a quarter to eight and Francine Carroll was the first to arrive. She unlocked the rear door and walked down the dark hallway toward her office with the confidence of experience, a heavyset lady with a firm mouth and iron-gray hair. But the closer she got to her office, the slower her steps became. She stopped outside the door, key in gloved hand, sniffing. She looked up the corridor toward the main entrance, then back the way she had come. Filing cabinets and the backs of lockers and big-bin storage shelves formed one wall of the corridor behind her. A low-watt ceiling light always left on overnight burned clearly; there was no drift of smoke. Maybe it was the pong of Charpentier's vile pipe gone stale over the weekend. She shrugged and unlocked the door to the office. She had already turned the knob before she realized it was hot.

There was a big, bright fire burning behind her desk, licking up the wall, casting orange shadows on her calendar, her telephone, her Rolodex file. She stood a moment, disbelieving, then heat and smoke entered her open mouth. She backed out, coughing, to slam the door. She turned and fled back up the corridor, bounced through an opening into the assembly area and hop-skidded to a halt at the foreman's desk. She snatched up the phone and dialed 911. "Fire!" she choked into the receiver. "Two-nineteen Forrestal, Lynn's Holiday Plastics, hurry!" She dropped the receiver on the desk so they could trace the call, turned and snatched the extinguisher with the long black cone and ran back up to the office, still coughing, yanking clumsily at the pin in it on her way. Her fingers were thickened by her gloves and stiff with terror.

She bumped the door open with a heavy hip and blasted the flames, already much higher than they had been when she first saw them, with a white cloud of carbon dioxide. The flames ducked and rebounded, then she remembered to aim at the base of the fire. By the time the first fireman came through the door, the fire was nearly out.

He grabbed her by the arm and pulled her out of the room. She was coughing so hard she could not speak. He led her around the corner and down to the main entrance. She was dimly aware of fire trucks with flashing lights; there seemed to be a great many of them. The fireman took her to one of them, made her sit down in the diamond-embossed step of it, and pressed a clear plastic mask over her nose and mouth. "Try to relax, hon," he said in a deep, comfortable voice. "Just relax and breathe."

Oxygen, she thought. I'm being given oxygen. Tears blinded her, and to her embarrassment her nose was running copiously. She fumbled for her purse, wanting the little pack of Kleenex she kept in it, then realized she'd left it on the foreman's desk. She hoped none of the firemen were thieves.

"Oh my God, oh my God!" It was Marty Lynn, her

boss. He ran up to them. "What happened? Who's hurt? Did anyone call an ambulance?" He bent and looked into her face, his own a pale and frightened circle. "Oh my God, Fran, it is you! And you're all burned, your hands are burned black!"

Horrified, she held them up where she could see them. They were not burned. It was her black cloth gloves, stained and, in one instance, split along two fingers. She yanked the mask away from her face. "Idiot! I'm fine!" She wanted to go on, but the coughing began again, and the fireman put the mask back and ordered Lynn away.

.   .   .

Brichter was going about fifty as he crossed the old steel-girder bridge that led to town. His radar alarm went off, but too late; he caught a familiar red flicker in his rearview mirror. He sighed, slowed, pulled onto the shoulder and stopped. The squad car pulled in behind him, and its passenger got out.

He frowned at the reflection in his mirror. There was something different about the cop approaching his car. Then he smiled; of course there was something funny about him, he was a she.

Cops don't normally get speeding tickets, but as part of his affirmation to the city that things were being straightened out, Interim Chief Cunningham had abolished even this most customary of perks.

Brichter rolled down his window with an unhappy grimace; honest he might be, but he had a leaden foot, and this was not the first time he'd been stopped. "Good morning, Linda," he said. It was Linda Ballard, Charter's only woman police officer, a big, brawny girl with a pretty face.

"Do you know why I stopped you, sir?" she asked, using the formula she'd been taught—but she was grinning.

"Yeah, yeah; I was in kind of a hurry." He handed her his driver's license.

"I clocked you at fifty-three, Sergeant. Do you know what the limit is across the bridge?"

"Thirty-five. Where the hell did you come from?"

She looked back over her shoulder and pointed. "The little dirt fisherman's trail that goes back and down under the bridge. It's real hard to see us even when we're only backed a yard off the highway. Not that you were looking."

"No lectures, okay? I'm late as it is."

He put the ticket, when she wrote it, into his map box and drove a sedate twenty-nine the rest of the way to the Safety Building.

.   .   .

He came into the squad room to find Ryder waiting for him. "Vigotti's gone."

"What do you mean, gone?" Brichter made his usual detour to the coffee urn.

"As in not here, departed, gone away. And you're late."

"I know, but I've got a ticket to prove I was trying to be on time. Where's he gone to?"

"That hasn't been determined yet. His wife called Missing Persons yesterday evening. Said he didn't come home Thursday night. Said he's not in the habit of going off and not letting her know where he is or when he'll be back. When did you talk to him last?"

"When Eddie and I asked him to come in last Tuesday."

"Not since?"

"No. I don't know if Eddie's talked to him since. I don't think so."

"How did Vigotti strike you when you interviewed him?"

Brichter sat down and thought. "Pretty confident. He knew what we wanted to talk to him about, and I don't think many of my questions surprised him. He knew there'd been a body found in Crazy Dave's basement, but he very emphatically didn't want to take a look at it, which is natural enough. I

110

didn't much like the pictures I saw in the ME's office." He sipped his coffee. "Do you think he cut and ran?"

"No indication of that; his car's in the driveway, and all his clothes are at home."

"If his car's at home, what did he do? Go for a walk and not return?"

"No, his wife said someone came by and picked him up. A friend, she thinks, but she doesn't know who. She said Tony told her he'd be gone a couple of hours. He left the house and never came back."

9

THIS time Kader smiled when he saw Brichter in his doorway. He'd asked around after their first encounter. Brichter was, he'd heard, acid-tongued and unforgiving, but gentle and compassionate; a hard-nosed pushover; a sexless playboy who had married for money, though she was not as rich as she was painted, and anyhow he was insanely in love with her, meanwhile being both after the Chief's job and about to quit the force. Everyone had an opinion about him, especially those who hardly knew him. The only thing everyone was sure about was his incorruptibility. "He wouldn't give the Pope a break," someone had said. That prompted the present smile; Zak was amused at the idea of a moral millionaire.

"Come in, Sergeant," said Zak, and he got out the file on Crazy Dave's TV and Appliance.

"Anything new on the investigation?"

"A few things. Mr. Wagner's inventory of loss is higher

than my estimate of what was in the store. He was holding a cash-and-carry sale at the time of the fire; between that and the loss of most of his records, it may be impossible to prove one way or another exactly what was in the store when it burned. His insurance company has sent one of its best investigators in, and he's being very helpful."

"Did Wagner have an appointment with his agent?"

"Yes, though the man says he'd told Wagner over the phone it wouldn't be possible to improve his coverage for the same rates."

"Does the same insurance company cover both building and inventory?"

"Yes. They're withholding payment, by the way, until more facts about the fire are discovered."

"What about the other tenants?"

"They were a dealer in rare editions—used books, really; a pair of marathon runners, gay, I think, who ran the sporting shoe store; and a young woman who would put anything you wanted onto a T-shirt or sweatshirt. They all say Wagner raised their rents twice in the past eighteen months and seemed about to raise them again. The bookstore man claims he was actively looking for a new location, and the shoe-store couple say they had given verbal notice, and were low on inventory in anticipation of moving. The T-shirt store was grossly underinsured; the woman who ran it is especially upset over the fire; she lost a brand-new heat-transfer machine that wasn't covered. So it appears none of them had a motive for setting a fire."

"Do you know if Sergeant Dahl has interviewed any of them?"

"I believe so; he asked for their names and addresses."

"When I talked with you before, you said this was the fourth suspicious fire you've investigated. Is there any connection you can determine between this fire and the others?"

"No. Though I think the other three may be connected."

113

Brichter looked interested, and Zak explained. "They all appear to be electrical in origin, they all happened in small commercial structures late at night when no one was present, and all the owners had recently raised their coverage. And they all happened within the last five months, which is well beyond the normal pattern of occurrence for this type of fire."

"Any fires before your time that fit the Crazy Dave MO?"

"I've searched the files. One, four or five years back, is close. Milbert's Paint Store, you may remember it. But the Chicago police caught a firebug at the scene of a fire. The guy's statement covered Milbert's fire, too. He was killed in a prison stabbing last year." Zak's phone rang and he picked it up. "Arson, Captain Kader."

"Zak, we got a little situation here I need your help on."

"Yes, Chief?" Charter's Fire Chief was a political animal, now as earnestly reform-minded as he had once been lax. Zak waggled his eyebrows at Brichter to indicate the caller was not a person who could be cut short.

"There was a fire this morning at Lynn's Plastics, over on Forrestal," said the Chief. "A secretary walked in on it, called for help, and then went back and fought it herself. Just about had it under control when our boys arrived. It wasn't a big fire, but the media's decided to give it some hype. The secretary's a tough old bird, real colorful. Her line seems to be the fire department wasn't necessary, though Tellerman says she was about to pass out from smoke inhalation when he got to her. I want you to go over there, see if you can't make a splash. Throw some jargon, determine the cause, make us look on top of things. Get us some good coverage for a change. Wear your hat, show the badge, be bright-eyed and bushy-tailed. Got it?"

"Yes, but I—"

"No buts. Get on it right away."

"Yes, sir."

Zak hung up and explained in terms he later hoped would not be repeated why he had to terminate their discussion.

"Well, look," said Brichter, "since it's not exactly a for-real investigation, could I come along? I'd like to get a look at what you do."

. . .

"Do you help your wife with the horses?" asked Zak a few minutes later, as they came up the harsh yellow corridor leading to the underground garage. His tone was friendly.

"A little," said Brichter, whose initial response to a hint of rapprochement was resistance. This reaction was the result of his years of unpopularity on the force, the profession itself—cop paranoia is a survival trait—and the countless lessons given to an undersized, overly bright, angry, abused child. Brichter hated no one, but the list of people he trusted was cruelly short.

"Would you believe I've never seen a horse close up, except on TV or in the movies?" said Zak, a smile lifting the corners of his droopy mustache.

Brichter said nothing, but opened the door to the parking ramp. People were always hinting they wanted to visit the ranch. He held the door for Zak, who took the silence as a hint and returned to business. "Have you got any idea why Tony Vigotti has dropped out of sight?"

"No. I wouldn't have thought he was the type to do a flit, but I don't know anyone who might have been mad enough at him to kill him."

"Perhaps a disgruntled customer? My car's this way."

"Why kill him when disgruntlement is coming to an end? He's being investigated by the police, and there's a witness willing to testify against him as a loan shark. What that should do is encourage his other victims to come forward—to testify,

115

not shoot him. Vigotti's disappearance doesn't make any sense, just like the rest of this case. What puzzles me most is that body you found. Who is he? And how did he end up dead?''

"Maybe he had a partner helping him set the fire, and they had some kind of quarrel, and the partner said, 'Hey, here's my chance,' and left him dead to burn up in the fire.''

Brichter turned the idea around in his head a couple of times and nodded. "It's possible."

"Mine's the green Datsun. I'm afraid it won't seem like much after driving that superb example of Dr. Porsche's engineering."

Brichter said, "Maybe you never saw the car I used to drive before I got married. If all four of your tires touch the ground at the same time and the bumpers aren't held on with clothesline, your present car is better than my previous one."

Zak chuckled. "That's right, I remember it now. A mottled sort of purple, wasn't it? Funny how quickly we forget. And how quickly we can accept a new situation when it happens to someone else. We're probably more used to your new car than you are." Despite himself, Brichter felt a thaw coming on. There was something comfortable about Zak. He had the air of a man who has taken measure of things, including himself, and come to terms with the results. He has been granted the serenity to accept the things he cannot change, Brichter thought, with a twinge of envy.

He got into the passenger seat of Zak's car and assumed the next-to-friendly role he felt most comfortable in: Lecturer. He said, "Horses are both very much like what you see on film and nothing like that. They can be stubborn, cantankerous fools, and surprisingly intelligent and cooperative. Humans tend, of course, to judge them by their own standards, a fact shown most obviously in the term 'clever,' which among the equine set means an obedient horse. Generally, they aren't as bright as the average dog—but few herbivores are as smart as the typical carnivore. How bright do you have to be to run down an oat? The Arabian horse is particularly beautiful; I used to laugh at my wife for the way she'd just hang on a fence and watch them in a pasture, but now, if I have a minute, I join her. They—pleasure the eyes.''

Zak started the engine. "That's a poetic turn of phrase. So they can be as beautiful in person as on film?''

"You should drive out sometime and hang on the fence with us and see,'' said Brichter without thinking. He looked out the window, glad—and a little surprised—when Zak did not instantly take him up on the offer.

As they drove out of the underground garage, Brichter said, "Why do you put up with that crap from your boss? You've got better things to do than go show the flag like this.''

"I am a man subject to authority. He says 'Go' and I go, he says 'Come' and I come.''

Surprised, Brichter said, "That's New Testament, isn't it?''

"A paraphrase, yes. And yes, I am Jewish. When I was a rebellious teenager, I would read the New Testament in my bedroom, making sure my parents knew I was doing it. I never seriously considered converting, of course, but some of it stuck.''

Brichter tried to imagine Zak as a rebellious teenager and failed. "You told me that you're glad you're not fighting fires anymore. Do you enjoy investigating them?''

"Yes, very much. I always took an interest in learning how a fire got started, and took some courses in it. I'm still learning, which can be hard on a man my age, and I haven't acquired the policeman's bravado, but I can tell you for sure, I'm as itchy as any cop to fasten handcuffs on the one who uses fire as a weapon to get something that doesn't belong to him.''

Brichter smiled and said, this time on purpose, "Maybe when you come out to hang on the fence you could stay to supper, too. Do you know where we live?''

117

"Out across the bridge, I think."

"Eerie River Road, yes. About six miles. The ranch is called Tretower. Here . . ." Brichter took a business card from his folder of them and drew something on the back. "This is painted on the sign. Big house, look for a racetrack circling the buildings. How about Sunday for dinner?"

Zak came to a stop at a red light and took the card. The design drawn by Brichter was a simplified drawing of three medieval towers, the center one taller.

"Thank you; I'll have to ask Miri. Is there some real connection between Tretower and three towers?"

"I don't know. Tretower is a Welsh place-name, and Welsh is a hellish language. It was the birthplace of my wife's ancestors. Her grandfather bought the ranch and named it Tretower."

Zak's mustache lifted to display his grin. "Would you call the symbol a brand? I'm assuming she brands her horses." The light turned green and he pulled away.

Brichter, smiling, shook his head. "The Tretower brand is stamped on her saddles, woven into her horse blankets, painted on her pickup truck, and printed on her stationery, but not burned onto the haunches of her horses; they're far too valuable to be mutilated like that."

"But the root meaning of 'brand' is to burn, isn't it?" said Zak, turning a corner. "Whereas 'logo' is from logogram, meaning a drawing that says a word." Zak grinned at Brichter, who was swiftly suppressing a look of surprise. "You forget, I'm a fireman. There are hours of waiting at a station house for the alarm to sound. One gets tired of cards and television, and turns to books. It would take a ladder truck at full extension to reach the top of the stack of books I've read, and no three of them in succession were on the same subject."

"Sounds like our library," said Brichter. "The books in there are sorted by size and color. Oddly enough, it seems to

118

work, so even though my wife has done over every other room in the house, I've managed to persuade her to leave the library alone. It's a wonderful room, very old-fashioned; a friend of ours says it looks like the sort of room you'd find Sherlock Holmes musing in."

"Funny how women love to redecorate and men hate it. My Miri says that as soon as the last of our children leaves home she is going to have such a housecleaning and a putting in order of our bookcases and furniture that it will be months before I'm able to come in late and get up to bed without turning on lights every step of the way."

"Sounds like Miri and my wife would have a lot in common."

After a minute of companionable silence, Britcher said. "It appears to have been a real-enough weapon that was used on the man they found after the Crazy Dave fire."

Zak replied, "We got lucky there. Considering its location, it's surprising the fire didn't have a better start on us. A few minutes more and there might have been a lot less left of him, and no way to tell he was killed before the fire."

"Does the fact that Crazy Dave himself was involved in discovering and reporting it cast a shadow of doubt on your suspicion that he's responsible for it?"

Zak shrugged. "As you pointed out, this is a real puzzle."

• • •

There was still a thin fog of smoke in the foyer of Lynn's Plastics.

"I thought the fire was out," Brichter said.

"It is, but it can take hours to clear the smoke, and days, even weeks, to get rid of the stink." With a grimace he hadn't displayed pulling on his boots, Zak put on his helmet, then turned his ID wallet inside out and tucked the back part into his handkerchief pocket so the badge hung out in plain view. With Brichter behind him, they walked down

119

the narrow passageway to an office at the corner of the building where a fireman stood guard. The smoke and stink were heavier here, despite a big floor fan that worked to move it along.

"Where is everyone?" Zak asked the fireman.

"Out back. The smoke was getting to them."

Zak led Brichter into the office, which was divided in half. The outer half, the secretary's area, was where the fire had occured. Great swatches of burn swept up the walls and blotched the ceiling. Blackened filing cabinets lined the back wall. A desk jutted out from the near wall, making a checkpoint past which any person entering had to walk. It was covered with a big plastic sheet stacked with file folders toasted brown around the edges. Someone had begun the cleanup by removing the contents of the filing cabinets. An old, unmarked wooden chair was behind the desk. A secretarial posture chair with charred fabric, metal showing an oxidized blue where the grime had been wiped away, occupied a far corner.

Zak, looking very alert, came around the desk, Brichter following. A melted plastic wastepaper basket stood on the remains of a fiberboard carpet guard, a crumpled telephone beside it.

Brichter suddenly realized he was standing in a puddle of filthy water and was grateful for the outsize boots Zak had insisted he put on. The mixed stink of burned wood, plastic, paper, paint, and carpeting made a thick soreness at the back of his throat, despite the fan-induced breeze that tried to move the vapors through the open door to the boss's office and out his open windows. Brichter began to wonder if coming along had been such a good idea. While not yet a clotheshorse, he was uncomfortably aware that he would take traces of what had happened in this place away with him.

Zak appeared not to notice the puddle or the stink. He was studying the walls, turning at last to focus on the wall beside

120

the secretary's desk. "This one's easy," he said. See the cone?"

"Cone?"

"Fire moves in a widening cone from its place of origin. And the area around where it starts is usually the area of deepest char. See, here the plasterboard is burned almost through, but up here it had only started to burn, and everywhere else it's just smoke."

Brichter looked and began to see what Zak was getting at. The file cabinets and desk spoiled the perfection of movement, but there was a general trail of decreasing concentration from the area behind and beside the desk to everywhere else in the room. There was a severely blackened electrical outlet at the bottom of the cone, down low on the wall, and the remains of two plugs and their cords were still attached. Without touching them, Zak traced one under the desk and up to the typewriter and the other to a small space heater. The space heater had been plugged into a long, heavy-duty extension cord; the excess, blackened with soot, was coiled neatly under the drawer section of the desk. The insulation on both cords had melted away near the plugs, and Zak, still without touching them, crouched over them for a closer look. Trying not to block his light, Brichter leaned forward to see what Zak was looking at.

"Who are you?" came a woman's sharp voice, startling them both upright.

The woman was above medium height, strongly built, with a formidable bosom and an old-fashioned navy-blue suit. Her hair was iron-gray and twisted into a no-nonsense knot, and her face was innocent of makeup—though any makeup might have been washed away along with soot and smoke, thought Brichter, realizing this was probably the heroic secretary. There were two grinning reporters and a photographer behind her.

"I'm Captain Kader, of the Arson Squad, ma'm," said Kader. "Are you Francine Carroll?"

"*Arson?* What are you doing here?"

"I was sent to see if I could determine the cause of your fire, Ms. Carroll."

"Miss Carroll, thank you! Well, what have you found out?"

"It appears, on brief examination, that the wire on the extension cord to your space heater is at fault."

"Nonsense! Both heater and cord are just three days old!"

"Very well, then, the cord was defective when purchased."

"So you say, but how can a fire start in a plug when the device it's running is turned off?" Miss Carroll came around the desk. Her tone was scornful, like a high school English teacher Brichter had once known and feared, and he moved unobtrusively out of her way, having no wish to have that tone of voice used on him.

"It can't," said Zak patiently. "The space heater was left turned on."

"Nonsense!" she said again. "I turned it off myself; I always turn it off!"

"I just looked at it, and it's turned on; what's more, the dial is turned up to high."

"You must be reading it backward; I never put it all the way up on high!" She stooped and began to reach under the desk for it.

"Excuse me, ma'm," said Zak firmly, "but I must ask you not to touch it." Reluctantly she obeyed, and Zak looked up at the trio grinning at him from the doorway. "You with the camera, could you take some pictures for me?"

"Sure, what do you need?"

"Without moving it, I want some shots of the space heater. Take an establishing shot of the desk, then one that shows where the heater is under it, then a close-up of the control dials. Then some of the cord near the plug, then overlapping views linking the cord with the heater. Shoot as much film as you need; I'll see to it you get reimbursed." He took Miss

122

Carroll by her elbow. "Here, let's get out of his way. I understand you behaved with great intelligence this morning on discovering the fire. Could you come and tell me about it?"

That struck the right note with Miss Carroll, who would rather have been accused of intelligence than courage any day. She softened slightly. "Let's go into Mr. Lynn's office, from which we may keep an eye on that photographer," she said, and Zak followed her into the inner office. Brichter stayed in his corner, out of her line of sight, and listened.

Miss Carroll gave a rapid and very clear description of her arrival and subsequent actions, making neither little nor much of them. At the conclusion, Zak said, "Well done." He went on, "You said the heater was new. Did you buy it?"

"No, Mr. Lynn did. He kept the office extremely cool all last winter, and I asked him repeatedly for a space heater, with no result. This fall I broached the subject again, only once, and he came in all smiles on Friday morning with this one. The plug would have reached the outlet easily enough from where I placed the heater, but he insisted on using the cord he'd bought with it, saying I might want to move the heater later. I don't see why he might have thought that, as it's my legs that suffer most, and anyway, that little heater would never have warmed the entire office."

"Is Mr. Lynn on the premises?" asked Zak.

"No, he went home. He said I should go home as well, and rest, but I don't need to rest. And the sooner we get started cleaning up, the sooner we can get back to our regular work. Frankly, this fire seems to have been the last straw for him. He is very depressed."

"What is your regular work?"

"We make Christmas and other holiday decorations for commercial use. Christmas wreaths and Santas for lampposts, pink Easter bunnies for card shops, shamrocks for florists, and so forth. Great fun, except we're always working in the wrong season. Our Christmas rush comes in the summer and ends just before Halloween, by which time nowadays the real season is underway, which can make the last weeks before December twenty-fifth very tiresome. Though it isn't as bad this year, since we lost our contract to supply street decorations for the city.''

"How did that happen?"

She sniffed. "Oh, they found some cheapjack company in Chicago that undercut our prices. Mr. Lynn was very upset, though I told him they'd be back and that now would be an ideal time to expand into parade-float coverings.'' She sighed. "It's been a real struggle the last year or so for us, and it's been a job keeping Mr. Lynn's spirits up. Though he did seem a bit more cheerful the last few weeks—until the fire, which, as I say, took all the stuffing out of him.''

10

ROSE Cunningham, Interim Police Chief Cunningham's wife, was a thin, bird-boned lady with a bawdy laugh. She hopped out of Kori's little white MGB in front of the Safety Building and, despite the rain, paused to say through the window, "Thanks for the ride. Send your sweetie my love and kisses."

Kori laughed; she liked Rose and was flattered that Rose liked her. Still, she hesitated. "Are you sure what we're doing is okay?"

And Rose said, "Honey, a little bit of the old political influence never hurt anyone."

"Well . . . ." said Kori, putting her car in gear.

"Shall I tell Malcolm you send him love and kisses, too?"

Kori giggled. "If you think it's proper for the wife of a subordinate to send love and kisses, by all means." She began pulling away.

Rose straightened and bawled after her, "Honey, whatever

it takes to get that promotion, right?'' Abruptly aware of the rain, Rose turned and trotted across the portico to the front door—only to have a man on his way out reach back and open it for her. She glanced at his face as she went by. ''Thanks, Eddie!'' she said.

''Any time, Mrs. Cunningham,'' replied Sergeant Dahl.

.   .   .

Brichter walked into his squad room to find Dahl waiting. ''We got an ID on the body in Crazy Dave's basement,'' he said. ''And I brought the widow in for us to talk to.''

A woman in a brown cloth coat was collapsed in Brichter's chair behind his desk, her face hidden in her hands.

Dahl glanced at his notebook and said, ''He was Jerry Cleaves, age thirty-one, a truck driver, lived and worked right here in town. And this's Mrs. Cleaves. Irene. Wife of the deceased.''

Brichter, feeling something should be said, went to touch the woman on the shoulder. ''I'm sorry.''

''W-we had a fight,'' the woman sobbed, making two syllables of the word. ''He was going out of town and we, we had a fight, so when he didn't call I just thought he was mad.'' She broke down again.

Brichter looked inquiringly at Dahl. ''He drives a semi,'' said Dahl. ''For Reliable Road Haulers. He was supposed to be in Miami Saturday evening, and when he still wasn't there Monday, someone down there called Reliable up here, and they did some checking along the route. When no one reported seeing him, they called Mrs. Cleaves to see if he'd called home to say where he was, and he hadn't. She called Missing Persons, who called Dr. Corbett, and here we are.''

Remembering the photos, Brichter asked, ''You're sure of the identification?''

''Oh, yeah. Corbett got hold of the dental records and she says it's a positive.''

Brichter stooped beside Mrs. Cleaves. "I know this is hard, but do you think you could answer some questions?"

"Y-yes, I think so." She made a serious effort to pull herself upright in the chair. A soaked tissue was clenched in one hand. Brichter looked, but there was no box of tissue in his desk, so he pulled a handkerchief from his pocket.

"Here," he said.

"Thanks," she said, using it to mop her face. She was a brunette, pale, disheveled, and red-eyed, but probably attractive under normal circumstances.

"Mrs. Cleaves," said Dahl briskly, "has your husband ever been in trouble with the law before?"

"He's not—" she stopped, blinking up at him. "No, never." She hiccuped, applied the handkerchief.

"Do you know what he was doing in the store where he was found?"

"No."

Brichter asked, "Have you ever bought an appliance from Crazy Dave's TV and Appliance?"

"I don't think so—no, I'm sure we haven't." She had stopped crying, but there was still a catch to her words.

"Does your husband know Dave Wagner from somewhere? Golf course, tavern, health club?"

She sniffed while she thought. "He never mentioned him to me."

Dahl asked, "How about Tony Vigotti? You know him?"

She shook her head. "No, neither Jerry nor I ever met him."

"How long did your husband work for Reliable?"

"Three years. Ever since we moved to Charter."

"Where are you and your husband from?" asked Brichter.

"Minneapolis, Minnesota. Well, Jerry's originally from Milwaukee, but I'm from Minneapolis. We moved here from Minneapolis."

"How long had you known him?"

"Nine years. We've been married seven—I mean, were—"
At this point she began crying again, big noisy sobs. She
yanked away from Brichter's tentative hand on her shoulder.
"No more questions," she moaned, "I want to go home."

. . .

Milwaukee Police agreed with Irene Cleaves's statement that
Jerry Cleaves had never been in trouble with the law. So did
Minneapolis—and St. Paul, which Brichter checked just in
case, as they were right across the river. Which could mean
Vigotti was out as a suspect; Vigotti, with his connections,
would have hired a pro; and a pro would have his name in a
police file somewhere.

On the other hand, if Wagner had hired Cleaves, why did
Wagner go out at a critical time, a time when he would have
known the arsonist was about to strike the match?

So it looked as if neither was responsible, yet with all the
movement so far, there was not the slightest indication of a
third suspect.

And no matter who hired him, why murder him?

Brichter pulled an ear and thought some more. If Cleaves
was a beginner, where did whoever hired him find out about
him? If he wasn't a beginner, and since he'd been in town
three years, why weren't there any other reports of arson fires
of this type?

Now would be the time for another talk with Vigotti. But
Vigotti was gone. Was he dead, too? Who killed him? Wagner?
Januschka? The infamous Person Unknown? Why?

Brichter had slumped into a discouraged slouch, his hand
resting on the receiver of his phone, when it rang. He picked
up the receiver and said, "Organized Crime Unit, Detective
Sergeant Brichter. May I help you?"

"I been trying and trying to get hold of Sergeant Dahl, but

128

he's never in, and he don't return my calls, so I'm calling you. What's the hell's going on here?''

"Dave Wagner?''

"Sure! And I wanna know how come Tony Vigotti's out of jail!''

"Have you heard from him?''

"Heard from him?! Hell, I *saw* him!''

"When was this?''

The sharpness of Brichter's tone made Wagner hesitate. "Thursday.''

"What time Thursday?''

"Afternoon. Two o'clock or thereabouts. Why? What did he do, break out of jail?''

Brichter's tone was relaxed now. "No, of course not. Tell me about seeing him. What happened?''

"I was at the grocery store, and I come around this corner and there he is, waiting for me. And when I turn my cart around, there's one of his muscle boys blocking me. I thought they were going to kill me right there in front of the Cheerios!''

"You recognized him?''

"Sure! I told you, I used to meet Vigotti once a week!''

"No, I mean the muscle boy.''

". . . Well, no. But it had to be one of them: He was a great big bozo, and he was grinning like a man who's gonna hit you grins!''

"Did he make any sort of move you could interpret as a swinging or punching gesture?''

". . . No.''

"Then how do you know the man is one of Mr. Vigotti's employees?''

"Because he was there with Vigotti, see? Who else could he be? Look, I want Vigotti arrested! He's gonna kill me if he gets a chance!''

129

"Mr. Wagner, I can well understand how running into him like that might frighten you. Have you ever seen Mr. Vigotti in that store before?"

"I never been in that store before, myself. I mean, I figured he was in jail, but I've heard how big shots like him can still give orders, so I've been changing my habits, you know? And I went to this store I never been to before, so if he knows where I usually go, he won't know where I am."

"Did it occur to you that you may have gone into Vigotti's usual grocery store?"

"No. No, it didn't." The idea that Vigotti might go grocery shopping at all seemed to startle Wagner.

"What store did you go to?"

"Captain's, that warehouse place: low prices, high ceilings."

The Captain's was a long way from either Wagner's or Vigotti's residences. "Neither of them said anything to you at all?"

"No, they just grinned. Then the muscle boy pulled his cart out of the way and I got by. I came straight home and I kinda thought Sergeant Dahl would be in touch again, but he hasn't; and I think we shouldn't just let it go, so I been trying to get hold of Dahl, only I can't. Where is he, do you know?"

"No, sir, I don't. Did you leave a message explaining why you wanted to talk to him?"

"No, I keep hearing that you guys have cleaned out the crud in the department—" Wagner caught himself, then with a shrug Brichter could almost hear, continued, "But who knows? Maybe there are still one or two left who will sell information to guys like Vigotti. Excluding you, of course. No one could meet your price, right? Ha, ha, ha! But I mean, Vigotti's one of the big ones. So I go registering complaints about him, and it gets back to him, and it won't be long before they find me in an alley with a bullet in my head. I'm sure you'd be glad

130

to nail him for murder if he kills me, but that'll be no help to me!''

.　　.　　.

A car pulled up behind a parked truck and semi trailer and Dahl got out. He checked the license number of the trailer, then walked forward and climbed up to peer into the cab. A clipboard was face-down on the seat, but on its back was a yellow foil medallion with red lettering: ''Reliable Road Haulers.'' The medallion matched the circle on the door of the cab and on the side of the trailer. And the license number matched, too. This was the rig assigned to Jerry Cleaves, all right. Parked three blocks from Wagner's appliance store and never noticed, because in a warehouse district there were always trucks parked, sometimes for two or three weeks—waiting for loads, to be unloaded, for drivers to come in from out of state.

If that don't beat all, thought Dahl. Right under our noses the whole time.

He went back to his car, got in wearily. This case is a mess. Someone cuts the alarm wires, breaks into a building, and sets a fire like a professional—only he turns out to be a truck driver who is clean as a peeled egg. And he gets murdered and the two main suspects got just the right kind of alibi innocent people have. This was beginning to look like one of those cases that never get unfolded all the way. And here he'd been hoping he could break it fast and find some way of giving Brichter all the credit. Right now it was more important than ever to exploit Brichter and his connections.

.　　.　　.

''I agree, Eddie, this looks like a real stinker,'' said Brichter into the phone. ''By the way, you'd better call Dave Wagner. He says he had a run-in with Vigotti on Thursday, and he wants to know why we turned him loose.''

''If the Supreme Court would just keep the hell off the cops' backs,'' fumed Dahl, ''we could handle people like Vigotti

131

the way they need to be handled. If he turns up and he ain't dead, maybe this time they'll let us keep him.''

. . .

Dahl came by the patrol officer's locker room at the end of the day shift and waited for Officer Ballard to come in. "I hear you gave Sergeant Brichter a speeding ticket this morning," he said.

"Yes, sir, I did. Second time, too."

"Don't you think that was a CLM?"

"What's a CLM?"

"Career-Limiting Move, Linda; a real dumb-dumb."

"Why? It's not like he can't afford them, and so far he hasn't collected enough of them so they pull his license. Everyone knows about him and that red-hot Porsche of his."

"Yeah, well, he's making his move for promotion. That job at Administrative Assistant to the Chief is open; and you can bet that if he wants it, he'll get it. Once he gets into that outer office, what do you think he's gonna do when your supervisor sends up you latest performance report for him to sign?" Dahl mimed opening a folder and scanning its contents. " 'Hmm, here's one from the cop whose hobby is giving me speeding tickets. That indicates poor judgment and a failure to learn from her mistakes.' " Dahl closed the folder. "You'll be up Shit Crick for the rest of your career."

"Brichter doesn't—"

"You mean Brichter never used to. He's sicced his wife onto the Chief's wife, and those two are like this." Dahl held up his right hand, fingers crossed. "I saw them together today and I heard enough to learn they're cooking up a campaign to help him move upstairs. So you do something about that ticket, hear? And let me know when you do. Him and me's partners now, you know; and I look out for my partners."

11

RATHER than going straight in the next morning, Drichter drove to Mrs Cleaves's house. She'd broken off the interview yesterday; he hoped, after a night to accept the situation, she might be willing to continue it this morning.

The house was a neat little white-sided cottage in a row of them on a quiet street. An older-model car in the driveway indicated someone was at home. He walked up and rang the doorbell. No answer. He rang again and leaned sideways to peer through a window. There was no light on in the house, but in the dimness there seemed to be a lot of disorder: clothing tumbled across the couch, a scattering of toys on the floor, a chair tipped over under the window. And there was still no answer, though he could hear the peal of chimes when he pressed the button again.

The procedure is, you go back down the sidewalk to your car and you request a backup unit to come by. That done, he went back and rapped loudly on the door. "Mrs. Cleaves?" he called, and tried the knob. It wouldn't turn. But the door wasn't pulled all the way shut. He pushed it open and called again. "Mrs. Cleaves, are you here?" No answer. He went in, stepping quickly to the side so he wasn't silhouetted against the open doorway, and listened. Nothing. The disorder had a fresh, hasty look to it; under it the carpet was vacuumed, the furniture dusted. Brichter unbuttoned his suitcoat jacket and reached for the Beretta semi-automatic 9-mm pistol under his arm. The house was very quiet.

Ahead, leading from the living room, was a narrow hallway. He started down it on noiseless feet; at the end he could see the sunlit kitchen. He went past the stairs going upward but stopped to look into the bathroom. There were two brown towels flung carelessly onto a bar by the shower and the medicine chest was open, empty except for a bottle of Maalox. The toothbrush rack had one adult-size green toothbrush in it. But no one was in there.

The kitchen was empty and in perfect order, everything put away. He opened a door to find stairs going to the basement.

There was a cat on the stairs waiting to be let in, a middle-size orange tiger with the inquiring, mildly wary air a well-treated cat displays to strangers. The basement was clean and empty.

There were two small bedrooms upstairs. In the adult bedroom, empty hangers were everywhere, and on the floor were a pair of jeans and a swimsuit. Two men's suits, shirts, and ties were hanging in the closet; a few women's garments were on the closet floor. There was a shelf with a suitcase-wide gap in it between two low stacks of jigsaw puzzles and board games.

Near the bedroom window was a chest of drawers, half of them open, and some of their contents draped over the sides: a bra, a pair of orange tights, a half-slip. An almost-empty bottle of perfume was tipped over on a bedside table, cap on. The bed was neatly made, its deep-rose bedspread brushing the cream-colored carpet. Brichter dropped silently to the floor, gun at the ready, then flipped the bedspread back. There was no one under the bed.

In the child's bedroom were more toys and a big spill of crayons, two of them stepped on. The little bed was not made and a mobile dangling in the corner where probably once a crib had stood had several of its little stuffed animals tangled around the wooden hoop from which they hung. To judge from the dolls, a girl child slept here; and by the size of the jumpsuit still in the closet, she was three or four years old.

"Hello?" called a man's voice from downstairs. "Sergeant Brichter?"

"I'll be right down!" he replied and, tucking his gun away, went grumping back downstairs to tell the pair of uniforms that whatever had happened was over.

. . .

"Well, yes," said a neighbor lady, pulling her quilted robe tighter around her skinny frame, "I did hear something last night, a little after midnight. Yes, next door. Doors banging, car doors slamming. And a woke-up child crying. I thought about getting up to take a look, but the car drove away and everything got quiet, so I went back to sleep."

"So you don't know if there was a man there or not."

"Of course there was! Mr. Cleaves and another."

"Mr. Cleaves?"

"Well, it had to be him, didn't it? Three years they've been in that house, and never a hint she's doing anything but what she ought to, even with him on the road half the time. Decent woman—and a fine man and a likable child, most of the time. Beth, her name is. Just turned four last month."

"Have you any idea why she should suddenly leave like that?"

135

"Death in the family, I imagine. Or someone sick like to die. Her mother, maybe."

"Did she ever tell you her mother was ill or frail?"

"No, she never mentioned her family at all, not to me. I sometimes wondered if there'd been a quarrel. But never mind, a woman will run to her mother's bedside, a man to his father's, if one is dying, no matter how long they've been parted or on what terms. Take my word for it: There's a dying parent at the bottom of all this."

.   .   .

Alison Fraasch, the young woman across the street, claimed to be Mrs. Cleaves's best friend. "She's gone?" Alison said, startled. "When?"

"Sometime last night. Did you hear anything?"

Alison, who was tiny, blond, about twenty-three, clutched a small bundle of something, an infant, judging by the creaking noises it was making, to her shoulder, and leaned sideways to look around Brichter at the house across the street. "I didn't hear a thing. I got up at three to give Julie her bottle, and I didn't hear anything. How could she be gone? Where could she have gone to? She was so upset about Jerry, she cried and cried. I was over there last night till she said she was all right and wanted to be alone."

"What time was that?" asked Brichter.

She looked up at him, her blue eyes wide and concerned. "About eleven, I guess, or a little after. I went shopping, new clothes for my new size, and bought some groceries and came home and put everything away and went across to see her, and she was all alone with Beth and the two of them were just about hysterical. She said Jerry was dead, killed in a fire. I thought he was driving to Miami, but she said he never got out of town, that he's been dead over a week. What a terrible thing! So I stayed, and got Beth put down for her nap, and we talked and cried. Then I came home and fixed supper and went right back over and made her eat some soup, and we talked and cried some more, then she said she wanted to go to bed. She said she'd be okay. I think she took a pill, the way she all of a sudden got calm and sleepy.''

"Did she get a phone call while you were there?''

"She got a lot of calls. Someone told the news people, and the phone kept ringing. She'd unplugged it in the living room so Beth wouldn't answer it—the poor thing only slept an hour, and she loves to talk on the phone, she's so *cute!* —so Irene had to keep getting up and running to the kitchen to answer it. I said she should unplug it in the kitchen, too, but she said no, she didn't mind answering just one or two questions. I couldn't hear what she told anyone or what they said to her, but she finally got tired of it after the last call at almost eleven, and unplugged it. I don't understand; where could they have gone?''

"Did she ever mention where the rest of her family was?''

"She said once her parents were both dead, killed in a car accident. I think she mentioned a brother . . .'' Alison frowned doubtfully.

"Do you know his name? Or where he lives?''

"No. Funny, when you think about it, isn't it? I mean, we're such good friends, we tell each other everything. But we never talked about our families except our husbands and kids. I don't think she's ever met my sister, and Barb lives right here in town.''

"If it were an emergency but she didn't want to disturb you, who else might she have called on for help?''

Alison shook her head. "No one. It's not just that we're best friends; I live right across the street, and we have a car. Her old car won't start half the time.'' She bit the inside of her cheek. "Well, I suppose she might call Mrs. Williams. She's a dear; she baby-sits for Beth when I can't.''

137

But Mrs. Williams was the lady in the quilted robe, and she had not even known Jerry Cleaves was dead.

"Do you have a photograph of Mrs. Cleaves, in case we have to start a search for her?"

"You think something happened to her, don't you?"

"No, I think she had to leave town very suddenly. But just in case, do you have a photo I can borrow?"

"Yes, wait here." For an instant he thought she was going to hand the bundle to him, and he went down a step off the porch. In his experience babies spit up a lot, and he did not want curdled milk on his lapel. But she was only shifting arms, and when she hurried off, the baby went with her.

She wasn't gone long, returning with a candid photograph of Gerald and Irene Cleaves in front of their Christmas tree, she explained—little Beth in Gerald's arms and Pumpkin the cat in Irene's. Gerald was a muscular individual, dark and Italian-looking, and Beth had inherited his ruddy good looks. The photo was not a good one; it had the poorly detailed, washed-out, sharp-shadowed look a flash cube and 110 film can create; but it was all Alison had.

He thanked her and asked, "Is it possible Mrs. Cleaves phoned here to ask for help, and your husband went over without waking you?"

She giggled. "Tom? Are you kidding? Since the baby came, nothing can wake him at night. He sleeps through phones, Julie crying, atomic explosions, everything."

.   .   .

Brichter wished he could go back and do a thorough search of the Cleaves house, but there was no way to justify a search warrant; his cursory inspection of the house had been technically illegal, although understandable under the circumstances. So after he talked to a few more neighbors and determined that no more information would be forthcoming, he went to the Safety Building and his squad room to phone Eddie Dahl.

"Screwier and screwier" was Dahl's comment. "Do you suppose she was kidnapped?"

"Could be," said Brichter, not as if he believed it. "But people living in this kind of neighborhood are virtually never kidnapped. The amount their families could scrape together for ransom makes it economically silly."

"You said the place was messy—maybe like there'd been a fight?"

"No, more like she'd packed in one hell of a hurry."

"Maybe she had to get someplace right away, like the old lady next door says. Someone had a heart attack or something."

"There's generally time even under those circumstances to tell a neighbor where you're going and why, and to ask them to take care of the cat."

"If it's an emergency, who cares about a cat?"

But it had been a friendly cat, only a little wary of the strangers in its kitchen. People who treat their pets well don't abandon them. The cat had a clean, if empty, food dish, a well-maintained litter box, and a seam under its belly fur that meant it had been spayed. It puzzled Brichter that a cat so obviously well cared for had been abandoned. How would Irene explain that to little Beth? He said irritably, "I wish I knew who the men with the car were who came and took her away."

"You think maybe it was the kind of help she didn't want?" asked Dahl. "Was this another version of Vigotti's disappearance?"

"No—well, probably not. She at least packed something. Vigotti went out for a quick visit and never came back. And he left his wife and son behind."

"Have you heard from Philadelphia about Vigotti?"

"No, and I suppose I should jiggle their line; it's been a while."

"You think Vigotti's dead?"

Brichter pulled the ear. "I don't know what to think. But I've got a feeling Mrs. Cleaves isn't. She took a suitcase and her kid."

"Maybe the killer didn't want any witnesses. And the suitcase was just a way to mislead us."

"Maybe."

"If not," Dahl said, "she left voluntarily. Why should she run?"

"You run because you're scared. Maybe both she and Vigotti were scared."

"Of what?"

"I haven't got the faintest idea."

. . .

Brichter pulled Vigotti's file and sat down at his desk with it and a cup of coffee. He made a notation that Vigotti was reported missing as of November 12, then began paging through the file, looking for leads. It is a fact that crimes committed by amateurs are most often solved by deduction and the development of clues; crimes committed by professionals are most often solved by informants. Vigotti's known associates were listed as Joe Januschka, Henry (the Undertaker) MacNeely, Nishan Amuseharian, Rebecca Worth, Buster King, Wayne (Hammer) Sokolovski, Dench LeBrett, Cherry Steen and Tami Galore. None of them were on Brichter's list of informants, but he wrote their names in his notebook and went to stand at McHugh's desk. McHugh tried to pretend he didn't see Brichter, but Brichter, used to the ploy, simply outwaited him.

"Okay, what do you want?" growled McHugh.

"The name of your new informant."

"Which one?"

"The one who says he knows one of Vigotti's strong-arm men."

"And why should I share him with someone who usually manages to spoil any informant he comes near?"

"I haven't spoiled an informant all year," said Brichter, not sure whether to pretend to be annoyed or to be really annoyed. He didn't like informants, but wasn't that hard on them. "I let you talk to Cal, didn't I?"

"Cal's got liver cancer; the only thing he's good for is the inside dope on hospital beds. In another month he'll be dead."

"Cris—"

"Look, I don't have time to argue with you; his phone number's right there on my calendar."

"Whose?"

"Tyler. He's the one you want to talk to, isn't he?" And McHugh immersed himself again in his reading. Brichter leaned over to copy down the phone number and as he did noted that McHugh was reading *The Anarchist Cookbook*.

"Does your mama know you're reading that?" he asked, eyebrows raised.

"My mama gave it to me for my birthday."

Brichter took his phone number and withdrew.

      •   •   •

"He was real mad at you, Sergeant." The speaker was a handsome, dark-haired young man with a sensual mouth and shifty eyes. His delicate narrow hands trembled from crack abuse.

"Vigotti was mad at me? Why?"

"Because," said Tyler, "Tony thought you were setting him up over this arson thing. Thought you were out to frame him."

"You mean he didn't set that fire?"

Tyler's eyes shifted. "Maybe he did, maybe he didn't. I'm only telling you what Nish told me." Nish was an enforcer. He was large as a sofa, mean as a cobra, bright as a brick.

141

Which put him on an intellectual level with Mr. Tyler of the delicate trembling hands. "Nish tol' me Joe was mad at Tony."

"Joe Januschka? Why?"

"Because Joe tol' us to lay off."

"Us?"

"Tony and Nish and everyone."

"Lay off what?"

Tyler shrugged and his eyes wandered off again. Brichter began to wish he had suggested they meet someplace indoors; a chill wind was blowing, and it was beginning to look as if this was going to be a long conversation.

Brichter tried again. "Why would Januschka tell Vigotti to lay off?"

"Not just Tony, everyone. All the made guys."

"Why?"

"Why you always asking me why? I dunno why. I could make up an answer, but you don't want me to do that, do you?"

"No, of course not."

"Sure. Hey, when you're in the outfit, you don't ask questions, you know; you just do what you're told." Tyler lusted after membership, probably for the prestige, but perhaps also because he would never again have to decide something for himself. Between some natural lack and his heavy doping, Tyler was even dumber than the other mopes, the hangers-on of the criminal element: too stupid to stay straight, too chicken to find his own way into hard crime.

"Where is Vigotti now?"

"Dead."

"How?"

"Dunno."

"Who?"

"Dunno."

"Come on, you want me to pay you for this? You're not telling me anything!"

Tyler's shoulders hunched inside his thin leather jacket. His muscular body was drying up under his abuse of it, though his large and handsome head remained unmarked. "I could lie if you wanted me to," he began.

"No, I want the truth," interrupted Brichter. "But I want all of it."

Tyler thought a while. The chill wind blew up the alley as if it were a funnel, and Brichter hitched his coat collar up. Tyler said, "Okay. People are saying Joe offed him."

"Did Nish say that?"

"No. Just people. Nish is hoping he just went out of town."

"If Tony's dead, where's the body?"

"Buried somewhere. With worms eating him." Tyler sniggered. "The worms crawl in, the worms crawl out," he sang, then looked sideways at Brichter, saw he wasn't amused and stopped.

"What is Nish saying?"

"That we all got to run cool until we find a way to—" Tyler stopped, his shoulders hunching again.

"A way to settle things with the new Police Chief?"

Tyler straightened. "So if you already know that, it isn't like I told you," he said.

"Where is Nish hanging out these days?"

"Dunno. He comes and he goes. When I see him, I buy him a Cherry Coke and he likes me and he tells me things."

Brichter sighed and reached into his handkerchief pocket for a twenty-dollar bill. "Hey," said Tyler, looking at the bill only after taking it, "I said fifty."

"You haven't told me enough to have earned that twenty."

"You cheated me."

"When you tell me more, I'll pay you more."

143

Tyler hesitated, then shrugged and pocketed the money. "If I wanna tell you some more stuff, how do I get hold of you?"

"The same number as Sergeant McHugh."

It wasn't the money that made Tyler turn informant; it was pride in having acquaintances in two different worlds, worlds that were enemies of one another. Tyler looked at his role as an opportunity to visit both sides of a serious question; that he had to be consecutively traitorous to the people in each to maintain his position was an idea beyond his comprehension —Tyler was as deprived ethically as he was intellectually.

.   .   .

It was time to go home. As Brichter unlocked the door of his Porsche in the Safety Building garage, Linda Ballard, in jeans and blue sweatshirt, came up and stopped on the other side of the car. Her auburn hair was in a pair of short ponytails, and her hands, clenched into fists, were shoved into her sweatshirt pouch. "I need to talk to you," she announced.

Brichter, surprised at her curt tone, put his keys in his pocket and asked, "What about?"

"You were on your way into work yesterday morning when I stopped you, right?"

"Yes."

"So that makes it official business, I guess. How about you give me that ticket and we'll forget I wrote you up."

"Are you sure about this?"

"Hey, don't look a gift horse in the mouth; just give me the goddamned ticket!" She looked angry and embarrassed.

Brichter cocked his head at her. "You doing an assignment for Internal Affairs? If so, you need to work on assuming a friendlier attitude."

"Look, Sergeant—"

"Anyway, you're barking up the wrong tree, and you know it, Linda. This is the second ticket you've given me; did I ask you to tear up the first one?"

"Yeah, well, you weren't up for promotion the last time."

"Promotion? Where did you hear that?"

She studied him, his surprised eyebrows, his angry chin, and said, "Maybe I heard wrong. You and Sergeant Dahl are partners, aren't you?"

"For this one case he's working on, yes." The eyebrows came down and he smiled, not his usual lopsided smile, but one that pulled his mouth back equally and looked, on his thinly fleshed skull, malignant. "I thought I smelled a rat."

Linda's fists came out of her pockets. "I always heard you were a by-the-book cop," she mumbled.

"Where did you get the idea I'm bucking for a promotion?"

"Not just a promotion; I hear you're aiming to work directly for the Chief."

"Come on!"

"Isn't it true Mrs. Cunningham and your wife are thick as thieves?"

Brichter frowned. "I'll grant you that my wife and the Chief's wife are friends. What of it?"

She shrugged and looked away.

He said, "Hey, so far as I know, all they're doing together is planning a church fair. But how does the rumor I'm trying for a desk job bring us to you and my speeding ticket? If you're hoping to gain some political influence, this isn't the way."

She said, still looking away, "I think we should just let it drop, okay? It was my mistake and I apologize."

"No, I'm not going to let it drop. I believe it's in the regulations somewhere that you don't offer to fraudulently cancel a speeding ticket."

That brought her blue eyes back around. "You son of a bitch—you'd report me?"

"Damn right. If not for your sake, then mine. Listen to me. I am married to a woman whose idea of a pleasant surprise for her husband is a sixty-thousand-dollar sports car. She has

145

friends and business connections among people who make the network news once in a while. Therefore, people think I'm just fooling around down here at the Safety Building. I have to be twice as good and four times as clean as anyone else to convince them otherwise. If word gets out I let one person do me a favor I don't deserve, inside of six months I'll have to quit in order not to be fired.''

"I didn't—I won't say anything.''

"That would be fine if taking care of that ticket was your own idea.''

"What makes you think it wasn't?''

"It was Eddie Dahl who told you to fix my ticket, wasn't it?''

She hesitated. "You think you're pretty clever, don't you?''

"Sure. Don't you?''

She made a gesture of exasperation. "Oh, all right. Sergeant Dahl told me to fix that ticket, and to let him know when it was done.''

"Then the next time he needed a cop to do him a favor, one just a little less legal than this one, guess who might find it hard to say no?''

Her mouth fell open. "He wouldn't!''

"You've heard the stories about him, haven't you? Never lean your badge on someone like him, Linda. It might fall over.''

She walked off around a fat concrete pillar, stopping on the other side to exhale noisily. Then she dealt the pillar a killer blow with her booted foot. "That scum-sucker!'' She came around, fists clenched, looking for something else to kick. "That low-down piece of pigshit!'' His car's rear bumper caught her eye and she drew back her foot.

"No!'' he snapped, stepping in front of her, catching her by the wrist. "Not my car!''

Surprised, she laughed and put her foot down. "It's true,

146

then, isn't it? You're in love with that machine. All right, I'm through.'' He released her and she said, "But what are we going to do about Sergeant Dahl?''

"We?''

"Hey, you better let me have a piece of whatever you're going to do to him. I got a reputation to protect, too, you know. Someday some other lady might want to be a cop in this town, and I don't want to be an example she's got to live down.''

"You on day shift tomorrow?''

"I'm on till Friday.''

"Could you find a reason to break off and come in tomorrow? About ten, say.''

12

BRICHTER drove up the narrow lane between the white fences, across the racetrack that made a neat one-mile circle around the house, cottage, barn, and outbuildings, and pulled into the garage. He had seen no lights in the barn; she must be in the house. He sat for a while, trying to think how best to approach her on this, but the more he thought, the angrier he got, and at last he just climbed out and walked up into the house.

He took his coat off in the hall, hung it in the big antique armoire, then removed his gun and locked it in the unobtrusive little drawer on top of the armoire. When he turned around, she was standing in the entrance to the dining room. Her welcoming smile died away. "Hard day?" she asked.

"Yes, and I need to talk to you about it. Can you put supper on hold?"

He never talked about his job. "Be back in a minute."

He went into the big living room and started to sit on the couch in front of the fireplace, then saw she had laid a fire for later and, just to have something to do, he knelt in front of it and lit it with one of the long matches from the box on the mantel. She came up behind him and put both hands on his shoulders. "What's wrong?" she asked.

He shrugged away from her hands and asked, looking at the flames licking up among the twigs, "Did you ever talk with Rose about getting me promoted?"

She hesitated and he knew what her answer would be. "Yes, why?"

"Because Eddie Dahl knows about it, and assumes I am now building a political base, one he would like to be a pillar of. He sent Linda Ballard to me with an offer to fix that speeding ticket she gave me yesterday."

"I don't understand." She backed off to sit on the couch. "Why should Sergeant Dahl think fixing a ticket is the right way to become your friend?"

"Because he thinks I've had a change of heart about the way I approach my job. He thinks I'm using you to gain the political clout to get a promotion I might otherwise not deserve."

"But—no, you're not!"

The fire had caught; it was growing steadily. He looked over his shoulder at her. "He'll believe that before he'll believe you've been going behind my back."

She looked at her hands, clasped in her lap. "How did Eddie find out?"

"Who knows? I don't think it's common gossip yet; I hope not. But it's put me in a real bind, and to get out of it, I'm going to have to make an enemy of him." He looked back at the fire, and held out his hands to the flames. "You'd better learn to be quicker on the pickup, *fy'n galon*, if you're going to dabble in police politics."

149

"What do you mean?" She was starting to sound indignant. "And why do you have to make an enemy of Eddie?"

"Because, the way he looks at it, between my wife's money and her excellent connections, I'm sure to get the cushy job as the Chief's personal assistant. And once I do, there's almost no limit to my clout. He wants a piece of that, so he's been doing everything he can think of to win my favor, including climbing all over my wife's maternity-shed roof on Saturday, and charming her with funny mouse stories over supper."

"Are you sure that's what he's up to?"

He turned around. "He is the Charter Police Department's official lickspittle, and our most infamous wheeler and dealer. Sergeant Edward Dahl, my erstwhile partner and would-be good friend, a fixer of tickets, is also a pimp, a fence, a bigot, and a liar."

"Oh," she said in a small voice.

His pale eyes, when he was angry, turned as cold as the ice they resembled. "When the hell did this start? I thought you and Rose Cunningham were planning a church social together!"

"We are! And that's all it was supposed to be! Only, we got to talking about our husbands, and how wonderful they are, and she said—and I agreed—that it's a shame you aren't a lieutenant, working indoors where it's safe." Color mounted her cheeks and her eyes dropped.

"So that's it," he said. "Why don't you just ask me to quit?"

"Because you don't want to quit!"

"I don't want to be 'safe,' either! Goddammit, I like what I'm doing!"

"Well, how am I supposed to know that?" she flared. "You never talk about it! I can only guess, and what I guess scares me. Every morning when you leave for work, I'm afraid until you come home."

150

And every morning before I even wake up, you are out in the barn bossing a nine-hundred-pound stallion around. drive thousands of miles a year to horse shows with horses hundreds of thousands of dollars, and you rely on a damn poodle to defend them, and you. Have I ever asked to quit?''

No, but—''

Remember the first fight we ever had? When I tried to fire ny and you told me in no uncertain terms that the ranch yours and I was not to interfere again?''

Yes.''

Good, because I'm telling you now, in no uncertain terms: keep your well-meaning fingers off my badge!''

'How dare you speak to me like that!''

'How dare you try to shove me into a promotion I'd hate!''

'You never said you wouldn't like a promotion! You took exam, didn't you?''

'Frank Ryder put my name in; I had to take the exam!''

'Yes, and Frank made you sit up late for weeks studying it!''

'All right, I wanted to pass it! I damn near had to pass it! e got enough problems as it is with people thinking I'm ly playing at being a cop; flunking the exam wouldn't have lped.''

''Who thinks you're playing at being a cop?''

''Anyone who knows we've got two million dollars.''

''What do you want me to do, give it all away?''

''Oh, that again! Don't be an idiot!''

They fell almost gratefully into a money quarrel, whose rms were familiar to them. Then, the real issue unre- lved, they gradually subsided into separate silences so osty that the dog Michael slunk around corners to keep out f their way.

.   .   .

Kori sighed and turned her pillow over. The truth wa
course, that over the four years of their marriage he
with her coaxing, come to be involved with the ranch
helped exercise the horses, assisted at breedings, was lea
more than he probably wanted to know about training
showing. He co-hosted parties for her customers and garn
helpful gossip at those few auctions and shows he was ab
attend.

And she had supported him in his career, turning up a
annual police-firemen softball game and barbecue, being
to his police friends when they chanced to meet, playing h
ess at Christmas dinners for them.

So it wasn't really fair, his speaking to her like that.

On the other hand, she could see how slimy it would be
him to find himself on the same side of the political suc
fence as the apparently infamous Eddie Dahl. She wished h
made it clear a long time ago what kind of person Eddie w
She wished she hadn't been so nice to him after dinner
Saturday.

She rolled over, seeking sleep. This whole thing was Ros
fault, wasn't it? Rose was the one who'd offered to he
making it seem like some kind of clever game, manipulati
the men into doing something important. Why couldn't Rc
have picked on someone else?

She rolled over again, onto her stomach, and Peter stirr
restlessly. She lay still until his breathing deepened again. I
had been seriously angry about this. Why? What was so terrib
about being promoted? Couldn't a lieutenant work the stree
as well as a sergeant? There were detective lieutenants on tl
street, weren't there?

But her slip had been absolutely Freudian. The idea ha
been to get him indoors, away from the pimps and dope addic
and "right guys" he dealt with every day.

She rolled onto her back and Peter said, "Hm?" She waite

152

until she was sure he was back asleep, then crept out of bed and the bedroom and down the stairs. Her back was aching anyway, and there was no need to keep him from his sleep. The clock on the mantel said it was almost half past one. With a tired but devoted sigh, Michael appeared and sat down beside her in front of the fireplace. There were still a few coals glowing under the ashes of the banked fire, and she occupied herself for several minutes, feeding it twigs and bark and sticks and then a log, until it was a real fire again; then sat, arms around her knees, watching it. She had brought a robe, but wore nothing under it, and it lay on her shoulders and open around her. It made her feel bold and sensuous in the big room to sit naked like this, after a glance confirmed the heavy curtains were closed.

This wasn't a lovers' quarrel; something had broken in their relationship tonight. He had never before ordered her not to do something. Of course, how much had he put up with up to now because he was in love with her? How much of this anger was from some locked-away store she'd finally managed to break into? Just as she never complained about his moods and his morning grumps, and put up with his belief that the horses were just an expensive hobby. She reached out and touched Michael's topknot. Just as she hadn't yet told him she was pregnant.

She heard a noise in the hallway and, clutching her robe closed, turned to see Peter standing in the doorway, looking scared.

.   .   .

He'd been vaguely aware of her restlessness for some unknown time, and finally reached out to comfort her—and she was gone. He let that thought percolate through his soggy brain for a few minutes. Was it time yet for her to be up and in the barn? He pried an eye open, and looked at the digital alarm clock on the bureau. No. Did she normally rise to use the

153

bathroom in the middle of the night? No. Maybe she was hungry; neither of them had eaten much at dinner. He waited long enough for her to finish a miniature carton of yogurt, her usual snack, but she didn't come back.

He was pretty sure that if she'd left the house and driven off he'd have heard her; the hollow snarl of the MGB was loud and very distinctive.

He'd really laid into her, hadn't he?

Sure, but she'd had it coming.

She was probably in the bathroom, sulking. Of course, for a sulk to work properly, one had to be sure the party of the second part was aware of the sulk. He was a heavy sleeper, so to make sure he woke and found her gone, she should have tipped something over, or slammed the door. He touched the sheets on her side. They were cold; she'd been gone some while. She must have used care not to awaken him when she left.

Just how mad was she? She was hard to read sometimes, and he wasn't always perceptive about her, though, God knew, he tried. What if she didn't come back?

He stretched out a leg to invade her space. The bed seemed unnaturally wide with her not in it. In less than four years he'd gotten used to her being there. More than used to it; when she was out of town at some damn horse show he had a hard time sleeping. Not that he'd mentioned it; he figured it was part of letting her run the ranch her way, as he'd agreed to do. They weren't snugglers, so it wasn't a lost-teddy-bear syndrome; it was just a lack of her presence in the bed, no one to share the air with.

Had he come down too damn hard on her? What if she was sleeping in the guest room? That had never happened before. Was this the beginning of some serious breach in their relationship?

Angry and scared, he climbed out of bed and reached for his bathrobe. He went down the hall, quietly opening doors, looking for her. Not here, not here, not here, not here. Not in the bathroom. Jesus, maybe she had gone out.

He padded down the stairs and saw the orange glow coming from the living room. Oh, God, and now we're on fire!

He hurried to the door and saw her sitting in front of the rebuilt fire, Michael beside her. She grabbed at her robe as she looked over her shoulder and saw him, but her face, now in shadow, was unreadable.

"Are you all right?" he asked.

"Yes. What are you doing up?"

"I woke up and you were gone."

"I was restless; I didn't want to disturb you."

He was so relieved he got mad. "I can't sleep any better knowing you're sitting all alone down here!"

"Michael's with me." Said smugly, as she rose onto her knees and belted the robe firmly in place.

"Damn the dog! Come back to bed!"

"Don't shout at me."

He exhaled, trying to cool his anger. "I'm sorry. Please, come back to bed."

She settled onto her rump again, and looked into the fire, away from him. Her expression appeared serene, though that might have been only an effect of the flames. "I'll be up in a while. You go ahead."

He came into the room. "Are you that mad?"

Her head bowed. "No, I'm that sorry. Peter, I should have known better."

His tension and anger lifted and he went to kneel beside her. "Yes, you should. But you won't do it again, I hope."

"No. Only . . ."

"Only what?"

155

"We don't talk enough. We should speak up right away when things bother us, not let things go on until they become too serious to ignore, and we have to shout at each other."

"I don't think I'm all that tolerant."

"Me neither," she said gloomily. "But I do tend to avoid quarrels. They give me a headache."

"I don't like them either. Is there something else on your mind, so long as we're talking again?"

She leaned against his shoulder and said nothing.

"Come on, out with it: What else about me bothers you?"

"You drink too much coffee."

He laughed. "I know. But I've been doing it for years. If I stopped now, I'd sleep for a month."

"You could cut back little by little. All that caffeine, coupled with the stress of your job, has got to be hard on your heart. Since you're twelve years older than I am, and a male, I think we should start now doing what we can to—to increase your life expectancy."

He wanted to laugh again, but it caught in his throat and instead he stroked her hair. "All right, if that's what you want, I'll cut back my intake: one less cup a day this week, two less next week, and so on, until I'm at what we agree is a reasonable amount."

"Thank you. Now it's your turn. Is there anything you want me to stop doing?"

"Eden Hills Country Club," he said without thinking.

"I didn't know you don't like the club!"

He almost took it back, so plain was her dismay, but he only amended it a little. "Well, maybe we could just not go as often. I like their racquetball court, and their Saturday-night menu is terrific. It's the members—some of the members. The ones who find out what I am and ask me to throw a scare into their delinquent children, or if I'll fix their wife's parking ticket."

156

"They don't mean anything bad, Peter."

"Do they ask to borrow Copper Wind to pass off as their own at a horse show?"

"No, of course not!"

"So why make a crook out of me? Is it because they think I'm already a crook? Or only that the work I do is unimportant? Whichever, it takes my ego a week to recover from an evening affair at the club."

She was silent, staring at the fire. "I didn't know. Honestly, they are very nice to me, always."

"That's because you are one of them. Your one eccentricity, and you seem to be allowed one, is me."

"You're exaggerating; they like you."

"I am not exaggerating. Joe Crossley-Holland asked me very kindly at the Harvest Ball where I'd rented my tuxedo."

She said indignantly, "That mean old man! As if his tailor were anything to boast of!" She grimaced, ashamed. "I'm sorry; I didn't know. I couldn't bear for someone to condescend to me that way." He recalled that some of her good friends were members.

"Not all of them are like that," he said. "But enough of them that I would prefer we not go to the Christmas Treat."

"All right, we won't. I'll send back our tickets. And I think I'll let it be known why. It's time they knew Peter Brichter is a member in good standing, not some handsome gigolo I rent for the occasion."

"Thank you."

"There, see?" she said, leaning against his shoulder again. "That wasn't hard. And much better than shouting."

"You're right. Anything else?" he asked.

She was silent a long while, and he thought she was trying to think of something, but she was only gathering her courage. When she spoke, it was so softly he had to lean in to hear her words. "Let me have your baby."

157

"I don't think we should do that. Not right now."

"Why not?"

"Because I don't know how to be a father. Hell, I'm still learning how to be a husband. I think our relationship is too fragile to stand the strain. Anyway, the idea of a child around the house scares me sick, literally."

She fell silent again, but he couldn't see her face to tell what kind of silence this was. She said, "Then share something else of yourself with me."

"Like what?"

"Talk to me."

He frowned. "I am talking to you; we're talking right now."

"No, I mean about your work."

"What, right now?"

"Now, tomorrow, next week. Come home from work and tell me what you did that day."

"I don't want to share my work with you."

"I know. But I need you to."

"Why?"

"Remember how we rented that old horror movie for Halloween at Anne and Geoff's? And how scared we were until we saw the monster—and then we laughed? Because our imaginations had cooked up a truly nasty creature, and the special-effects man just wasn't up to our imaginations."

"And your imagination is, you think, much worse than the reality of my job."

"Yes."

He stroked her upper arm through her robe. "In your worry about my safety, it probably is. I don't engage in shoot-outs more than once a week, and I haven't been involved in a high-speed chase since last Wednesday."

"Don't patronize me."

"I'm sorry. *Fy'n galon*—may I call you *fy'n galon?*"

"Well . . ."

158

"Thank you. *Fy'n galon*, there are things about my job that would disgust you. Things that would break your heart. Things that would change the way you look at the world. And I need sometimes to look at the world through your eyes, borrow a little of the hopeful outlook you maintain. Our home sometimes seems to be my one clean place in a sea of filth, and I just can't see breaching the seawall on purpose. You only think you need to share it." He tightened his grip on her shoulder and put fatherly authority into his voice. "Therefore, I hereby assert my status as the senior partner to order you: No more asking about my job. I think it's at least as bad an idea as your allowing Rose Cunningham to work on my promotion." He gave her shoulder a little shake to sink the lesson in. "Now come on, let's get to bed."

She pulled away to look at him, and he saw tears in her eyes. "How dare you speak to me as if I were a naive child! As if I've never seen nastiness! As if Uncle never happened! Here I thought we were making progress, and you start sounding like a male chauvinist pig!"

He didn't agree, of course. In a few minutes the quarrel reheated, and by the time they quit for what remained of the night, Michael had taken refuge on his most distant strip of carpet, behind the furnace in the basement.

159

13

BRICHTER wasn't whistling when he came into the squad room the next morning. He took the coffee urn down the hall to the janitor's closet to rinse it in the deep sink and fill it, brought it back, put a new paper filter in the bin, put in two more scoops of ground coffee than the instructions called for, and plugged it in. While he was waiting for it to perk, he picked up his orange mug, noting for the first time in a long time the bristling lettering around it. *Illegitimi non Carborundum.* It was, his wife had once assured him, very bad Latin, though its meaning was clear: Don't let the bastards wear you down. "Huh!" he snorted. Or the women.

The door opened and a cheerful voice cried, "Good morning, everyone!" even though Brichter was the only one present. McHugh came into the squad room like the sun coming from behind a cloud, right into your eyes.

Brichter turned his back and went to his desk. He sat down

and opened the fattening manila folder labeled "Wagner-Arson-Murder," and wished he hadn't tried to eat breakfast. The half an egg and one slice of toast seemed to have stopped halfway down. He forced himself to concentrate. The Wagner case was getting unwieldy, even for two investigators. For example, he had not yet found time to interview Mrs. Vigotti. That had better go to the top of the list today.

"How's it going, Pete?" asked McHugh.

"Just fine." Brichter heard it come out wrong and noted McHugh's approach with despair. His paternal interest in Brichter's personal life could be helpful or wearing, depending on Brichter's mood.

"What's wrong?" asked McHugh.

Brichter flipped a page in the folder and tried again. "Nothing."

"So where's the merry whistle?"

"How about we be cops today, instead of goddamn social workers?"

McHugh stopped unbuttoning his topcoat. "What's that supposed to mean?"

"Nothing, not a thing."

"You and Kori still having that fight?" McHugh seemed surprised.

"That is not any of your business."

"There have been times you've asked for my advice on your domestic situation."

"A mistake I won't make again."

McHugh, coat hanging off his shoulders, came toward Brichter. "Has she talked to you recently? Maybe I should call her. I mean, when I was out there Saturday, I noticed—"

Brichter could think of no way to stop this conversation without baring some bad-old-days teeth at McHugh. "I thought I told you to stay the hell away from her, you goddamned, fat-ham interfering slobgobbet!"

161

McHugh made a comedy of shrinking back and scuttling off to the coatrack, but he said nothing more to Brichter.

.   .   .

An hour later, Brichter drove alone to the Vigotti residence and sat out front for a minute to discipline himself into a patient frame of mind. There was a tightness around the back of his head he knew to be a danger sign. The interview was already off to a bad start.

Mrs. Vigotti had agreed to answer questions only if Brichter would come to her house rather than meet on some neutral ground, and if he would allow the presence of a lawyer. This could mean nervousness, and Brichter would have to be careful not to alarm her further. Or it could mean guilty knowledge on her part, and careful tiptoeing around on his part might simply conclude the interview before he got anything of value from her. Right now, he didn't feel capable of ordinary care, much less tiptoeing.

He tried an old trick. He made a picture in his head of a huge bank safe, put his fury into a heavy metal canister, trundled it on a two-wheeled cart into the safe, came out, and with great effort closed the door, giving a hearty twist to the dial. Satisfied, he got out of his car, went up the walk and pushed the doorbell.

The house was a butter-colored split-level with pale-blue trim, beautifully maintained. Nice juniper bushes along the front.

Mrs. Vigotti was also beautifully maintained, a short woman of obvious Italian parentage, her salt-and-pepper hair tucked into a fat bun at the nape of her neck, her kind dark eyes guarded. She wore a violet knit dress, adorned, and clutched a small white handkerchief with very fine crocheted lace edging, also violet. A silver crucifix gleamed at her throat. She merely nodded at his ID display and led him up five steps to a formal living room done in putty and pale lavender. There was a smell of coffee and, more faintly, Italian cooking.

A man stood in front of the striped velveteen couch. He was of medium height and build, with a tanned face surmounted by a lot of curly dark hair. His suit was black pinstripe, padded at the shoulders and pinched in at the waist. The handkerchief in his pocket was vivid yellow. "Sergeant Brichter, I believe," he said, extending his hand.

"Mr. Lazarre," said Britcher, taking it. Lazarre's presence set off an alarm: he was the criminal defense attorney Joe Januschka kept on permanent retainer.

"Would you like some coffee?" asked Mrs. Vigotti.

"No, thank you, ma'am," said Brichter.

"No, I'm fine," said Lazarre.

"Well, then," she said, and sat down on the couch. Lazarre sat beside her and Brichter took the matching chair. "What would you like to ask me, Sergeant?" Her manner was like her living room—formal but not uncomfortable.

Brichter brought out his notebook and a pen. "First, I suppose, when did you last see your husband?"

"Friday evening about eight P.M. He went out and didn't come back." Mrs. Vigotti's Philadelphia accent was stronger than her husband's.

"Did he say where he was going?"

"To see a friend."

"Did he say which friend?"

"No."

"Did he say when he would be back?"

"Not in so many words, no."

"But you expected him back in an hour or so?"

"Maybe longer. I didn't think he'd be gone overnight or anything like that."

"When did you become concerned?"

163

"When I woke up the next morning and he hadn't come in, I got scared."

Her husband was not with any of their friends, she said, wringing the little handkerchief in her plump hands. Nor had he contacted any of his family back east. Yes, she'd called to check. No, they hadn't had a quarrel the night he went out. No, he hadn't been worried, anxious, or upset.

"How old is your husband?" asked Brichter.

"Fifty-two."

"Does he have any medical problems?"

"High blood pressure. He takes pills. But I called the hospital and he's not there and he hasn't been there." She twisted the little handkerchief into a rope.

"Mrs. Vigotti, is it possible that something happened to your husband, that he's dead?"

She stared at him and he thought she was merely surprised at his question until the tears began spilling over.

· · ·

Brichter went back to the squad room and began typing up his notes on the interview. The phone rang and he scooped the receiver up and said, "Organized Crime Unit, Detective Sergeant Brichter. May I help you?"

"Brichter, that's the man I want. This's Martinson, Intelligence Division, Philadelphia Police. You called here some while back asking what we got on one Anthony Vigotti, right?"

"Yes, and I—"

"Yeah, I know, I know. We apologize for mislaying your inquiry card. Now, here's what we got. He's a reputed member of the Fordero bunch, or rather, was. Fordero's doing twenty to life at Danbury—a night watchman died in one of his fires."

"Fires?"

"Fordero was running a great big arson ring, all up and down the coast, from Baltimore to Jersey City. Don't tell me it didn't get into the news—where are you, anyhow?"

"Just north of East Overshoe, West Dakota. Was Vigotti mentioned in the indictment?"

"No. He'd moved out of town some time before this broke. He wasn't directly involved in the arson operation; he was Fordero's bodyguard for a while, did some loan-sharking and enforcing on the side."

"He left before it got started?"

"Before it got big. The federal investigation covered the past six years, from the time it went interstate. We were running our own investigation, which went back ten years. Got the usual cooperation from the fed; namely, none. They managed to turn one of the participants around. He wore a wire and testified at the trial, blew Fordero and six others right out of the water, and got put into the witness program. Fordero's big, and he's got some very heavy connections."

"And Vigotti's name didn't come up."

"Not at the trial. Let me tell you what we got on him. He did time for agg assault back in the fifties, for larceny and for auto theft in the sixties. Then he hooked up with Fordero. Was his bodyguard and enforcer, did some loan-sharking on the side, but nothing provable. No outstanding wants or warrants on him at our end. Come on, where are you really, somewhere near Chicago?"

"Nearer than I like sometimes," said Brichter. "In your opinion, was this arson ring operating while Vigotti was still in Philadelphia?"

"Hell, yes. I don't think Vigotti was directly involved, but he had to know what his boss was doing."

"What do you know about his wife?"

"Constancia? Comes from a pure Sicilian mafia line. Her father was Fordero's uncle, born in the Old Country. Half her cousins are connected—hell, her brother's doing time in Danville for racketeering. A nice Catholic lady, but very loyal to her husband and the company he works for."

"The arson fires, can you tell me about them?"

"What about them?"

"For instance, was gasoline used in starting them?"

"Sure, why?"

"Because we've got an arson fire here that used gasoline."

"Shoot, that don't mean diddly. If they don't use gasoline, how do you know it's arson?"

.   .   .

A little after ten Dahl was at his desk. Brichter had called to say he wanted to speak with him, so Dahl pretended to be busy with paperwork while he waited.

The Homicide squad room, on the second floor, was long and narrow, with crayon-green walls and gray carpeting. An outside window running its length was covered with narrow-gauge green blinds. Four gray metal desks faced each other in pairs, and a fifth, Dahl's, was up against the wall of the lieutenant's office opposite the door.

The door opened and Officer Ballard came in. She glanced along the row of desks, saw him. Still by the door, she called, "Sergeant Dahl? I want to talk to you about Sergeant Brichter and that ticket of his you asked me to fix."

That got everyone's attention—and all the desks were occupied. Two of them even had visitors, investigators from other squads. Dahl stood and said, as much to them as to her, "Hey, what are you talking about? I never—"

"I talked to him after work last night and he about took my head off," she interrupted. "I thought you said he'd appreciate not having to make a court appearance. He seems to think I was trying to do something illegal and he's pissed as hell." Dahl was on his feet and walking toward her, both hands up in a shushing gesture. She seemed to think he meant he couldn't hear her, so she raised her voice and pointed a finger at him. "You said he was on official business! If he makes an official complaint and I get a visit from Internal Affairs, I'm going to

166

tell them it was you told me to take care of that ticket, you hear me?'' It was possible the guys in Internal Affairs could already hear her. "So maybe you should explain to him next time you see him that it was a mistake on your part, not mine, and see if you can calm him down, okay?''

Without waiting for an answer, she turned on her heel and slammed out. The door had barely ceased vibrating when it opened again and Brichter came in, a slip of paper in his hand. He walked up to Dahl and held it too close to his nose to be read, and asked in a cold, quiet voice, "You know what this is?''

Such was the fascinated concentration of everyone in the room that he was as audible as Ballard had been.

"No, what?''

"My receipt for the fine I paid on that speeding ticket I got Monday morning. I earned that ticket, Eddie. And I paid for it, just like I pay everything I owe. I don't know where you got the idea I don't, but you're wrong. And hear this, fart eater: If you stick your nose into my personal affairs again, you will lose that nose and maybe some other elemental portion of your miserable anatomy!''

And two seconds later, the door received its second jolt of the day.

. . .

Zak was reading a report from an electrical engineer who did analysis work for the Arson Squad.

The fire at Lynn's Holiday Plastics, it said, was caused by a defect located near the plug end of the extension cord, at the precise place where internal wires are broken by people yanking on the cord to pull the plug.

However, the engineer noted, it normally took time for this sort of flaw to develop. This cord wasn't particularly old— nor was it new: There were scratches on the prongs and inside the other end, indicating it had been connected and discon-

167

nected a number of times. There were some scratches and wear marks on the insulation, too; but again, not a great number.

Zak made a note on his pad. Miss Carroll had said Mr. Lynn had brought cord and heater to her, saying he'd just bought them both. "Ask Lynn re cord," he wrote.

There were virtually no scratches on the prongs of the heater's plug, continued the report. There was evidence the heater had a defective thermostat, but was too damaged in the fire for that to be determined with certainty.

Zak was no electrician, but he'd been to enough fires in his time to know the danger of worn electrical cords. A cord abused in the manner described could seem just fine, but have enough of the internal wires broken that it could no longer handle any kind of load. The remaining wires would heat until they melted, causing a short, which would send the wires and burning insulation flying. The circuit breaker would blow, but by then the fire would be started.

The analyst had an alternate theory for how the cord might have been damaged, and Zak had to read it twice before he understood what the engineer was getting at. But the real bombshell was on the last page. Winding up smaller details, the engineer had made a drawing of a logo he'd found stamped on the cord. Zak muttered a startled expletive, pulled out his wallet and from it took the business card Brichter had given him. Given the difference natural to amateur hands, the three-tower design the engineer had found on the cord was an exact match for the Tretower logo.

14

THEY hadn't talked much last night; they were too busy being careful not to set off the quarrel again. She had sent the housekeeper home and cooked supper herself; he had cleared the table and started the dishwasher. Then they had sat in the library reading separate books until it was time for bed. Michael had stayed in the kitchen; silence didn't fool him.

But in the morning there was a residue of peace from the quiet evening before. "More coffee?" she offered.

And he, wanting to nurture the fragile peace, said, "No, I'm trying to cut back."

Her eyebrows lifted, then her polite smile turned real and his heart went sideways. He'd do anything to keep that smile coming. "I'll make a deal with you," he said. "If you won't mention having a baby for one year, then during that year I will talk to you about my work."

For some reason the offer amused her. "I don't think I can wait a whole year."

"Six months, then? And I promise, six months from today we will reopen the question."

"Unless you mention it first?"

"I'll try not to do that."

"All right. And you don't have to bring home all the gory details, you know. Just things like how you and Sergeant Dahl are getting along."

He didn't reply until the waiting silence had gone on long enough for him to realize what she meant. "Ah," he said, "apart from the fact that my gorge rises every time I see him, pretty well."

"When I came home from shopping yesterday, he was here to see me."

"What did he want?"

"For me to pass along his apology to you. He's sorry you misunderstood his trying to help you with that ticket."

"Not as sorry as he's going to be."

"He seemed sincerely anxious that his mistake not ruin the investigation you're doing together."

"There's nothing to ruin. We're not really working together; he's working his list of people, I'm working mine."

"But if he comes to you with information or questions about this case, would you please not leave pieces of his ego all over the wall?"

"Ego on the wall?"

"That's what he said happened to him yesterday."

A satisfied smile tweaked the corner of Brichter's mouth, and he settled back in his chair to tip his cup high for the last of his coffee. "No, I won't lay into him again so long as he behaves himself—not after this next time, anyway. I don't like him coming out here uninvited." He looked at his watch

170

and stood. "Now I'd better get going, if I don't want another ticket."

"I'll see Rose this afternoon. I'll tell her no more secret plots, okay?"

Thinking of the terms he intended to use on Dahl, Brichter said, "Uh, you won't make her mad, will you?"

"I'll be the very soul of tact."

She walked him to the door and they exchanged a long hug before he set off to the squad room.

·   ·   ·

A jogger huffing steam into the chill, damp morning air along the Eerie River slowed to a halt when he saw the big bite taken out of his customary path.

The river, swollen by unusually heavy autumn rains, had been undermining its banks along the bluffs of Riverside Park, and the jogger had encountered several earthfalls. But this was a big one, and he had to work his way between some thornbushes and the missing segment of path to get by. Safely past, he turned to peer over the edge at the fresh raw earth of the bluff, fuzzy with tree roots. Nine feet below was a swirl of muddy water. Halfway down something drooped out of the riverbank like a science-fiction-size slug. It was a muddy sheet, and a second glance told what filled it. The jogger set a new personal record for the half mile as he ran for a public phone to report his find.

·   ·   ·

Ryder came in shortly after Brichter did and gestured at him. "I want to see you, right now." His tone was curt.

Ryder frequently joked about his minuscule office, but he didn't look about to crack a joke as he sat down at his small desk and leaned his chair back until it touched the wall behind him. He studied the thin, wary-looking man standing before him, his own rumpled face serious under its white thatch. He barked, "What's the matter with you, anyway?"

171

Brichter, pressed, responded, "I have a mild congenital stoop, am missing a piece of lung from an old Navy incident, and suffer a bit from male-pattern baldness." Ryder still didn't smile and Brichter added, more sincerely, "And I occasionally drive too fast. Is that what this is about?"

"No."

"Ah, Eddie Dahl."

"While officially I frown on your filleting him in front of his fellow officers, here in the privacy of my office and off the record I say he had it coming."

"Then what have I done?"

"You handed Cris his head yesterday morning."

"I did? Oh, hell, that's right, I did."

"Why?"

Brichter pulled an ear. "He was asking me about something I didn't want to talk about."

"What?"

"A personal matter."

"Peter, are you relapsing into an old problem? First Cris, then Eddie?"

Brichter shook his head. "No, sir. The Eddie Dahl incident was staged. Only Cris was real."

"What kind of personal thing is eating you so bad you came down on Cris like that?"

If anyone else had asked that question, the gates would have slammed shut as bowmen appeared on the battlements. But Ryder had been firm and patient with Brichter five years ago, when Brichter badly needed someone to be firm and patient with him. A bond had formed that had yet to be broken. Brichter's acknowledgment of Ryder's special authority over him—a concession consciously given and rigidly adhered to —was Brichter's contribution to the bond.

"Katherine and I have been quarreling over something," Brichter said. "We were up late night before last, shouting it over. Cris thinks he ought to be allowed to intervene. I warned him, but he kept coming, so I let loose at him."

"You want to talk to me about it?"

"No, sir. We're working it out."

Ryder studied Brichter for a moment and gave a little nod —his knowing when not to press was his contribution—and Brichter sighed, relieved.

"Straighten things out with Cris," said Ryder. "And quit allowing your domestic problems to cause trouble in the squad room."

"Yes, sir." Brichter started to reach for the doorknob.

"By the way," said Ryder.

"Yes, sir?"

"That lady officer—what's her name?—Ballard. She came to Eddie over this ticket thing, too."

"Yes, sir, I know."

Ryder grinned. "I thought you might."

.   .   .

McHugh was at his desk, humming "Joe Hill" as he typed a report. He was wearing an old Army jacket with sergeant stripes on it. Brichter wondered how this might connect with anarchism, but decided not to ask. He simply stood and waited for McHugh to acknowledge his presence. McHugh let him stand a good fifteen seconds, then held out a stiff-armed hand. "I'm only taking insults in writing from now on," he said.

"Why, so you can publish them in the goddamn paper? Why did you have to go crying to Frank over a simple insult?"

"Simple? 'Interfering fat-ham slobgobbet,' and I believe I am quoting correctly, is not a simple insult. You came in primed with that one, Pete. 'Slobgobbet' is a first-class neologism no one, not even you, can dream up on the spur of the moment."

" 'Slobgobbet' is the name of a demon in a book by C. S. Lewis, and is, so far as I know, his neologism."

173

"Oh? Oh. Well, for the record, I didn't go to Frank, he came to me. He noticed when he came in that the temperature in the squad room was ten degrees lower than usual, and you know how he is about his people getting along. I thought you gave up collecting insults when you gave up insulting people."

"I haven't given up insulting people; they just don't take me as seriously as they used to. My latest acquisition, by the way, is a replica edition of a book published in 1811, a dictionary of underground slang. Did you know that 'pig' was slang for a cop among the pre-Victorian criminal class?"

"No, I didn't. And so what? Are you saying the next time some snotbrain calls me a pig I should be honored to be part of a long tradition?"

"No, I'm just making conversation while I nerve myself up to apologize."

McHugh jerked his head in the direction of the door to Ryder's office. "On orders, I suppose."

"Yes. But on the other hand, maybe I'm aware that I owe you one."

"Maybe?"

"All right. I owe you an apology. I shouldn't have slashed at you like that. I'm sorry."

"I accept your apology. And when I finish typing this, I want to tell you something you maybe don't know."

"Fine," nodded Brichter. "But if it's to the effect that my wife and Mrs. Cunningham are cooking up a promotion for me, or that they're priming the Chief to move me into that opening as his assistant, that is a false rumor."

"I must be spending too much time on the street; I hadn't heard that one. What's the source?"

"Eddie Dahl."

"Ha! After yesterday morning, nothing that bastard says about you will be believed." McHugh sat back and looked up at his friend. "You know he was out toasting his new pal Peter Brichter Saturday night."

"No, I didn't."

"That's my fault, at least partly. Last week he asked me how to make friends with you. He seemed serious, so I told him to play it cool and be nice to your wife. I said that when you were won over, you'd tell him to call you Peter. I should've known he'd play fast and loose with that. But it'll be a long time before he'll think he can fool anyone by dropping your middle name." McHugh chuckled his deep, rich sound of amusement. "So long as you aren't aiming it at me, I purely enjoy hearing casualty reports when that howitzer you call a mouth goes off." He sat forward and put his hands on his typewriter keys. "By the way, Crazy Dave Wagner may indeed be a problem gambler."

"Where did you hear that?"

"There was some talk around a poker table last night. He's banned from Dench LeBrett's games because he told the cops about LeBrett steering him to Vigotti."

"Wagner said he met LeBrett at a party."

McHugh sat back again. "LeBrett was the party in question, and his game is craps. LeBrett steered Dave Wagner to Vigotti when he lost big and couldn't pay off."

"So Wagner is a high roller?"

"He may be high elsewhere, but he's grounded in Charter."

Brichter sat on a corner of McHugh's desk. "Let's talk some more about Vigotti. So long as the subject came up at your poker game, did anyone have any opinions as to where he's gone?"

. . .

Marty Lynn of Lynn's Holiday Plastics was a fat man with little round eyes. His curly brown beard and thick brown hair were lightly sprinkled with gray. He looked as if he'd modeled

175

for one of his Styrofoam elves, as if he were normally funny and gregarious; but Miss Carroll had been right, the fire had taken the spirit out of him, leaving him with bags under his eyes and a nervous habit of fiddling with his beard, combing it with his fingers while thinking up answers to Zak's questions.

"Well, yes, I guess I did buy the cord and heater in the same place," he said.

"Where was that place?"

Lynn's fingers rummaged in his sideburns with a ferocity Zak found interesting. "Why do you ask?"

"Are you saying you don't remember where you bought it?"

"No, no. But I don't want to get someone in trouble for stocking defective merchandise."

"It would be the manufacturer, not the store owner, who got in trouble if an appliance was defective, Mr. Lynn."

"Oh, yeah." Silence.

Zak said, "Who sold you the cord and heater, Mr. Lynn?"

"Huh? Oh. Well . . ." He stopped playing with his beard and clasped his hands on his desk. He looked at Zak with unhappy eyes. "Do I have to tell you?"

"Do you have a reason for not telling me?"

"No, no. I mean, yes." Lynn sat back and bit savagely at a hangnail. "Shit," he muttered. "What brought on this sudden desire to know where I bought the cord and heater, anyhow?"

"A preliminary lab report indicates the cord was not new."

That truly seemed to surprise Lynn. "Not new? Sure it was. Ask Miss Carroll."

"I did. She said she didn't examine it closely, but assumed from what you told her the cord was new. But I have reason to believe it was in use somewhere else before you brought it into your secretary's office."

"Huh!" said Lynn, frowning. He began to search his chin for some explanation.

"So you see why I'd like to know how you came by a cord that appears to have belonged to someone else."

"I told you, I bought it. I bought it with the heater, both at the same time and the same place. As new. And I brought them into my office and I got down on my hands and knees and plugged them in my very own self. And it set my place on fire, almost killed my secretary, and now I got to put up with you treating me like I'm some kind of criminal, asking me all these questions."

"Which you are curiously reluctant to answer, Mr. Lynn."

"Am I?" Lynn turned around in his executive chair to look out the window. The clouds had finally cleared away; it was a pretty late-autumn day. A small flock of Canada geese were circling low over a man-made pond across the street—Lynn's was on the edge of an industrial park. The honk of the geese could be heard faintly through the office window, and they watched until the geese settled onto the water.

"Oh, all right," said Lynn, swiveling the chair back around. "I bought the cord and heater from a man who told me the cord was new and the heater was a factory reject he'd rebuilt himself. That's why I find it hard to believe the fire was caused by the cord. In fact, I still think the heater is at fault. Miss Carroll said something about the heater not being very efficient. I just took it as her natural critical attitude. She is a peach of a secretary, but when she dies and goes to heaven, she is going to have a few words with the Creator about His sloppy methods. Since the heater is a rebuilt, and since there was a fire, I think you should have another look at that heater."

Zak pretended to write this down. "Who sold you the cord and heater?" he asked, trying to make it sound like a new question.

177

"A cop. A friend recommended him as a guy who does electrical re-wiring and stuff around town for extra money. Underground economy, takes cash only. So you see why I don't want to tell you his name."

"Something he sold you nearly cost a human life, Mr. Lynn. I think you have a greater responsibility now to tell me who it is."

Lynn looked sick, then turned away to watch another short string of geese circle in. "Yeah, sure. And then he'll be pissed at me, and he'll tell all his cop friends, and I'll never be able to park my car or have a party or shovel my walk clean enough again. I've told you all I'm gonna—too much, in fact. Go on, get out of here. And next time you want to ask me any questions, see my lawyer first."

.   .   .

The door to the squad room opened and a hatchet face poked around the edge. "Obie, they found him," said Dahl. Armed with this important bit of news, Dahl nevertheless was prepared to retreat.

"Found who?"

"Vigotti."

"Where?"

"Riverside Park. Someone buried him in the bluffs, but all the rain we've been having undermined it along there, and a jogger found him sticking out."

"Come in," said Brichter. "I've got a couple of things I want to tell you, too."

Dahl, encouraged, walked to Brichter's desk, grabbed a chair from McHugh's desk on his way, flipped it around and sat down on it, inspiring a jolt of déjà vu.

"Was Vigotti shot?"

"Garroted. Still had the wire around his neck. So I guess that tells us what we wanted to know, huh?"

"What do you mean?"

"Well, this means it was Vigotti set the fire. Or, rather, hired Cleaves to do it. And Januschka was pissed at him because his boys are supposed to be running quiet right now, so he sicced that weirdo bodyguard of his on him—a wire's his favorite toy, you know. I told you all along it was Vigotti. Shit. I was hoping to bust his ass good for this. Now we might as well stick it in the files, because why bust our buns to prove a dead man did it? I don't know about you, but I got enough live perps to run down."

"What makes you think Joe Januschka is a better investigator than we are?"

"Huh?"

"We haven't found any real proof it was Vigotti. Has Januschka? Vigotti put two people in the hospital last week for failing to pay their debts despite Januschka's orders that his people lay off. That alone may explain Vigotti's presence in a riverbank."

Dahl hitched himself around on the chair, clearing his throat. "Well, yeah, when you put it that way. I just figured Januschka must know something we don't."

"He knows a lot of things we don't. Maybe one of them is that Vigotti's guilty. Until I know it too, I'd like to continue the investigation. Maybe it's someone we haven't come across yet."

"Aw, you're always doing twice the work—" Dahl caught himself, scratched under one ear with a forefinger. "What the hell, maybe you're right. So okay, we don't write this one off just yet. Now, what is it you wanted to tell me?"

"That from now on you are going to call me Sergeant Brichter and I am going to call you Sergeant Dahl. That you will refrain from telling people what good friends we are. And that you will not visit my home again for any purpose without a written invitation, which it will be a cold day in a hot place before you receive. Is that clear?"

179

Dahl, surprised and embarrassed, said, "Sure."

"Not 'sure.' I want to hear 'Yes, Sergeant,' said with some indication I'm getting through to you."

"Yes, Sergeant. Loud and clear."

"Good. Now, is there anything else you wanted to talk with me about?"

Dahl gamely followed the swerve back to business. "Well, if we're gonna keep looking, what do we look at next? I've been over everything I can think of, some of it two, three times."

"Have you spoken with the cops who patrol Wagner's district? They know the area. Even if they haven't seen anything themselves, maybe they know someone who did, or could have."

Dahl made a hasty note. "Right."

"And have you visited the neighborhood at night, at the time the fire occurred?"

"No, why?"

"Even in a business district, there are people who work nights. Janitors, for example. Embezzlers cooking the books. Workaholics. Go there at eleven, look around, see what lights are on. You may find someone who was there that night and saw something."

"Damn," muttered Dahl, writing that down, too.

Brichter had his own notebook out. "Do you know anything about some muscle named Hammer and Nish?"

"Great big guys? One of 'em's a Turk or something?"

"That sounds like them."

Glad to be on the giving side of the information booth for a change, Dahl said, "They used to hang out at The Shamrock. I tried talking to them once, but whether it was because I'm the heat or because they been taking 'ludes by the bushel, it was like . . ." He tapped his temple. "Nobody home, boss."

"I understand they worked for Vigotti."

Dahl nodded. "Yeah, but they're free-lancers at heart. Do kneecaps for fifty bucks a leg. You ever met them?"

"No."

"Scary types. Not just big; they don't listen when you talk to them, so you can beg, threaten—anything, and they just keep coming. You get this feeling you could shoot them, hell, you could run over them with a truck and not slow them down."

"Any idea where they are now?"

"Uh-uh. I was in The Shamrock last night and someone was saying he wondered where they got to. Maybe Joe told them to hit the trail after he had their boss taken care of. I wonder why?"

⋅ ⋅ ⋅

"Sergeant Brichter? This is Alison Fraasch. Remember me? Irene Cleaves's friend."

"Have you heard from her?"

"No, and I was wondering if you'd found out anything."

"No, I'm afraid not."

"Well, I've got a problem sort of related to that, and I don't want to get rid of it until I talk to you first."

"What kind of problem?"

"It's Pumpkin. My Julie's allergic to Pumpkin."

Brichter almost asked what that had to do with him, then remembered Pumpkin was the Cleaveses' cat. Still . . . "I don't think I understand why you're calling me about that."

"Well, Tom said I should just take the cat to the pound, but I decided I better ask: Is she evidence?"

"Of what?"

"I don't know; you're the policeman!"

"All right, you're right. No, I don't think Pumpkin is evidence."

"Well, I'd keep her anyway, but Julie wheezes something

181

terrible when they're in the same room. The doctor said the cat has to go, and then I get to scrub down the whole house to get rid of the dander, he calls it. I've asked everyone I could think of and no one will take her. So then I thought I should check with you, because I don't want you to be all mad when you find out she's been . . . put to sleep.'' There had been an article in the Sunday *Clarion* about overcrowding at the Charter County Animal Shelter, and how it would be necessary for some heavy culling to be done, especially among the cats, to bring the numbers down.

"And you want me to find her a new home?"

"Oh, could you? Thanks! She's had her shots; Irene was really good about that, because of Beth. Really, thanks! Bye!"

Brichter hung up and sat back in his chair. Slick lady. He was tempted to call her back and ask her why she thought she could pull that stuff on him; but there was no need to condemn Pumpkin to an early death just to show a little blonde she couldn't push a big bad cop around.

There was an easy solution to this, maybe. Any farm has its clowder of cats, and Tretower was no exception. It would not be politic just to turn up with an addition, but he could call and ask. And he was not averse to hearing her voice in the middle of the day.

He had to let it ring awhile, and the tinny quality of her voice when she answered told him she was in the barn. He asked, ''Are we very overstocked in the cat department? There's an orange female that needs a home. Spayed, and shots up to date.''

"Who's asking this time? Honestly, just because we have a barn . . .'' What did she mean, ''this time''? He'd only brought a cat home once before; she was the one who was always taking in strays. But he didn't voice his thoughts; she was sounding hassled already.

"I'm sorry to call when you're busy, but the cat goes to

the shelter if I can't find a home for it. It's a nice cat and they don't want to dump it, but a baby's allergic."

"Oh, well, I suppose one more won't matter. But I hope you aren't going to ask me to come and get it."

He discarded that idea also unvoiced. "I'll bring it out. Thanks, *fy'n galon*." He hung up, but left his hand on the receiver in a kind of caress. It was as well she hadn't objected to his resumption of the endearment, because he'd have to be very careful to avoid a slip; he thought of her in his head as *fy'n galon*. It was a Welsh endearment that translated to "my heart." Her father had called her that; it had been for a long time virtually her only memory of him. Brichter had taken it up when he discovered Kori was a nickname given her by her wicked uncle and therefore not a word he cared to find on his tongue. Katherine was for formal occasions, and for when they were quarreling. But even then, in his head, she was *fy'n galon*. When she was mad at him, it was as bad—and scary—as having angina. He shook himself, picked up the phone, and called Alison back.

15

"WHY did you want to see me?" asked Dahl, lowering himself into the blue plastic chair in front of Zak's desk. He leaned back in a calculated, insolent pose, his little mouth in the hatchet face smiling and his small dark eyes partly hidden behind white lashes. Zak particularly disliked the man, which made him all the more determined to be fair.

"I just got back from seeing Marty Lynn of Lynn's Holiday Plastics. He had a fire Monday morning, you know."

Dahl shrugged indifferently. "No, I didn't know." He lifted his chin and frowned. "You think there's a connection with the Crazy Dave fire?"

"No. Mr. Lynn says a policeman, a detective, sold him a rebuilt space heater and an extension cord last Thursday."

"So?"

"The cord was the cause of the fire."

"And you think it was me sold it to him? No, I never met the guy."

"He says this policeman does electrical repair work for people."

Dahl shifted in the chair, crossed his legs. "Now that sounds like me. But I do it just for my friends. How did he know about it?"

"Did you ever do any work for Sergeant Brichter?"

"What's Brichter got to do with it?"

"Maybe nothing. Have you ever done any work, outside of the department, for Sergeant Brichter?"

"Not electrical work. Me and Sergeant McHugh did some repair work on a shed roof out at their ranch on Saturday. I do carpentry, too."

"Did you see any evidence that he might be more skilled in electrical work than people might think?"

"No," said Dahl, puzzled.

"Is it true that you and Brichter have quarreled since you did that work out at the ranch?"

Dahl's lipless mouth stretched into another small grin, but his eyes shifted nervously. "Yeah, we had a misunderstanding. But it's over, and we're still partners."

"How serious was this 'misunderstanding'?"

Dahl scratched his cheek with a forefinger. "I wish you'd just tell me what you're after. How does my having a little spiff with Pete—with Sergeant Brichter—connect with a fire at Lynn's Plastics?"

"It may be very relevant. How serious was this 'spiff'?"

"I don't think it was very serious. I mean, I was trying to do him a favor, save him a minor courtroom appearance, and he took it wrong. Wrong, hell, he was cold-ass pissed, but I explained and we're okay now. I was just down to his squad room for a meeting and we got along fine."

185

"Is Brichter aware that you do electrical work?"

"Hell, I don't know! He may be. Why?"

"I was wondering why a fire that appears to be arson, that by some evidence points to you, should by other evidence point to Sergeant Brichter."

Dahl was suddenly alert. "What do you mean?"

"Mr. Lynn refused to name the police officer who sold him the cord and heater, but the remarks he did make about the man point quite clearly to you. On the other hand . . ." Zak opened a file folder and handed over a five-by-seven glossy photograph. "This is a close-up of a mark on an electrical cord that caused the Lynn fire."

Dahl looked at the photo. "What is it, a manufacturer's mark?" asked Dahl.

"Don't you recognize it?"

Dahl looked again, frowning. "No, I don't think so."

"It's the Tretower Ranch logo."

"Well, I'll be dipped," said Dahl. "So it is. But I still don't get what you're after here."

"The Lynn fire was arson."

Dahl made a little circular motion with the photo. "And this cord was part of it, somehow."

"Someone interfered with this cord so that it started the fire."

"And what this Lynn person says makes you think it was me." Dahl studied the photo. "But the cord came from Tretower Ranch, right?"

"It appears that it did."

"And maybe Lynn was primed to say those things by the person who really did bring him the cord and heater. So why aren't you talking to Brichter, too?"

"I will be. Do you still deny you sold Lynn the cord?"

"Absolutely. What kind of 'interference' are we talking about here?"

"My lab man says it could have been done by bending the cord over and over at one spot until the wire inside the insulation started to break. A cord damaged like that would not be able to handle the heavy drain of a space heater; the weak spot would heat up enough to start a fire. This is a sophisticated method; the wires must be strong enough to carry the current for a while, yet weak enough so that a predetermined load will cause a fire within a certain time, which might be after normal working hours, when no one is around. Bent too often, the wires break altogether and the cord won't work at all. It would take skill to bring cords to that point reliably—this is not the first fire someone has set with this method, though in this case a defect in the heater kept it from working as planned."

"Did he open it up to see if it was just damaged enough?"

"Neither Lynn or his secretary noticed the cord was dam aged; in fact, they both seem to think it was brand new. My expert suggests the arsonist used a highly sensitive ohmmeter to measure increasing resistance in the wires as they began to break."

Dahl nodded. "Yes, I see. But I wouldn't've thought Obie knew enough about electricity to do something like that. He's always letting on he's got the mechanical aptitude of a teddy bear. Of course, he also lets everyone think he's lacking in the brawn department, too, but I happen to know something different about that."

.　　.　　.

Dahl beat a hasty trail down the inside stairs from Zak's office to the parking garage, trotted to his car and squealed his tires up the steep ramp to the street. "Damn, damn, damn, DAMN!" he muttered. That'll teach me to pay goddamm attention. That goddamm mark on the cord, I never saw it. This is Brichter's fault, he must've given me the wrong cord. If that heater had only worked like it was supposed to, there wouldn't've been enough cord left to find a mark on.

187

Dahl took a corner on three wheels and shoved the accelerator down hard. But it's okay, I hope, he thought. That stupid fireman was already primed to believe Brichter framed me. Everyone knows he sicced Linda onto me about that ticket, so why shouldn't they believe he took the opportunity to frame me for an arson he committed, too? But now I got to move fast. I left my own cord out there in that exchange on Saturday. If I can get it back, I'll be home free. He took another corner too fast, tires yipping.

Whoa there, *compadre*, he thought, slowing down. Fireman Zak isn't bright, but he ain't all that dumb, either; it may take something more to tie the can to the Tretower tail. Think, dummy, think!

. . .

Dave Wagner walked into the shabby liquor store, to the cooler box in back, where he took out a six-pack. He slowed as he went by the snacks, but didn't pick up any. He went to the front cash register and put the beer on the counter.

" 'Lo, Ogden."

"Afternoon, Mr. Wagner. Got your usual, I see."

"Yep." Wagner pulled his wallet out of his back pocket. "By the way, I really owe you one. If it wasn't for you, I'd be in jail right this minute. It was you remembering I was in here for beer and cheese curls that Thursday night that gave me an alibi." Which was why he was here, of course. On the slim thread of Ogden's memory hung his freedom, and he was anxious to strengthen that thread.

"So they still think it was arson at your store, huh?"

"Yeah. And everything's in limbo till they get some kind of handle on who did it. But at least they aren't looking at me anymore."

"Well, you mentioned poker when you came in that night, and it was Thursday you played with your friends, so there you are. I suppose you want a *Racing Form*, too?" Koch reached for one on a stack beside him.

"No, thanks. I've sworn off gambling until the insurance company comes through. I got so close to being cleaned in a poker game last night that this six-pack represents the last of my discretionary income." Which was an exaggeration of sorts. He was buying the six-pack with fully half of what remained of his resources.

.   .   .

Storm Wind was definitely lame now, and the vet said her pregnancy would only aggravate it. So it would be heat treatments and confinement until the middle of February. They wet her side with the special lotion for the ultrasound scan, and the news was bad again: the mare was carrying twins.

The farrier, meanwhile, was having his own problems with Chinook, who was being fitted with special shoes to control a tendency to paddle-foot. The yearling, who had a low boredom threshold to begin with, and more imagination than was desirable in an animal whose biggest daily worry was the size of her morning flake of hay, decided to play the farrier's visit for all it was worth. The farrier was a horse thief, and his forge a dragon; his hammer an instrument of torture, his hand on her flank an unendurable insult. It had taken the vet, Kori, and Danny, all three, an interesting and flattering time to calm her, and almost as long to persuade the bruised and angry farrier to finish his job.

And through it all, Danny, who had asked for a couple of hours off and to borrow the pickup, had become increasingly impatient.

But at last it was all over. Danny was gone, and she was hanging up Chinook's bridle after replacing a buckle broken in the mixup with the farrier. She was looking forward to a nap before helping Mrs. Morales start supper.

189

This new desire to sleep in the middle of the day had worried her until the doctor had said it was a predictable symptom of early pregnancy. Indulge it, he had said; it has its purposes.

And then Eddie Dahl came in, anxious to recover a stupid extension cord.

"I know it's a bother, but I thought you might want your own cord back, and I know I'd like mine." In honor of the sunny day, Dahl was carrying his topcoat draped over one arm. There was something about the way he was standing with it that suggested a hat also doffed.

So she politely concealed a sigh and said, "Of course, I understand. The cords are in the equipment shed, I think. Will you wait here?"

"Sure. Take your time."

She left him in the barn's tack room, where he'd come looking for her.

.   .   .

Brichter rang the doorbell at the Fraasch house and Alison answered. She was wearing a blue ruffled apron and had tied the matching headscarf at the back of her head. "Hi, I was hoping it was you. I'm already starting on Julie's room, cleaning. Just a sec, I'll get Pumpkin." She hurried off, leaving him standing on the doorstep, and was back very promptly with the orange tiger cat in her arms.

"Someone told me orange female cats are rare," she said, "so maybe it's a shame this one has been fixed." The cat was lying very comfortably on its back in her arms, and regarded him with a complacent eye. "You be a good kitty, and catch lots of mice for your new mommy and daddy." She held out the cat and Brichter took it. "You don't think she'll mind living in a barn?"

"Our barn is heated and insulated, and there's no lack of high perches and interesting company."

"Good, because she loves to sit up on high things. Thank

190

you for taking her," said Alison. She looked away, listening. "Oh, there's Julie, up for her playtime. Bye-bye, Pumpkin."

.   .   .

Dahl pulled out a handkerchief, shook it out and tossed it up in the air so it came down over his hand. With the covered hand he reached under his topcoat and pulled out his Keithley 580 ohmmeter, putting it on the floor under a wooden work-bench. He stepped back to see how visible it was, then bent and moved it farther back. Satisfied, he put the handkerchief away and heard the barn door open.

He went to look, saw Kori coming back with an orange extension cord coiled in one hand, her big black dog at heel beside her. The sun streaming through high small windows made a series of spotlights on the dirt floor which she kept walking into and out of, as if she were Jimmy Durante on a stage. But she didn't look or walk anything like Jimmy Durante. She was slim and neat in her white shirt with the sleeves turned back, knit vest, and tan riding pants, not hiding her figure, but not making a sexy display, either. What a classy dame, thought Dahl. Too bad I never got a break like that; no one I ever encountered in the line of duty turned out to be worth my attention afterward.

And that included wife number two, who retired from her job as streetwalker to marry him, and then expected him to remain faithful. Last he heard she was dealing blackjack in Reno, where she'd gone to get the divorce. Mrs. Brichter probably didn't know blackjack from a candy bar. No wonder Brichter had grabbed her with both hands. All that class—and all that money.

This is the way I wanted my life to turn out, thought Dahl. Living in the country with a classy wife who rode horses that won blue ribbons, walking toward me with a kind of smile on her face, just like this one. But the dog at her side should be a cocker or an Irish setter, not an oversize poodle. At least

191

she hasn't got it clipped like you sometimes see pictures of them, big in front and nothing behind, with a fuzzball on the tail. With that all-over-curls look, the dog might almost be some kind of mutt. Dahl blinked himself out of his musing, came out the door and started across the arena toward her. He didn't want her to come into this room while he was still here. "Your cord's in the trunk of my car," he said. "I'm sorry, I should have waited outside for you to come back."

"That's all right," she said, but not as if it were, and turned on her heel to lead the way back out.

"I didn't want to get it out and give it back to you until I was sure you had mine," he said, stepping over the high sill at the door. "I use it all the time."

They went across the gravel together, and to the rear of his car.

"Nice-looking dog," he said to her. "You told us his name on Saturday, but I forget."

"Michael D'Archangelo." The dog, hearing his name, looked up at her, and his mouth fell open in a silly grin, tongue lolling. Between the grin and the curls coming down over his eyes, he looked like the kind of dumb dog you'd see in a Burt Reynolds movie.

"Excuse me," Kori said, "but could I have my cord back?"

"Huh? Oh, sure." He twisted the key in the trunk lock and hoisted it. The cord was not in sight. "Well, I'll be damned!" he said, lifting a blanket as if to look for it. "It was here; I put it in here myself yesterday! I think," he added, frowning.

He gave Kori his best rueful smile. She was looking frankly exasperated. "I'm sorry," he mumbled, closing the trunk. "I guess I should've checked before I came out to see if it was there. I'll go home right now and get it, bring it out."

"No, don't bother," she said. "Here, take yours and bring ours to Peter at work."

He put his cord in the trunk of the car, apologized again

and left. He was crossing the Eerie River Bridge on his way back into town when he saw the red Porsche going the other way. But he didn't think Brichter saw him.

.   .   .

She struggled up off the bed when she heard his voice addressing Mrs. Morales downstairs. "Taking a nap?" he was saying, surprised.

"She's been having a hard day," said Mrs. Morales.

"Peter?" she said from the top of the staircase. "What are you doing home?" She was tying her robe on, having decided to face him that way rather than chance he might discover from Mrs. Morales why the nap had become a feature of her day.

"I brought the cat," he said, lifting it a little. "Was Eddie Dahl out here again?"

She started down the stairs. "You really are a detective; how did you know?"

"I passed him on my way out. What did he want?"

"We gave him the wrong extension cord last Saturday, and he came out to trade back. Only he forgot to bring ours. You'll probably find it on your desk when you get back to work. Oh, what a pretty cat!"

Brichter held the creature out to her. "She sat on her own side all the way, no roaming, no yowling for rescue at the windows, no trying to help me steer; I never saw a cat behave like that before."

Kori came the rest of the way down and took the cat into her arms. Pumpkin accepted the transfer docilely. She had a white nose and chin and white paws. She also accepted being tucked on her back into Kori's left arm, and studied Kori's face as earnestly as Kori studied hers. "You have a nice face, Pumpkin," said Kori. She ran the back of her fingers up the cat's forehead, and Pumpkin captured them in her two paws, sniffed them, then began to wash them with an emery-board tongue. Kori pressed one paw gently between thumb and fore-finger.

"Peter, we can't put this cat in the barn."

"She's on the small side, I know, but—"

"She's not just small, she's got no claws. The others always pick on newcomers until they find their place in the cat hierarchy, and poor Pumpkin would be cat number last forever with no claws to defend herself with." Poor Pumpkin stopped licking long enough to look adoringly up at her new mistress and trill a query.

"So what are we going to do with her?"

"I don't know yet. We'll think of something, won't we, little one?" Pumpkin trilled again, then resumed licking. She also started to purr.

"Do you want me to wait around while you decide?"

"No, no. You go on back to work. I'll take care of it." She turned and walked toward the kitchen, dipping her head to coo at the cat. "Is the little one hungry?" Which made Brichter smile. If she continued like this, in a day or two she'd forget who foisted it on the household.

· · ·

To explain the time he'd spent away from the squad room, Dahl made a couple of quick calls. The patrol officer who covered the area that included Crazy Dave's TV and Appliance said the store's big front windows had been covered with giant white paper signs announcing a sale for the last few days before the fire. They had obscured the interior of the store, which was why it was a practice not recommended by the police, and which was why he remembered them. But he knew nothing bad about the owner or his tenants, or of anyone who might have something of interest to say.

An informant said none of the other tenants were into anything illegal he knew about, except the shoe-store pair. They were gay, which was illegal, wasn't it? But no, they didn't do drugs or handle hot merchandise, or star in porno movies, so far as he knew. Nor did the bookstore fellow or the lady with the T-shirts.

On his way back to the Safety Building, Dahl stopped at a pay phone and called Syverson's Laundry and Dry Cleaners. "The deal's off," he said to the owner.

"What do you mean, the deal's off? I just increased my coverage!"

"Tough. Call and cancel it."

"Come on, why is the deal off?"

"Because I said it is."

"What's the matter, I'm not paying you enough?"

"No, the money's fine. Look, I wish I could do it, but I can't, and I'm not going to stand here and argue with you about it. And don't try to get in touch, okay? You stay away from me, or you got troubles you won't believe."

. . .

Brichter noticed the difference in Zak's attitude as soon as he walked into the office. Where there had been an increasing friendliness each time they met, now there was a distinct chill.

"Sit down, Sergeant," said Zak.

Brichter obeyed. "I'd ask if I've worn out my welcome, but you're the one who asked me to come by."

Zak said formally, "I have information on the Lynn Holiday Plastics fire that involves you."

"Me? What is it?"

"Remember the orange extension cord that connected the electric space heater to the outlet?"

"There was a cord under the desk; I don't remember it being orange." An alarm was sounding in Brichter's head and he sat up straighter.

"You looked at the cord, as I recall. Had you ever seen it before?"

195

"I doubt it, but I also doubt if anyone would have recognized it in that condition."

"You remember a discussion we had in the car on our way to the scene of the fire?"

Brichter frowned. "About horses?"

"About trademarks and brands. You drew one for me, one that connects directly to you. Have you any idea if the Tretower logo is used by anyone else?"

"To the best of my knowledge, no."

"I want to show you a drawing made of a mark found on that extension cord." Zak opened a file folder and took out the same drawing he had shown to Dahl. He handed it to Brichter.

Brichter took it and drew air just audibly through his teeth. "You're going to tell me the cord with this mark on it caused the fire."

"Mr. Lynn says he bought that cord and a space heater from a policeman. The cord has been tampered with in order that it would start the fire."

Brichter handed the drawing back. "I have never met Mr. Lynn or, so far as I know, anyone else who works at Lynn's Plastics. Did he name the cop?"

"No, he said he was afraid of reprisals if he did."

"Am I the only person you've questioned about this?"

Zak didn't answer, and Brichter said, "Do you want me to guess the other person you've talked to?"

"If you think you can."

"Eddie Dahl."

"Why do you say him?"

"I don't know what other evidence you have, but let me tell you this: Eddie Dahl was at the ranch last Saturday, helping repair a shed, and when we needed another extension cord, he had one in his trunk he let us borrow. It was the same color as our two, and when he left, he took an extension cord with him. But two hours ago he was out at the ranch again, saying we'd given him one of ours by mistake. And he didn't bring ours back; he said he'd forgotten to bring it."

"Had he in fact left his own behind?" asked Zak.

"My wife found an unmarked cord and gave it to him. And I told you how careful she is to mark everything. So I'd say yes, there was a trade. Accidental, as I was the one who handed him the cord at the end of the day. Did you talk to Eddie about this just over two hours ago?"

Zak checked his watch. "Yes."

Brichter sat back with an audible sigh of relief. "Then that's why he turned up so anxious to get his own cord back. And he didn't forget ours; he used it in the Lynn fire."

"But," said Zak, "Lynn said he bought the cord and heater on Thursday, before this alleged switch took place."

"All right, to establish that everything was working fine, he gave Lynn a good cord to use. Saturday he was at our place and Saturday night he was out on the town, so it was probably sometime Sunday that he took the doctored cord over. Has Lynn increased his fire insurance lately?"

"Yes, and at a time when he's been cutting back on other expenses, too."

"How do you fix a cord so it will start a fire?"

Zak explained the method. "Have you got a Keithley ohmmeter at the ranch?"

"I don't know. There's all kinds of equipment out there. I can tell a hacksaw from a monkey wrench if you give me three guesses, so I couldn't tell you if we have a meter for ohms. Would a Keithley be useful around a ranch?"

"No."

"Then we probably don't have one. Have you got an expert who will testify to the cause of the fire in court?"

"Yes, but not that the cord was deliberately interfered with. It could have been damaged through careless use. What I'm thinking is that Lynn will break. He's very upset about this, I think because Miss Carroll might have been severely injured or even killed fighting that fire by herself.''

"You aren't telling me he's fond of her, are you?"

Zak permitted himself a smile. "No. She's an interesting person, but hardly the sort to stir warm feelings in the heart of a man. I used to have a history teacher like her.''

"Me, too," said Brichter. "Only mine taught English.''

Zak said, "What I meant was, if a person dies in an arson fire, the charge becomes murder.''

"Yes, I know that. Oh, I see. A 'successful fire' is one thing; murder is another.''

Zak asked, "Can you account for your movements this past weekend?''

"Yes. I was with someone the entire time—" He winced. "No, she went to church Sunday morning, and I don't go to church; so there's an hour and a half unaccounted for. Danny was on the ranch, but he was in the barn, and I stayed in the house. On the other hand, Sunday afternoon we had company, about twenty people, and three of them stayed late for wine and conversation. They are Geoffrey Marshall, his wife Anne, and their son Benjamin, though I doubt if the kid will be very helpful; he's only eleven months old.''

"I'll have to ask Eddie Dahl to confirm the story of the mixed-up extension cord.''

"If he realizes why you want to know, which he will if he's guilty, he'll deny it. And if I'm lying, he'll deny it. So there's no joy there. But if you decide to charge me, you'll be hard-pressed to prove I need money badly enough to be tempted into felony—repeatedly, as I assume this is one of that series you told me about, electrical fires in small companies more than adequately insured. Shall we try for a better alibi for one of the other fires?''

"Later, maybe," said Zak, and Brichter knew Zak had accepted his story.

"I don't know how to test the resistance of an electrical cord with an ohmmeter," said Brichter. "On the other hand, I'm sure Eddie does. You might see if you can discover if he owns such an instrument."

.   .   .

Wagner was driving home in his "new" car, a battered and rusty Mustang. It was mostly a faded apple green, but the passenger door was blue and the front fender on that side was black. On the other hand, it had a V-8 engine and a four-barrel carburetor, and kept scooting out from under him at stop signs. Every time it did, the gas gauge dropped a little.

The back seat held a meager supply of groceries and the six-pack of his favorite beer. The rest of the money he'd gotten from the sale of his LeBaron made his wallet a comforting presence in his back pocket.

He hadn't wanted to sell his car, but he needed a chance to get well. He'd put the groceries away and drive over to Terre Haute and find a game there. Not craps; craps ate money at a breathtaking rate, and he wanted something that would last. Poker, maybe.

His luck was in, he could feel it. He'd win a few big pots, then switch to craps and win some more, and this time he'd bring the money home in bucketfuls.

His nerves were heated up like big antennas, thinking of the game to come. When his luck was in, it was as if a sixth sense told him which cards to hold and which to discard. A memory of one game swam up in his memory. The sweet tension of picking up the dealt cards and fitting them together in a perfect pattern, hand after hand, his struggle to keep the face neutral, his surreptitious glances at the faces of the other players, looking for signs they, too, held good hands. He had picked up his cards one at a time, to prolong the tension, but was quick and generous in betting, tossing the money into the pot as if he could not wait to get rid of it.

One hand, everyone had stayed in, everyone raised and raised again. Then, at the last unbearable moment, when the last raise had been called and the cards had to be shown, the tension peaked, then flowed away like water. It had been better than sex.

Had he won that hand? Yes, he thought he had. Funny how he almost never remembered whether the best hands ended in his winning or losing. He only knew it was the tension that he loved, that he could never get enough of it, that he came home only when he was out of money and had to quit.

A car's honk brought Wagner back to the present. The light had turned green, catching him unawares, with his hands gripping the unfamiliar steering wheel too tightly. And the stick shift was not where it should be, so the car behind had to honk again before he could put the Mustang in gear and pull away with a squeal of rubber.

This time it would be different; he'd clean out everyone and come home joyous. This time he couldn't lose.

Terre Haute. Tonight.

16

"EDDIE Dahl is an *arsonist?*" Kori did not believe it.

"Captain Kader has reason to think that if he isn't, I am." Brichter recounted his conversation with Zak. "I admit I wouldn't have thought it of Eddie," he concluded. "There have always been rumors about him, though when you know what they used to say about me, it's hard to take rumors seriously."

Diverted, she asked, "What did they used to say about you?"

"That I nearly got married once, but they couldn't figure out how to do a blood test on the *Encyclopaedia Britannica.*"

She giggled; there had been a time when she herself had wondered if there was any limit to his knowledge of esoterica.

"That the world will end when I die because God and Satan will go to war over who has to take me."

The giggle faded into a smile. "That's not nice."

"That I piss 10W-40 and shit road ice."

She frowned. "Who said that about you?"

"Mr. Anonymous, on a bathroom wall. But that was a long time ago."

She'd been looking over photographs of Copper Wind, one of which would form the centerpiece of an ad next spring for Tretower Ranch. She put the current favorite down and turned in her chair to look at him lounging against the wall by the door. "That's why you didn't like that talk on Saturday about dirty tricks, isn't it?" she asked. "You were given much more than the usual rough treatment back then."

"I asked for it, probably; I have what is sometimes called a personality problem. It's better since I met you."

"Well, I like you just fine," she said. "And if Eddie Dahl is typical of the people who were picking on you, then I'm glad they didn't like you!"

"He is, and he isn't. There's a lot of corruption in our department, which anyone who's read our newspaper or watched the local TV news for the past sixteen months knows. And Eddie has been more blatant than anyone—which is why he's been able to stay on the force when the others had to quit."

"I don't follow."

"The coward who makes a comedy act of his cowardice gets to stop being ashamed of it and still be cowardly. Eddie talks constantly about all the places he knows of that give free lunches, of the special deals he can arrange in the purchase of merchandise, and so forth. No one can be as constantly on the make as he pretends so be, so people tend to discount even his actual dishonesty, even while they know he's a crook. It's hard to take someone seriously while you're laughing at him. Whenever anybody asks who's a crooked cop, somehow Eddie's name is left off the list. But Eddie is rotten in other ways, too; with that alibi gun in his sock, and that goddamn sap glove he calls his 'attitude adjustment tool,' and—"

202

"Sap glove?" she interrupted.

"A leather glove with lead weights sewn into the knuckles. To make sure that when you hit someone he stays down, and that witnesses don't see you use a weapon on him." He offered his wry smile at her shocked expression. "You did say you wanted me to talk about my work."

"Yes, and I still do. What's an alibi gun?"

"A second gun, carried hidden in case you shoot someone who turns out to be unarmed. You can put it on your victim and claim he pulled it on you."

"But if everyone knew he was crooked, why didn't he get fired?"

"Lack of evidence. There were damn few complaints about him, considering, and most got dismissed, which sent a message to prospective complainers. And despite his cruddy behavior, he was—and remains—a decent investigator, making his share of arrests. Oh, he's on his way out now; but a cop is a civil servant, and the firing procedure is lengthy and complicated. And Eddie has to wait in line. Under the old Chief, the atmosphere positively encouraged people like him, each of whom has to go through the tedious firing procedure. Ex-Chief Donaldson's own fingers were stained, so he had to be careful lest he stir up his own pond, if I may mix my metaphors."

"Did the responsibility lie entirely with Donaldson? Why couldn't the rest of you have done something?"

"The rest of us were either lining our pockets with what the crooked ones dropped, or trying to find a safe bit of high ground to be standing on when the flood of reform hit."

"Including you?"

"Including me. I've told you, *fy'n galon*, I like being a cop. I wanted to go on being a cop. A cop who loses his job in a reform sweep may find it hard to be a cop somewhere else."

203

"All the newspaper stories about that grand jury summoning cops to testify about corruption. Why didn't they call you?"

"Because I was known to be clean, and I didn't know anything about the corruption."

"But—"

The lopsided smile was painful. "Personality problem, remember? Nobody talked to me; I had no tales to carry."

"Ha, you know all sorts of things about all sorts of people who go to great lengths to stay out of your way. You knew plenty about those corrupt cops, too, I bet. Suppose you had been summoned. What would you have told them?"

His face closed down. "I wasn't summoned, so it doesn't matter."

She, too, knew when to stop pressing. "Is Eddie under arrest for arson?"

"Not yet. It may take a while for Zak to gather the evidence. Meanwhile Eddie and I are still working together on the Crazy Dave arson case."

"How can you work with him, knowing what he is?"

"I'll breathe shallowly."

. . .

Dahl sopped up the last of his eggs with a corner of toast. The Coffee Cup Café, out near the freeway, featured a full menu, but served breakfast twenty-four hours a day, and offered half-price breakfasts to peace officers. A pair of highway patrolmen came in and stopped two stools up. Dahl nodded at them when their glance came his way.

"Hell, everyone knows about fingerprints nowadays," the younger one was saying. "I bet they haven't broken a case with fingerprints in fifteen years."

"Bullshit. Sure, everyone knows about fingerprints. But they still leave 'em behind." The pair tugged up their trouser legs and sat.

204

The waitress came by and refilled Dahl's cup, and he rewarded her with a wink.

The older one continued, "I know of a case where some kid broke into an old lady's house and beat the shit out of her with his flashlight. He stole some jewelry and her purse and she died three days later. By then they'd found the flashlight in a garbage can, with the old lady's blood and hair on it, but no fingerprints; the kid knew enough to wear gloves. But he'd put fresh batteries in it a week earlier, and forgot to wear gloves to do that. He had a record long as your arm, and even though his mama cried on the witness stand and said he'd spent the whole evening at home with her, the jury said he was guilty and the judge gave him life without parole—which he should have done two convictions back no matter how hard his mama cried. But the point is, fingerprints can still make a case."

Dahl opened his mouth to make a contribution to the conversation, then shut it again. He'd just remembered something about some batteries of his own. He'd opened up the Keithley right after he got it, to see what kind of batteries it used. They were nickel-cadmium, recharged in the meter as he ran it on house current, so he'd shut the case and never thought about it again. Today he'd wiped all over the outside before leaving it at the ranch, but in his impulsive hurry to get rid of the evidence, and in his glee over the clever idea of planting it at Tretower, he'd neglected to open it up and wipe the inside.

Of course, it was possible no one else would think to open it, either.

Except Brichter. In reviewing the Crazy Dave case with him earlier today, Brichter had humiliated him twice. A man who could so casually come up with two solid suggestions about places to look in someone's else's investigation was not a man who, when faced with a felony rap against himself, would forget to look absolutely everywhere for a way out.

He'd have to get back out there and fix things.

Michael D'Archangelo sat up on his strip of carpet outside his mistress's bedroom door. Just when he had thought things were settling down after a period of tension, they had to go and bring a cat into the house. Michael didn't mind cats, so long as they kept to their place, which was the barn. A cat in the house was a Disruption of the Natural Order of Things, and Michael liked everything nice and orderly. He had been forbidden to worry or tease the cat, even when it had sneaked into his food dish and left cat snot all over his kibble. His mistress had neglected to replace the kibble and Michael had, naturally, sulked the rest of the evening, finally filling the emptiness of his belly with water. And so now he had to make a trip outside.

He sighed and got up. He listened at the bedroom door to see if anyone was awake and so might be persuaded to come with him, but they were asleep. One of the rules was, Sleeping People are Not to Be Disturbed Except in Emergencies. (The cat had rules of its own, and had earlier created an awful ruckus right there in the bedroom, a place Michael was forbidden to enter, and was later allowed to make a prolonged growly noise while she stroked and spoke love words to it, another grievance stored away for rectification someday when only he and the cat were at home.) Since he had his own flapper door cut into the backdoor, having to go outside was not an Emergency.

Michael trotted down the corridor and the back stairs to his private exit.

. . .

Dahl pulled his car into an almost invisible lane at the eastern end of the ranch and left it there. No one passing by this time of night could see it. He waited until his night vision was in full bloom, then set out at a brisk walk for the ranch, prepared to duck off into the bushes if he saw approaching headlights.

But he'd waited until nearly three-thirty in the morning, an unlikely hour for traffic, and he didn't see another car.

A large pale square with dark printing loomed up, and beyond it a big silver mailbox marked the break in the white rail fence that was the entrance to the ranch. There was a barnyard light at the end of the lane, but otherwise the place was completely dark. Still, caution bid him to keep low and stop frequently to check for signs of life at the end of the lane.

.   .   .

Clouds were breaking up overhead; a half-moon was cradled in streamers of them. It was chilly, but not really cold. The air was moist and full of wet-earth and dead-leaf smells. Michael came off the porch and marked the northwestern corner of the little greenhouse, then a cement statue of Pan, and, in two places, an enormous old white maple that grew near the back rail of the racetrack. Feeling better, he decided to wander around the front and see if anything was stirring.

He visited, and marked, the oak tree where a squirrel he hoped to capture sometime lived, then snuffled idly along the border of a freshly spaded flower bed. The barnyard light down near the barn made it possible to see up here, but Michael was using his nose to trace the passage of a field mouse— His head came up. Someone was approaching the house. A human, on foot, walking a few steps bent-kneed, then rising to listen, then stooping to walk some more.

"Whuff," said Michael, but very softly, because the movement of the person very much resembled the way certain people moved, people he had been encouraged to jump on and bite during the wonderful Game his mistress had helped him learn. And during the Game, he was not to shout a warning unless ordered to do so.

Michael, pleased and excited, began trotting quietly down the sloping front lawn.

207

Dahl crossed the racetrack and found himself at the edge of a big, gravel-covered barnyard. There was no sign of anyone up and moving, but the idea of all that open space made him nervous. He took a couple of deep breaths, then set off at a run. He was halfway across when he was knocked down by something heavy slamming onto his shoulders, throwing him forward onto the gravel.

He lay half-stunned a few seconds, then tried to roll over. But the heavy something was on his back. It blew hot air across his right ear while saying, "Urrrrrr." Dahl, considerably enlightened, lay still again. He could identify pressure points now, forepaws on his shoulders, hind paws near his buttocks. A dog, a big one. That goddamn big black poodle.

His hands and knees began aching with the aftereffects of landing on stone. The dog's hot breath blew again across his ear, as it explored the side of his face. So where was Kori? He waited, but she didn't come to call the dog off. All right, the dog was operating on his own. And he, Dahl, was smarter than a poodle, he didn't care how big it was.

"Good dog, nice doggy," he said, and felt a heavy tremor in the animal. He almost laughed. It was wagging its tail. "Atta boy," he said, and the tremor increased its rhythm. "Okay, game's over. Let me up." He moved his arms, and the dog nipped him sharply on the ear and said, "ARRRRRrrrrrrrrrr!" He lay still again. All right, this wasn't going to be easy.

What did he know about the dog? An image rose in his head, of it sitting beside Kori this afternoon. A big dog with a silly grin and a silly cap of curls and a silly tongue hanging out of the side of its mouth. All of which served to distract from what the tongue had been hanging over. Teeth. Big teeth, now inches from his jugular.

Don't panic, he told himself. Think. What else about the

dog? He'd seen it sleeping in front of the fireplace last Saturday evening. It had allowed anyone who wanted to pat it, but it hadn't come around soliciting pats. And when Dahl had asked it to shake hands, it had slouched away and not come back, a snub he'd been glad Kori hadn't noticed.

Michael D'Archangelo, that was the dog's name. He recalled the way it had stayed close to her today, and had sat without being told when she stopped. Basic obedience moves, but with a crisp reliable look to them, not the sloppy, say-it-twice obedience of most "trained" dogs. Michael D'Archangelo, for Michael the Archangel, the general of God's army, the number-one guardian angel. What an ass he'd been not to pay attention to that. Because here he was, at going on four o'clock in the morning, face-down in a barnyard, held prisoner by a professional guard dog.

Fifteen or so minutes went by, and Michael was showing no sign of boredom. But neither had he bitten Dahl again. Maybe he wasn't a killer. Dahl was prepared to suffer a few nips on the ear in order to get loose.

In his sock was his alibi gun, which he carried even off duty. If Dahl could get to the gun, he could handle the dog. "Good dog, Michael," he said, "Atta boy." Again the tremor started up. So you think this is a game, do you, Mikey? We'll see what kind of player you are when the game is hardball.

He planned out every movement in his head: Roll sharply to the left, tipping the dog off, pull knees up, yank out the gun, roll back onto feet with a handthrust to help the legs, and be running before the dog recovered. He would probably slam the barn door in the dog's face before it could get to him, and that way not have to shoot it until he wanted out of the barn. Or unless it started barking.

Dahl began to tense his muscles in anticipation of the move, but the change in muscle tension earned him a sharp bite on the ear. This time the blood flowed freely down his cheek.

209

"Goddamn you!" he said, and the dog growled, a serious, heavy rumble Dahl could feel through the bottom of the dog's feet. But the tail was still wagging. "Stupid dog," Dahl muttered.

.   .   .

In the house, Kori stirred, dreaming of jumping in a show on Copper Wind, going for the blue with a faultless round, only to be disqualified when the judges saw Coppy's wings spread to help him over the triple bar.

Pumpkin, curled into a ball near her feet, stirred, raised her small head in a yawn, then settled back into sleep again.

.   .   .

His leg muscles were cramping with cold and his fingers were starting to hurt. His back would never be right again. Dahl gave up hope of freeing himself and began praying for rescue. He was beginning to shiver from cold, and Michael kept misinterpreting the shivering. He would have yelled for help except when he started to take the extra-deep breath, Michael didn't like that, either. How long has it been? he wondered. Hours seemed to have passed, though there was no dimming of the big yard light, which would indicate dawn was coming.

A tiny, warm, vexing drop of moisture struck Dahl on the back of his neck. Not the first. On and off the dog would pant, and when he did, he dripped spit. And he wouldn't let Dahl wipe it off.

.   .   .

Kori was puzzled not to find Michael waiting for her outside the bedroom door, and even more puzzled not to find him downstairs in the kitchen. Pumpkin had "helped" her dress and followed her down the stairs, and was now spraddled protectively over her milk, managing to purr and lap at the same time. But Michael was not downstairs anywhere. His nose really is out of joint, thought Kori. I'll have to be especially nice to him, until he and Pumpkin make friends. She put grounds into the Mr. Coffee machine and started the brew cycle, so Peter would wake up to the smell; then grabbed a jacket and went out the front door, down the big lawn toward the barn. It was not yet light, though the stairs were fading and the sky in the east was deepest blue. The nighttime clouds had gone away, it was going to be another beautiful day.

She was so busy looking at the sky, she was onto the gravel before she saw Michael. And then she saw that the dog was standing on someone lying prone, a man in jeans and dark jacket. She stopped short. Michael was wagging madly, anticipating praise.

"Who have you caught, Michael?" she said.

"Thank God!" said the figure. "Call him off!"

"Who is it? What are you doing here?"

"It's me, Eddie Dahl. Call your dog, will you?"

"Sergeant Dahl? What are you doing out here at this hour of the morning?"

"Lemme up, okay? And I'll tell you."

"No, tell me first."

"Jesus sufferin' Christ! Your husband told me not to come out to the ranch again, okay? But I left something out here this afternoon, in the barn, in that room where you keep the saddles. I put it on the floor and I walked out and forgot it. It's something I'm using, and rather than bother him about it, I decided just to come out and get it. Only your dog here caught me, knocked me down, and he's been standing on me ever since. And I'm cold and whenever I shiver he bites me."

"Out, Michael!" she said and the dog jumped off and came bounding to her. "Good dog!" she said, thumping his ribs. Dahl rolled over with a groan. She said, "Michael, watch him!" The dog came around, alert all over again. "You can get to your knees, Sergeant," she said. "But no further."

Dahl said, "Come on, okay? Let me up! All my joints are crying for me to move around!"

211

"On your knees, no further!"

"Aw, for Christ's sake!" Dahl rose onto his knees. "All right, see? Come on, these rocks are killing me!"

"Unzip your jacket, Sergeant," she ordered.

"Are you kidding? What's the matter with you? I'm freezing to death as it is! I'm not a horse rustler or a goddamn tramp!"

"I know perfectly well what you are. Unzip your jacket."

"What for?"

"So I can see if you're carrying a gun," she said.

"What would I be doing with a gun? I'm off duty!"

But Peter carried a gun even off duty. "Show me."

Grumbling, Dahl unzipped his jacket and pulled it apart so she could see under his arms and around his waistband. "See? Now can I get up?"

"It's in your sock then, isn't it?"

"What's in my sock?"

"Sergeant Dahl, you will sit back and lift your trouser legs by pulling them up at the knees, or I will set Michael on you."

Dahl sat down. "Shit," he grumbled. "I'm sorry, but shit." He pulled at the denim until he had lifted his trouser legs high enough to expose heavy gray socks. There was a large bulge in the outside of one of them.

"What's that over your right ankle?"

"A Smith and Wesson Chief thirty-eight-caliber revolver with a two-inch barrel." He had meant to say it snottily, but he only sounded depressed.

"You will remove it very slowly and put it on the ground beside your foot. Then you will lean backward on your hands and move away from it."

Dahl hesitated. After all, she was an amateur. Yeah, but that dog wasn't. And he'd heard too many stories about dogs even with bullets in their hearts tearing up some poor sucker before dying. And he had a feeling that she'd be right in there swinging, backing up her dog. Which meant he'd have to shoot her, too. Which meant he'd have to deal with Brichter, and he didn't want to deal with Sergeant Brichter after having shot Mrs. Brichter. He sighed. "Oh, all right, what the hell."

She waited until he had moved several yards from the gun, then asked, "Do you have another gun on your person?"

"No, ma'm!" He said it as firmly and honestly as he could, having no wish to hint she might profit from making him strip further.

"Very well. You will get up very slowly and lead the way to the house. Your hands will remain well away from your body, and you will not turn or look around."

"I'll try," said Dahl. "But honest, I'm all stiffened up."

"If you feel yourself falling, just let it happen. Michael won't attack you if you merely fall down. But if you turn around or attempt to run, I'll release him."

Dahl looked at Michael. "Hell, I couldn't run if I wanted to." He staggered to his feet. "And why should I? I don't know why you're acting like this toward me. I haven't done anything."

"Get moving."

She was speaking with authority, and he didn't like that. She'd be easier to handle if she were a tiny bit unsure, or amused, or feeling a little sorry for him. Maybe if he could get her talking . . .

He started across the gravel. "Have a heart, Mrs. Brichter. I'm cold and I'm tired and I'm dog-bit. And all that's going to come out of this is that your husband is going to slice me up for breakfast, then tell me to take my goddamn meter and get the hell off the place."

There was the briefest of pauses, then she asked in a slightly different, interested voice, "Is that what you left in the tack room? A meter?"

He leaned forward to meet the sloping lawn. "Yes, ma'm; did you find it? It's an ohmmeter, says 'Keithley' on it, and

213

it's a light color, beige or cream. I set it on the floor in that —what did you call it?—tack room. And I just plain dumb forgot it.''

"Why didn't you call and ask me to send it in with Peter?''

"Well, Obie was kind of emphatic about me not talking to you anymore, either. I thought I could just get it and go away and not have to bother him or you about it. But your dog here had other ideas. That is about the most stubborn dog I ever did meet. I tried everything—sweet talk, orders, playing dead even, and he just wouldn't get off me. What is he, an ex-police dog?''

"No. Up the steps, then through the door. Go to the middle of the hall and stop.''

"Yes, ma'm,'' he said, discouraged. She was sounding bossy again. He opened the door and was greeted with a rush of warm, coffee-laden air. He walked into the middle of the big entrance hall and stopped, eyes half closed in pleasure. "God, I was praying someone would come and invite me into the house,'' he murmured.

"You will sit on the floor over by that door. Michael will watch you while I go get Peter. If you move or attempt to get up, he will attack you.''

"Anything you say.'' He lowered himself in the place indicated.

"Guard him, Michael!'' she said, and the dog lay down about eight feet from the soles of Dahl's shoes and focused in on him. She went up the stairs and a few seconds later Dahl heard a door open and close. Bedroom, he thought. Brichter must still be asleep.

He looked at the dog. "Atta boy,'' he said, but there was no answering tail wag this time. He put his hands in his lap and his head back against the wall, then looked across his cheekbones at the dog. It had not moved. He put one hand back on the floor. Nothing. He leaned on the hand and the dog got to its feet, so he put the hand back into his lap, but the dog did not lie down again.

"Good dog," he said, clasping his hands in his lap, but Michael growled softly and began to move restlessly to the right, then back to the left again, as if looking for an opening, or an excuse. Dahl began to sweat. He sat very still and hoped she would not be long upstairs.

· · ·

Brichter was on the deck of a big ocean liner bound for Europe. He had just noticed that the deck was made of rabbit fur when Kori called him. "Peter? Peter, wake up!" He hadn't been aware that he was asleep, but now he was in bed and she was sitting on the edge of it with her hand on his shoulder. He reached up and stroked the hand.

"Wake up, Peter."

"Wha'sit?" No good, try again. "Wha' time is it?"

"Six-fifteen. Peter, Eddie Dahl is downstairs."

"Tell him go away."

"Listen. Michael caught him trying to sneak into the barn to retrieve something he says he left behind when he was here this afternoon, and stood on him for hours, he claims, and held him until I went out to feed the horses and found them."

There were too many pronouns in that sentence. He rolled onto his back. "Run that by me again."

"Eddie Dahl was trying to sneak into the barn."

"Our barn? Why?"

"He says he left something in there. A meter, he says. He says you ordered him to stay away from the ranch, so he came in the middle of the night; only Michael caught him."

"What was Michael doing out in the middle of the night?"

"I don't know. But that's not the point."

"The point is that Michael caught Eddie Dahl sneaking into our barn, right?"

215

"Yes, and knocked him down and stood on him until I went out to feed the horses."

"Why didn't he just bark when he saw him? Michael, I mean. Saw Eddie."

"I don't know. But listen, Eddie says he left an ohmmeter in the tack room yesterday when he was here for the extension cord, and he wants it back."

Brichter grabbed at that and came awake. He smiled. "Where is he?"

"Michael's holding him in the hall downstairs. Eddie's very stiff and sore, and I made him leave his gun out on the gravel."

"Gun?"

"It was in his sock."

Oh thou excellent lady, that rememberest all thou art told, he thought. And thank you, God, for setting me up to make that deal to tell her about things like that.

She said, "He says you're going to be mad at him, but all you'll do is tell him to take his meter with him when he leaves."

"He's half right." Brichter sat up. "Hand me my robe, please."

She did so.

"Did he say what kind of ohmmeter it was?"

"A Keithley. Isn't that the kind Captain Zak mentioned?"

"Yes." He heard the smugness in the word, a savage sort of smugness, and he paused in the act of putting on pajama bottoms to savor it. "Keithley, by God."

"Do you want me to go get it?"

"No, don't you touch it. And let's make sure no one else touches it, for now."

.   .   .

Dahl was sitting on the floor beside the door to the parlor, legs extended, hands in lap. He was looking nervous. Michael was

216

pacing back and forth in front of his prisoner, head low, and did not look up as they came down the stairs.

Kori stopped by the carved baluster at the bottom of the stairs as Brichter went to the lockbox on top of the armoire and took out his gun, putting it into his robe pocket. He turned and said to Kori, "Call him off."

"Out, Michael!" The dog immediately came to her, and she stooped to hug him. "Oh, you brave, smart dog!" she murmured into his ear, and he wriggled with pleasure. She straightened. "Shall I go out to the barn now?"

"Is that coffee ready?" he asked.

"It should be."

"Could you bring us each a cup first? We'll be in the parlor." He looked at Dahl. "How do you take yours?"

"Black with two sugars. And I thank you."

.   .   .

Dahl sat on the front edge of the champagne-colored couch to show he was aware that it was clean and he was dirty. There were bruises on his hands, and the knees of his jeans were powdered white from the gravel. There was blood on his right ear, trailing forward on his cheek, and some had dripped onto the shoulder of his jacket. He held his coffee mug with both hands and groused, "I thought she'd never come out. It's bad enough being stood on by a dog, but when it's a goddamn French poodle—"

"They're German, actually," said Brichter, from the matching couch opposite.

"German?"

"The name was *pudelhund,* meaning a dog that splashes— a water dog—in German. Same root as our 'puddle.' They were originally used by duck hunters."

"I don't get it."

"He's not a clown, Eddie; his ancestors were hunters. We

217

just turned down an invitation to enter him in a national obedience trial, not because we didn't think he'd do well but
because we don't want to advertise his expertise.''

"He looks like a clown."

"That's so a prospective customer won't be afraid to get
out of the car when they see him in the yard."

"Yeah. Yeah, I can see that."

"Now, Eddie, I want to talk with you about some things.
You don't have to answer any of my questions, you can stop
me at any time, and you can ask me to wait until you've talked
to a lawyer. If you want to consult with an attorney and can't
afford one, I'll arrange to have one assigned to you. Do you
understand?''

"I'm under arrest?"

"Yes, you are."

"For what?"

"Trespassing, to start with. But I think Captain Kader will
want to add to the charges later this morning."

"Shit."

"Do you want to tell me about the Keithley you left in the
barn?''

"What Keithley?"

"Eddie . . .''

"You're so goddamn smart, you figure it out. I ain't sayin'
another word. Oh, except this. Handcuff me to something
while you go get dressed, will you? I don't want to go another
round with that frickin' German puddle dog.''

17

RICHTER took Dahl into the jail and had him booked for trespass with intent, phoned Zak to come in, then went out for a quick breakfast. He came back and found Zak waiting in his office. They talked and then Brichter came down to the squad room to find Ryder waiting.

"You're still hard on partners, aren't you?" said Ryder.

"It's more like partners are hard on me," retorted Brichter. "That bastard was out to frame me for arson." He went to draw a mug of coffee and explained while he drank it. "So," he concluded a few minutes later, "the meter is now in custody as well, while we try to find out why Eddie wanted it back so badly."

Ryder smiled. "I got a call just before you came in; they found his fingerprints inside it, on a battery case. There's a message on your desk that says, 'You were right, Obie.' I assume that means you suggested they look there for the fingerprints."

Brichter shrugged. "I suggested they look everywhere. I

219

knew it was a last-minute decision to plant the thing out there, and a man in a hurry can make stupid mistakes.''

"How do you know he decided at the last minute? Is he talking?''

"Not to me. But why should he get rid of a tool of his trade unless he knew that game was over? Which wasn't until he found out Zak had the goods on him. That Lynn fire was one of a series, and there's no reason to think it would have ended with Lynn. No, he probably stopped by his house and grabbed it on his way to the ranch. He was in one hell of a hurry; he needed to get his extension cord back before Zak talked to me and I called home to see if it was there. Once he had it he could deny he ever left it out there, and any story we told about his coming to get it could be dismissed as a cover-up. Planting the meter was just an added touch, to confirm what the Tretower cord had started Zak thinking, that I set the Lynn fire. He was hoping it would be handled by one or more people at Tretower before its link to the Lynn fire was discovered. You'd have thought, since the idea was to get my fingerprints on it, he'd have remembered about the battery case. But he's one of those A to B folks.''

"A to B?''

"You know, he can reason from A to B, but doing so doesn't fire off additional synapses in his brain. Like when you're thinking about one thing and suddenly another pops into your head, and if you care to, you can run back the connections from the new thought to the old one.'' He sipped his coffee. "Do you think I should wait for a call from Lieutenant Urban or should I head out? I've got a couple of places to go.''

Ryder laughed. "I see what you mean.''

"What do I mean?''

"Sparking synapses. Eddie was your partner, you'll need a new partner; Gary Urban is head of Homicide, he'll want to notify you about your new partner, hence your question. He's already called me, said to send you up when you were ready. He's assigned Sweeney to the case. Bring your file, he said.''

Brichter pulled what information he had from the file cabinet and went upstairs. Captain Urban wasn't in, but Lieutenant Sweeney was.

Pat Sweeney at forty was a large freckled redhead with a faint brogue and a habit of wearing knit vests under his tweed sport coats. His small grin over a substantial chin was all puckish Irish charm, but his eyes were small, green, and cold. He'd been a brawling rookie—his nose still bore the signs of combat—but he'd learned to control the temper even as he developed a fondness for seeing his name in the paper or on the ten-o'clock news. For all his flamboyance, he was a hard worker and a deft investigator, a collector of nighttime postgraduate degrees, incorrupt and very ambitious. Brichter wondered how Captain Urban felt knowing Sweeney was after his job, and that he considered it just another rung on the ladder to the Chief's chair. Sweeney got him a cup of coffee, then prepared to listen.

''Late on Thursday, November 5,'' Brichter said, ''someone broke into the back of Crazy Dave's TV and Appliance Store, poured gasoline in three places, laid gasoline-soaked toilet paper between the places, and lit a candle he'd placed in the middle of the basement floor. Right about then he, or someone with him, or a stranger he found there, was struck a heavy blow on the back of the head and left to die in the basement.''

Brichter continued his succinct review of the case, concluding, ''There's all kinds of movement, but none of it in a single direction. I can't remember the last time I had a case with this much evidence uncovered and no solution apparent.''

Sweeney had been taking notes during Brichter's narrative, but now he sat back in his chair and closed his freckled eyelids, a pencil held horizontal between his fingers. After a moment, he opened them. ''That's a foine summation, Obie,'' he said in his best brogue—Brichter had heard that the accent waxed and waned with the season, the company, and the amount of whiskey flowing in Sweeney's veins. "I wonder if solving the Gerald Cleaves mystery mightn't break this case wide open. You say Mrs. Cleaves hasn't sent so much as a postcard to any of her former neighbors here in town?"

"No one we know about. Her disappearance got a certain amount of publicity; it should have brought a report if anyone knows where she is."

"That house she left behind, was it a rental or did they own it?"

"Owned it. She also left furniture, a number of unpaid bills, a six-year-old car, a cat, and three hundred dollars in a savings account. Things were tight, but hardly tight enough for her to abandon ship. She has twenty-five thousand dollars in life insurance coming to her, more than enough to restore her fiscally."

Sweeney made a note and shifted ground. "What does Mrs. Vigotti say about her husband's murder?"

"Nothing; since we found the body she won't talk to us at all. I saw her before we found it, after she'd reported him to Missing Persons. She broke down when I asked if she thought he might be dead, so I don't think this was entirely unexpected. Philadelphia says she's loyal to the firm her husband worked for. Joe Januschka is being very supportive; he sent Butch Lazarre to hold her hand while I interviewed her."

"Does she know that much about the firm? For example, who Januschka is?"

"Philadelphia PD said her brother is in the rackets there, and so were her father and half her cousins, so it's hard to think she doesn't. It's possible she's allowing Januschka to assist her as a form of recompense for killing her husband, though that is pure speculation and may be a calumny on a nice lady. She did seem honestly ignorant about Crazy Dave's fire."

"Hmmm. Is it possible that Crazy Dave's poker-playing friends are covering for him, that he was gone from the game longer than they're saying?"

"I suppose. They started off covering for him, saying he'd never left at all. Then one of them got nervous about lying to the police, and his change of heart scared the rest into agreeing that Wagner had gone out after all. Dahl told me he interviewed them separately, and they all agreed when and for how long he'd been gone; there was some kind of bet on it. One claimed he'd timed him, and that he was gone exactly twenty-two minutes."

"So what do you think?"

Brichter pulled an ear. "I don't know what to think. On the face of it, I'd say Vigotti was responsible for the fire. But then how does the amateur Cleaves figure? Or is he not an amateur, but an incredibly lucky pro? I agree, we need to find the Cleaves connection before we can finish this one."

"Have you contacted the FBI?"

"Yes, but they've got nothing on him."

"So what are your plans for the rest of the day?"

"I'm going out to the trucking company to see if they'll let me look at Cleaves's personnel file. Maybe there's something in his résumé that will give me a lead. Then I thought I'd talk to Joe Januschka, if for no other reason than I haven't turned his rock over in a while. And I want to talk to some others among Vigotti's ostensible victims, to see if they might be willing to talk about Vigotti, now that he's gone.

"Foine. I'll talk to Wagner and the poker players again and try to find time for one or two of the tenants in Wagner's building. What do you think of our arson investigator—Kader?"

"He seems to know his stuff. And he's easy to talk to."

"Good. I'll run your file past the copier and put the original back on your desk. And I'll send you copies of what Eddie had in his file. Could you copy me on any reports or other paperwork you generate from here on? And I'll reciprocate. Because it may be hard to find time to meet. I know this isn't your only case, and God in heaven knows it isn't mine. But call if you get anything you think I should know immediately."

"Yes, sir." Brichter stood and so did Sweeney.

"I've heard what a bright chappie you are, and the reports seem accurate, now that I've met you. I think we'll do all right together."

. . .

Brichter went back to his squad room and found among his slender stack of messages one from Chief Cunningham, and the block next to WANTS TO SEE YOU was checked. He looked over at McHugh. "What's this?"

"You forgot how to read? Or maybe you want to call my attention to how important you're getting, with your messages to go see the Chief?"

"Jesus, Cris, I only asked!"

"I know, I know. It's me. My game came all apart last night. One of the turkeys recognized me, high-signed his friends, and not only did they all get away, they took a thousand bucks of the department's money with them."

"Oh, hell, that must've really hurt."

"Yeah, well, they tell me tomorrow's another day." Cris sounded as if tomorrow were six months away. "Tell Malcolm I said hello, and if he happens to mention it, I'm sorry about his thousand dollars."

. . .

Brichter went up and found himself cooling his heels in a paneled, lushly carpeted anteroom—no raw cement painted primary colors on the third floor. After twenty minutes of waiting, with only the Chamber of Commerce's cheap quarterly for entertainment, he was getting annoyed. Then the door opened and the Chief came in. He nodded at Brichter, signaling him to follow. Chief Cunningham was a tall man, beginning to thicken in the body. He had very long legs with bad knees, so that when he walked, the leading knee snapped outward, then inward, was passed by the other knee, which snapped outward, then inward. Walking behind him was like walking behind a dancer doing a miniature but vigorous Charleston. Brichter was interested in this phenomenon, but he did not smile. Cunningham's bad knees were the result of being shoved off a roof by a cornered bank robber, and the reason the injuries had not been more severe was that he'd brought the robber along as a cushion.

A police department is a paramilitary organization, so Brichter stood at a sort of attention in front of the Chief's massive desk while Cunningham went around to sit in the high-backed leather chair behind it. Cunningham's graying hair was cut short on the sides and lay in a flat wave across his forehead. He had deep-set eyes in a long, narrow, deeply creased face. He did not look up as he said, "At ease, Sergeant."

"Yes, sir. Thank you, sir," said Brichter.

"I mean it. Please sit down. I'm glad you could spare me a few minutes."

Brichter bit his tongue and sat down in one of a pair of cushioned armchairs in front of the desk.

Cunningham continued to search among the few papers on his glass-topped desk as he began, "About Sergeant Dahl—" and stopped.

"Yes, sir?"

The shadowed gaze came up. "What is your opinion of the man? Private and personal, not to go beyond these walls."

"I haven't known him personally until very recently, sir."

"But you've heard stories?"

"Yes, sir."

"And based on your short personal acquaintance, were those stories confirmed?"

"Pretty much."

"In your opinion, has he always been a crook?"

"As I said, I haven't known—"

"This is not a court of law, Sergeant. I am asking for your personal and private opinion, and I say again, it will not be repeated to anyone, at least not with any sort of attribution."

225

"He is two years my senior on the force, and by the time I joined, he already had a reputation for being first in line with his hand out for any shady offer."

"Do you know personally of any illegal dealings he engaged in?"

"No, sir; since I wasn't interested in getting involved, I stayed out of his way."

"Why do you suppose he picked you for a partner in this arson-murder case you're working on?"

"Did he?"

"He asked his captain to ask your captain to assign you to the case. And I understand he tried to involve you in it before the assignment was made."

"Well, yes, he did."

"Why do you suppose he did that?"

Brichter saw the way this conversation was headed, gave a mental shrug and let the chips fall. "He thought I could protect him."

"From what?"

"Internal Affairs. You, ultimately."

"I don't understand."

Sure you do, you tardy son of a bitch; that's what this conversation is all about. "My wife and your wife are working together on some church affair, and have become friends. Dahl discovered this, and assumed somehow that you and I are friends, or will be. He thought that if he could get to be my friend, that I'd get you to call off the investigation of his activities. Which, as it turned out, was a much more important thing to him than I imagined."

"You believe he is culpably involved in that arson fire at Lynn's Holiday Plastics, and therefore the three preceding it?"

"Yes, sir."

"But you have no idea whether or not he was involved in illegal activities prior to that."

"I know he's always walked very close to the line between

226

unprofessional and illegal conduct. But I've had no firsthand knowledge of his crossing the line.''

"But you'd hear things."

"People would say things and I'd hear them."

"Give me two examples."

Brichter thought. "A few years back he threw a bachelor party for a fellow officer and hired a woman to perform fellatio on the guest of honor in front of the rest of us. Rumor had it she was a prostitute, one of several whose pimp was Sergeant Dahl." He thought some more. "I saw a patrol officer confront Sergeant Dahl in the locker room, demanding Dahl give him his money back for a ring Dahl had sold him. I later heard it was an engagement ring that was supposed to be new, but the officer's girl threw the ring back at him because someone else's initials were inside it."

"Who was the officer?"

"Alex Spelling. He was run over by a drunken driver four months later. Rumor had it that Dahl could get you all kinds of merchandise at very low prices."

"But you know nothing firsthand."

"The first time I seriously thought he was doing something wrong was when Captain Kader told me about the extension cord with a Tretower Ranch stamp on it. Dahl was one of a very few persons who could have gotten hold of that cord, and his later actions proved to my satisfaction that he was guilty of arson."

"What about your speeding tickets?"

This was asked as if it were not a change of subject and Brichter was nonplussed momentarily. He felt a pulse begin to beat in his jaw. "I received a speeding ticket on Monday, sir. Not my first."

"Did you pay the fine in person?"

"Yes, sir, the next morning."

"Did Dahl fix any other ticket for you?"

"No, sir, he did not."

227

"Had you asked him to?"

"No, sir."

"Then why did you go to him and insist he stop fixing tickets for you?"

Brichter frowned. "I didn't . . ." he began, then, confused, he stopped and waited for a prompt from Cunningham. There was a funny glint in Cunningham's eye, as if he were both daring him to explain and warning him not to. Brichter hated these games, mostly because he was very bad at them.

The glint faded and Cunningham gave a curt nod, then did change the subject. "Mrs. Cunningham says she will no longer bring me love and kisses from your wife, and that you are henceforward cut off from Mrs. Cunningham's love and kisses."

Brichter kept his face neutral. "Yes, sir."

"I'm glad we had this conversation, Sergeant."

Brichter stood. "I'm always pleased to be of service to you, Chief." The two shook hands, Brichter did a paramilitary about-face and walked out.

·   ·   ·

"I don't understand why he's saying these things," complained Dahl. "All that happened is a practical joke went wrong. I was gonna smear dirt all over his fancy sports car and write 'Wash Me' in the dirt and leave. I told her that, I told him that; hell, I tried to explain that to their dog when he knocked me down out there! But no one would listen. And now you aren't listening. I don't know anything about a goddamn meter."

"Do you own an ohmmeter?" asked Zak.

"I own two ohmmeters, a G.E. and a Hewlett Packard."

"But not a Keithley 580."

"What the hell would I want a Keithley for?"

"I understand it's a very fine meter."

"It's a laboratory meter, for scientists and engineers. I see them advertised in catalogs now and then, but I got no interest in buying one; I'm an amateur electrician, for Christ's sake!

228

I replace light sockets, outlets, rewire a lamp now and then; what do I need with milli-ohms?''

"So you now deny you left a Keithley 580 ohmmeter in the Tretower Ranch barn?''

"Absolutely.''

"And you deny you were out there very early this morning trying to retrieve it?''

"Yes, I do.''

"Were you at the ranch yesterday afternoon to retrieve an electrical extension cord that was accidentally exchanged for a cord marked with the Tretower logo?''

"No, and that's another thing. I don't know why those two cooked up that oddball story—''

"Don't you?''

"What?''

"You're a real de-tec-uh-tive, Sergeant Dahl. Why do you think they would conspire to 'cook up' such a story?''

"That goddamned, tale-carrying son of a bitch!'' Dahl shouted. "He's been bad-mouthing me all along, hasn't he? Poisoning everyone against me!''

"Now, Eddie, if anything, he's been excessively careful not to say anything bad about you to me. You are, after all, a fellow cop, and I'm only a fireman. No, I overheard the remark the day you came to my office to take Sergeant Brichter away. A sign of carelessness, Eddie: You didn't close the door all the way. Like your leaving your fingerprints on the battery case of the Keithley meter. Internal Affairs has made its file on you available to me, and I have an appointment in the morning with a gentleman from Vice. You are, or have been, a pimp, an extortionist, and a fence, as well as an arsonist. Do you want to amend your statement, or shall I have them take you back upstairs to the jail? My patience with you is at an end.''

Dahl looked around the room, as if saying goodbye to it and the life it stood for. "I hereby assert my right to silence,'' he said.

18

BRICHTER crossed the oil-stained blacktop parking lot next to the small brick office of Reliable Road Haulers. It was a single-story building, with limestone trim around the windows and a black pipe railing going up the four steps to the entrance. Stickers on the glass door proclaimed allegiance to a fuel additive and a brake lining, to law enforcement, to the rebel flag, and to keeping on truckin'. Inside, he was directed to a vulturous, mean-eyed woman who lurked behind a desk in an enclosure made of green filing cabinets. When he showed his badge the meanness was tucked away and she became conspiratorial.

"We always cooperate with the police," she murmured, leaning sideways to look for eavesdroppers before continuing, "They know their business, and I'm sure they can make life very difficult for uncooperative people." She sounded as if she had a list of names she'd like to compare with his.

He explained what he was after, and she scooted her posture chair back to move a knobby finger down a filing cabinet until she found the drawer she wanted. "I have my own private system here; I'm the only person who can find anything. If I'm sick even one day, the office gets all in an uproar." She pulled open the drawer, walked her fingers along the row of file folders, stopped, backed up, found one and pulled it out. "The day they go computer, that's the day I retire," she concluded, handing the file to Brichter, who wondered why no one had taken her up on the offer. He looked for a place to sit down, and she said, one thin eyebrow raised significantly, "I think it's time for my coffee break. Shall I?"

"Fine," he said, and she flapped out of the enclosure, no doubt to spread poisonous hints about what he was doing all the way to the lunchroom.

Brichter took her place at the desk. The file was neatly kept, up to date, and ended on top of the right-hand side with a copy of the death certificate.

Jerry Cleaves had worked for Reliable for nearly three years, accepting a position as a truck mechanic on condition he be moved up to driver when a slot opened, which happened after four months. He had received pay increases at regular intervals and grudging compliments from his work supervisor. He had joined the Teamsters and the bowling league and the state credit union. He had life insurance, medical and dental coverage. He had, for an additional sum, given medical coverage to his wife and daughter. He had put in a claim for treatment of a stomach ulcer and for two annual physicals. Wife Irene had been treated for bronchitis last winter. Little Beth had been given immunizations against measles, whooping cough, polio, and diphtheria. Brichter noted down the name of the doctor and the clinic; and because such things helped speed the process of file-finding, he noted down their clinic

231

ID numbers. The clinic used its adult patients' social security numbers as ID numbers, a practice allegedly illegal but nevertheless very common. Jerry's number was one digit lower than Irene's.

One finds signs of the human story in the most bureaucratic of places; he could almost see Jerry and Irene going down hand in hand, teenagers in love, applying together for that sign of dawning adulthood.

He flipped past the pages, looking for and finding Jerry's original application for employment. He had been born in Bowie, Maryland, but had moved first to Baltimore, then to Milwaukee, Wisconsin, in time to enter South Division High School, from which he graduated. He had also graduated from the Professional Truck Drivers School of Wisconsin. He had worked for two trucking firms, both now out of business, before moving to Minneapolis, where he'd leased a rig and worked as an independent. He was familiar with most standard routes, particularly in the east and south. He was married, one daughter, and in excellent health. He was willing to travel. An old friend of the family in Maryland and an attorney in a Philadelphia law firm had both offered to vouch for his character. There was no indication that Reliable had contacted either of them, but Brichter, made cynical by experience, wrote down their names and addresses. He was about to close the file folder when memory nudged him, and he hauled out his fat notebook and flipped back through the pages.

She had said she was from Minneapolis. If he hadn't moved there until well into his working career, how had they managed to go down together to apply for social security cards? And if they hadn't, how had they acquired sequential numbers? He underlined the numbers to call his attention to them, closed the manila folder and left it on the desk for the vulture to refile.

•   •   •

There is a routine to investigation. It's tedious, but it's routine because it gets results. Brichter called the Intelligence Division of the Baltimore Police Department. "Yes, Lieutenant," he said, "I'm looking into the background of one Gerald Henry Cleaves, age thirty-one, white male. He is supposed to have lived in Baltimore with his parents, John and Margaret Cleaves, from the age of four until he was fourteen, when they moved to Milwaukee. I want anything you can find." He gave the Baltimore address Cleaves had listed on his résumé. "Also, can you see if there's a record of his birth in a town called Bowie?"

"You sure that Baltimore address is right?"

Britcher looked at his notebook. "Unless the résumé had a typo on it."

"No, I mean is the name of the street right?"

"Isn't there a North Avenue in Baltimore?"

"Sure there is. But it runs through the heart of our ghetto, which has been black as far back as anyone can remember. Didn't you say this man is white?"

"Yes, I did."

"Well, ain't that strange. I'll check it out and call you back. Maybe he's passing as white."

Brichter consulted a standard reference work kept in the squad room that listed all American corporations and didn't find Professional Truck Drivers School of Wisconsin listed. Maybe it, like the trucking companies Cleaves had worked for, had gone out of business.

Then he called a man in Police Intelligence in Milwaukee to see if Cleaves had indeed graduated from South Division High School and from the truck drivers' school. He had spoken to Magovern on other occasions; though the two had never met, they were on friendly terms.

"He would have gone to the old school, which was torn down some years back. But they transferred all the records to the new South Division when they built it right across the

233

street, and they'll tell you, he didn't graduate from South; in fact, he never was enrolled at that high school."

"You know that off the top of your head?"

"You called me a few days ago asking if he had a record, remember? And you sounded pissed and puzzled when I came up empty. You said he was from here, so I dug a little deeper, and there's nothing on a Jerry Cleaves that matches your man at all. He didn't go to high school here; never had a phone, a job, or credit at any of our department stores; he never bought property, borrowed money, or opened an account at a local bank. Are you sure he lived here?"

"He was born in Maryland, but his résumé says he graduated from South Division High School in Milwaukee, and that he worked for two Milwaukee trucking firms, both now out of business." Brichter consulted his notes for the names of the firms and gave them to Magovern.

"I heard of one of them; it was bought out by a national company a few years back. I'll see if the old personnel records are being kept at the new company."

"See if there used to be a Professional Truck Drivers School of Wisconsin up there, too, will you? Cleaves supposedly graduated from it."

"I never heard of it. And I probably would have; my oldest boy checked out every one in three states before he signed up. He's now got hemorrhoids and a bad back, but he owns his own rig and made forty grand last year, so what can I say? I'll check it out and get back to you."

.   .   .

"I can't help it if the cops are so damn-dumb slow!" shouted Wagner into the phone. "You've seen the papers, haven't you? He did it, he's dead, so why they don't just mark it closed, I don't know! The facts are, he got his hooks into me for a whole lot of money, and when I couldn't come

234

up with more, he burned me down. The cops were gonna arrest him, so his boss took care of him, probably so he couldn't cut a deal. There's no mystery here, I know it, you know it, the cops know it. So there's no longer any reason for you guys to be dragging your feet over paying what you owe!''

He listened, but interrupted: "No, no, you're not paying attention! I want you to sit down right now, this minute, at your little portable and write a letter to the corporate head: We owe David Wagner two hundred thousand clams!''

He slammed the phone down. He was getting sick and tired of this. All those months of running scared, of watching the debt pile up, helpless to slow its progress, all that was over now. He'd risked his neck telling the cops about Vigotti, and now Vigotti was dead. The result was, Dave Wagner was free.

Except the insurance company didn't want to admit it. They kept taking him over ground he'd covered countless times, making him fill out forms identical to those he'd filled out three and four times already, making lamer and lamer excuses for keeping the file open.

Maybe what he needed was to look up those two goons of Vigotti's. They were unemployed now, right? And sic them on whatever his name was, the chairman of the board, the chief executive officer of American Eagle Insurance. He smiled; the mental image of two large thugs marching across deep-pile carpeting into the august presence of some silver-haired CEO, lifting him by his elbows from his large, tufted-leather executive chair and walking him out past the astonished face of his very executive secretary was a gratifying one. The smile faded. Because it wouldn't work, of course. You might scare the piss out of the CEO, but you didn't scare American Eagle. Big corporations were immortal, and there was always another silver-haired man willing to appear in the brochures and annual stockholders' reports as the kindly personification of your friendly insurance company.

Wagner went into the kitchen and opened his noisy old refrigerator's scuffed door. One lonesome beer left.

No, terror worked on little people, like David Wagner. Nothing scared giant corporations. He picked up the beer, but stopped in the early motions of popping it open and put it back, his face pulled into a thoughtful frown. Nothing? Maybe there was one thing the little guy could use to scare money out of a giant corporation.

.   .   .

Edward James Dahl appeared in District Court and, through his attorney, entered a plea of Not Guilty to charges of criminal trespass, arson, and conspiracy to commit arson. Bail was set at fifteen thousand dollars. On his way out of the courtroom he was advised that he was suspended, with pay, until his case was settled, news he took without comment.

.   .   .

Sweeney went into Ogden's Liquors. Behind the counter was a tall man with a tired face. Even his beer belly looked tired. He sagged further when he saw Sweeney, who had never looked like anything but a cop. "What can I do for you." It was a greeting, not a question.

"Just a couple of quick questions, Ogden."

"What about?"

"Crazy Dave Wagner."

"Oh, Christ, that again?" Koch parked a buttock on the little shelf behind the cash register and recited, "He was in here twice, on Tuesday and Thursday. On Thursday he bought two six-packs of Schell's Deer brand beer and a big plastic bag of cheese curls and said, 'I got to get back to my poker game' and he left."

Sweeney opened his notebook and pretended to consult a note in it. "You're sure it was Thursday?"

Koch sighed. "Your Sergeant Dahl asked that exact same question, except it was Wednesday. Yes, I'm sure it was Thursday."

"Except what was Wednesday?"

Koch sighed again. "Okay. Dahl comes in and he tries to rook me out of a six-pack of that Schell's, and he says was Dave in and I says, 'Twice, Monday and Wednesday,' and he says, 'Are you sure it was Wednesday?' and I say no. So it turns out it was Tuesday and Thursday."

"Why did you think at first it was Monday and Wednesday?"

"How the hell do I know? I just thought it was."

"Then how did you come to change it to Tuesday and Thursday?"

"Because he asked me if it could be Thursday, and I said yes, and if it was Thursday, then it had to be Tuesday." Koch caught something in the little green eyes and he raised his hands placatingly. "Now don't get mad at me, it's not my fault, okay? I only answered his questions. Dave Wagner mentioned the poker game the second time he come in. I'd swear to that, he said he had to get back to it. He didn't play poker on Wednesday, he played poker on Thursday. So it had to be Thursday."

"Suppose I told you he played poker on Wednesday night, too?"

Koch turned away, rubbing the back of his neck. He turned back, leaned on the counter with both hands and said, "Then I don't know when the hell he was in here."

. . .

"Wagner didn't play poker on Wednesday," said Sweeney on the phone to Brichter. "But it just goes to show."

Brichter said, "If I were a very clever man, I might go in

237

on Wednesday and mention a poker game I had to hurry back to. Of course, I'd have to know they'd run out of beer. Can that be arranged?''

"I take it you don't play poker on a regular basis with the same group of people," said Sweeney.

"No, I don't. Do you?"

"Not since the department got religion. But I recall a strong pattern to those games. We'd meet at a certain time and talk for X minutes, then one of two guys, always one of the same two, would sit down and we'd all sit down. A certain guy would always get bored around the same time and start calling for weird hands when it was his turn to deal. It was all predictable. And we'd stop about the same time to stand and stretch and pop open a cold one. Wagner himself says it was his turn to buy, so that means his game was one where they took regular, predictable turns to supply beer and a munchy.''

"What you're telling me, Sweeney, is that Wagner left the condo at a critical time, was gone twenty minutes, and we no longer know for sure where he went."

. . .

Januschka was very angry, but he was determined not to lose his temper, which created a terrible tension in his voice and manner. "*Someone* has to know where he is."

"I checked just a couple minutes ago; he isn't at home," said Undertaker, who ran the ladies. "He hasn't visited any of my girls or massage parlors. And Hammer was alone when he caught that bus out of town." His cool voice was belied by the high set of his shoulders and the sheen of perspiration on his brow.

"I got the bartender at Chauncey's and the other places he hangs out all primed to call if he turns up," offered Smith, Januschka's subordinate in charge of drugs, twisting his thin body into a combination bow and lean toward the phone at Januschka's elbow.

"I want to talk to him," said Januschka softly, and the two trembled. "You can find him; it ain't like he fades into the background of any place he goes."

"We'll go look some more," offered Smith, and there was a murmur of agreement from Undertaker. Januschka gestured dismissal and they fled.

. . .

It was almost bedtime. Talking things over with her hadn't helped, nor was Brichter yet convinced this business of talking about his job was a good idea. He'd taken the Porsche out for a run, a distraction that lasted only as long as the drive, and had come home still irritable.

"Let's turn on the news," she said. "Maybe if you see how little of anything makes any sense, you'll feel better."

The program started with the usual assortment of state politicians piously defending their latest outrage, and the daily ration of bad news from Chicago. Then came Crazy Dave applying for food stamps in a carnival of friends and reporters. He was at the welfare office, he said, because the insurance company refused to pay what it owed him for the loss of his business. He wore raggedy jeans and a gray sweatshirt liberally spattered with white and the motto "Goddamn Seagulls" on it. He couldn't get a job anywhere else, he said, because all he knew was selling household appliances and he was too closely identified with his own late lamented business to get a job with a former competitor.

"Them bums at so-called American Eagle Insurance should change their name to American Buzzard!" he shouted, shaking his fist at the cameras. "They think that if they delay payment long enough, I'll starve to death out here, and then they won't have to pay at all! Well, this is Crazy Dave, and you all know I got no pride, not where money is involved! By God, I'll eat government cheese and live in the projects like the rest of the welfare bums until I get what's coming to me!"

"Is he serious?" asked Kori.

Brichter shrugged. "About what? Getting the insurance company to quit stalling and pay up? Doubtless. Failing that, he wants to force our hand, get arrested and tried now, when there's not enough evidence to convict."

"Will it work?"

"I don't know about the insurance company, but we cops have no pride, either. Sweeney's not about to arrest him."

"Well, if Tony Vigotti did it, why is Crazy Dave asking to be arrested?"

"Because it may never be proved that Vigotti is guilty. Wagner realizes that proving himself innocent at a trial would put the insurance company on notice to pay up."

"But you aren't going to help him out."

"My job is to find out who did it, not help Crazy Dave collect on his insurance."

She wanted to ask who Zak thought was the guilty one, but the commercial break was over, and the news continued with a rerun of Eddie Dahl firmly declaring his innocence outside the County Courthouse, an introduction to an "exclusive interview" with Chief Cunningham about police corruption and, specifically, Eddie Dahl.

"I'm surprised you didn't fire Fast Eddie when this broke, Chief," said the reporter, showing the back of his perm to the camera.

"Sergeant Dahl, like any other citizen, is innocent until proven guilty," replied Cunningham calmly.

"Do you think he's innocent?"

"I don't feel it's appropriate to comment on that at this time."

"If you think he's innocent, why did you suspend him?"

"I didn't say I thought he was innocent." He held up a long-fingered hand with a grin that transformed his bloodhound looks wonderfully. "And I won't tell you I think he's guilty, either. But with so much publicity surrounding his case, I don't think he'd be able to function in his role as investigator."

The camera showed the reporter's sincere face. "There are a lot of stories going around about Fast Eddie. That he abused his authority, particularly in cases involving minorities, that he ran illegal businesses in the community, that he was involved in illicit dealings within the department. For a minor but recent example, he fixed a traffic ticket for another officer"—the reporter glanced at a sheet of paper in his hand underlining the implication that he had more information than he was giving about the other officer involved—"who, by the way, has not been suspended as of this time."

"Sergeant Dahl is—was—an aggressive police officer. I will not deny that Internal Affairs is looking into his activities on and off the job, and I expect a report on my desk shortly. However, I will speak to that specific rumor you have brought up about fixing a ticket. Doubtless with your sources you know who the other officer is, and that he has had a number of speeding tickets. However, If you had checked further, you would have discovered that he has never tried to have a ticket downgraded or dismissed, much less 'fixed.' He denies that Dahl came to him with an offer to fix a ticket, and as he is one of the more honorable members of our department, I believe him. And I hope he will continue behaving just as he has—except maybe driving a little slower."

"He's talking about you!" said Kori.

"Yes, he is," said Brichter, and at her look of inquiry shut the TV commentator off in mid-stride to tell her about the odd conversation he'd had with Cunningham.

She said, "So that was partly what he was after, getting a statement that was the truth, that he could repeat to the reporter, and that got you off the hook. I'm glad he's on our side; he's a very clever man. But it's too bad I won't be getting any more love and kisses from him." She poked her underlip out

241

to show how disappointed she was, a difficult maneuver, since she was smiling at the same time. She leaned over against Brichter with an exaggerated sigh. Her hair smelled of her perfume, and one of her breasts was pressed warmly against his ribs.

"Maybe you could request an increase in your ration from another source?" he suggested, and she lifted her head to accept the offer. Things moved on from there.

Later, as he carried her up the stairs, he wondered if this wasn't some sort of bonus for keeping his word. She didn't often initiate lovemaking, his appetite being quicker than hers. But why should he concern himself with the logic behind a delicious emotional experience? And there was a bonus of another sort: He discovered that it is impossible to remain depressed while making love to a beautiful woman.

19

B RICHTER came in to ask McHugh to lunch, and found a phone message on his desk saying that Tom Tyler wanted to talk with him. Since he was not prepared to pay another twenty dollars for a minimally productive conversation, he ignored the message.

When they came back, there was another pink message, this one having the square next to URGENT as well as WANTS TO HEAR FROM YOU and WANTS TO SEE YOU checked. He sighed and dialed the number indicated; Tyler insisted he drop whatever he was doing to meet him in a nearby doughnut shop. "There's someone wants to talk to you," he said. "It's real, real, real important; you got to come."

But at the doughnut shop there was only Tyler. He herded Brichter to a booth near the back, where two Styrofoam cups of tepid coffee and a plate with two chocolate-covered doughnuts waited. "Have a doughnut," invited Tyler. "Free."

"No, thanks, I just had lunch. Why did you want to see me?"

Tyler selected one himself with a shaky hand and took an enormous bite out of it, and they both had to wait until he had chewed and swallowed. "It's Nish," he said.

"What's Nish?"

"The guy who wants to talk to you. It's Nish. You know, my good friend, Nishan Amuseharian." Tyler said the name in a careful sing-song: Nish-ahn Ah-moose-ah-HAHR-ee-an, and Brichter wondered how long ago the boy had learned his good friend's real name.

"He's going to meet us here?"

"No, I got to take you to him. Only"—Tyler took another bite and there was another wait—"there's conditions."

Brichter wasn't liking this. "What kind of conditions?"

"Like just you alone can come to him. And like you got to call in the FBI right away."

"The FBI? Why?"

But Tyler had put the last of the doughnut into his mouth and while he chewed as fast as he could, Brichter pulled the plate toward himself, hoping that laying claim to the second doughnut would keep Tyler from further delaying the conversation. At last Tyler was able to continue. "I wish you wouldn't all the time be asking me why everything. I dunno why. I could lie and make something up, but you don't want me to lie, do you?"

This was a reprise from last time, and Brichter responded with the expected chorus. "No, Tom, I don't want you to lie." He pulled an ear. "Where is Nish?"

"I can't tell you, I gotta take you."

"Uh-uh. No, no way. I don't play those kinds of games." Brichter slid out of the booth. "I'm going back to the squad room. You have Nish call me when he's ready to meet."

Tyler, greatly alarmed, said loudly, "No, no, you don't

244

understand! I gotta take you to him now!'' He scrunched down in his seat, looking around. Since it was shortly after lunch, there was no one in the place but the cashier, and after a bored glance their way he went back to his magazine. Tom slowly emerged from his crouch. ''You don't understand,'' he murmured. ''He's scared, life or death, and he's depending on me to help. I'm supposed to take you to him now, right now. Otherwise, the deal's off.''

.   .   .

They sat parked across the street from an abandoned gas station on the edge of the black section of town. ''He's around here somewhere,'' said Tyler, ''but I don't know where.'' Tyler glanced at the gas station, whose boarded-up windows were covered with gang graffiti. There was a giant faded FOR SALE sign bolted to a flaking brick false front.

''Then how am I supposed to find him?''

''What you do is, you go across to that for-sale gas station. Knock on the front door and the door to the men's room. You should maybe look like you're thinking you want to buy it. How come this car smells like a shoe store?''

''Because the upholstery is leather. Then what? Nish will come out and talk to me?''

''No, you come back and sit in the car and he'll come along and get in.''

''Are you coming with me?''

''Uh-uh, I get out now and I go away and don't look back.'' He rolled down the top of the white paper bag containing the leftover doughnut. ''You should wait until I'm all the way gone before you get out, okay?'' He sounded very anxious that Brichter obey this part, and Brichter, liking this less and less, nodded comprehension. Tyler seemed to think he should say something else, but since he wasn't asking for money this time, he couldn't think what it might be, so he shrugged and said, ''Bye,'' and got out. He walked up the sidewalk looking

245

straight ahead and turned the first corner he came to. Brichter gave him another ten seconds, then got out.

It was a quiet neighborhood, with a lot of sedate three- and four-story apartment buildings whose occupants were mostly at work. Besides himself, the only humans visible were a couple of pre-schoolers quarreling over a plastic three-wheeler. Brichter crossed the street and strolled as casually as he could across the concrete apron of the station. The gas pumps had been removed, and dried weeds stuck up out of the cracks in the cement. He went to try the door of the station, and though there was evidence of previous break-ins, it was currently locked. Feeling exposed, swearing fluently at himself for agreeing to such a stupid arrangement, he knocked; then, without waiting for an answer, walked around to the side where the rest rooms were. Boards covered the signs indicating which was which, so he went to the nearest one and knocked. There was no answer. He went back across the street and got into his car. He started his engine and lifted the radio microphone off its hook, laying it on his thigh.

A long two minutes later the passenger door was wrenched open and a man got in. A very large and dark man, pungent with old sweat, he had fresh sweat streaking his scarred cheeks, though he wore no jacket and it was chilly out.

"Drive," he said in a high, thin monotone, and Brichter pulled away from the curb.

"Nishan Amuseharian, you are under arrest," Brichter said, still not sure this wasn't a setup. But Nish was glancing out the windows for threatening faces, so Brichter continued, "You have a right to remain silent. If you give up this right, you have a right to consult with an attorney before any questioning. Do you understand?"

Nish said, "You're Brichter, right?"

"Detective Sergeant Otto Peter Brichter, Charter Police."

"I hear you're okay. Where we going?"

"The Safety Building."

"I don't want to go to jail until after we talk."

Brichter chose to focus on the second half of that statement. "Are you willing to waive your right to silence?"

"That means talk, right? And I'm talking to you now, ain't I? Ask me anything you want."

Interrogation is a delicate process. To do it well calls for experience, wisdom, tact, nerve, tenacity, intelligence, and empathy, most of which Brichter had. It is a skill enhanced by natural talent or, as in Brichter's case, study. It was not something Brichter cared to do while driving a sports car, which makes use of many of those same qualities. "How about we go park somewhere and talk?"

"Pick someplace safe and private."

Brichter decided that a safe, private place to park and talk was the underground garage of the Safety Building.

"You got to be kidding," said Nish.

"Why? You get only city servants through there, no one else; no civilians. And they're all on their way to or from somewhere, so they aren't likely to be hanging around—and this is the wrong time of day for a shift change. Anyway, my parking place is way in the back." And if you get spooked, there's all sorts of help available.

Nish, slow in the idea-processing center, was unable to refute any of this, so he consented; but he ducked and put an arm across his face when he realized there was a closed-circuit TV camera looking at the car when they arrived at the bottom of the steep entrance ramp. He did not uncover until they were parked.

"Joe Januschka wants me dead," he said, straightening and glancing around.

"Why?"

"Dunno."

"You must have some idea!"

"Sez you."

Brichter almost laughed at this old-time comeback, but Nish's high, expressionless voice had an icy quality to it that stifled humor. "Are you sure, then, he's put out an order to hit you?"

"Hammer called me."

"Your partner, Wayne Sokolovski."

"He says he's talked to Joe, and Joe said he'd pay him fifty big ones to off me next time he sees me. He says he was scared that if he don't agree, Joe will put out a hit on him, so he says to me, next time he sees me he'll have to try it, but to keep that from happening he's leaving town. He was crying, Hammer was." Nish knuckled a nostril and sniffed.

"Have you and Hammer been partners a long time?"

"We got thrown out of the Army together when we was just kids."

"Did Januschka give Hammer a reason for wanting you killed?"

"Joe says to Hammer, never you mind."

"Have you done anything to or for Januschka lately?"

"Uh-uh."

"Has Hammer done anything for Januschka lately?"

"We mostly do everything together."

"Mostly? Have you done anything lately without Hammer?"

Nish was silent awhile, then said, "I dug a hole."

"For whom?"

"You gonna call the FBI for me?" In his thin monotone, the question sounded like a demand.

"What do you want to talk to them for, Nish?"

"Listen, if you're gonna go back on your word—"

"I need to give them a reason to come and talk to you."

"Mr. Vigotti loaned some people in Terre Haute some money. Terre Haute is close to here, but it's another state, right?"

"It's a city in Indiana, Nish. And yes, Indiana is another state."

"Yeah, well, that makes it interstate, and interstate makes it a federal offense, right?"

"That's substantially correct."

"Well, I can hand the feds Mr. Vigotti all tied up in ribbons then, 'cause I know about an interstate thing. I beat up two guys in Terre Haute for him. Deadbeats."

"Mr. Vigotti is dead, Nish."

That startled the big man. "What happened?"

"He was strangled with a thin wire."

"Jeez! Who'd do something like that to Mr. Vigotti? He was always fair to people. Even deadbeats, because he let them keep asking for it until he hadn't got no choice but to send me or Hammer. Jeez, dead." Nish thought a bit. "So?"

"That makes your information much less valuable to the FBI."

"Oh."

"Was Dave Wagner one of Mr. Vigotti's customers?"

Nish frowned, deepening natural clefts in his forehead. His face was covered with a close pattern of small lumps and craters. "Wagner?"

"As in Crazy Dave."

"Used to be on TV. He was littler than I thought he'd be, we had to be careful not to break him by accident. Went to his store and brought him to Mr. Vigotti, and brought him back after."

"Did Mr. Vigotti burn down Mr. Wagner's store?"

"I heard the guy who set the fire got burned up."

"Did Mr. Vigotti hire someone to set the fire?"

"He was crazy mad at Mr. Wagner for saying he did."

"This hole you dug. Why did you dig it?"

Nish shifted uncomfortably. "You got to take care of me, you understand?"

249

"I understand, and I'll do everything I can for you. Why did you dig the hole, Nish?"

"To put a body in."

"Whose body?"

"It was wrapped in a sheet and I didn't like to open it and look."

"Where did you dig it?"

"On the riverbank, in the park."

"Jesus, Nish, haven't you seen any TV or read any papers in the past few days?"

"Uh-uh. Why?"

"Because that's where they found Tony."

Nish was silent a long time. He said at last, his voice sad, "He was all wrapped up and I never looked." He made the nostril-touching gesture again. "I wish I'd known. Jeez."

"Who told you to bury the body, Nish?"

"Is this why Joe's after me?"

"Did Joe Januschka tell you to bury the body?"

"Uh-uh. Helgerson."

Helgerson was reputed to work for Januschka. "Yes, I think this is why Joe's after you."

"I been living in the basement of a burned-out house, and I ain't et since Sunday. I heard about this deal you can get into, where you help them send away a wise guy and they send you someplace nice and you get a new name. Even fix your face." Nish touched the scars. "But you say Mr. Vigotti's dead—"

"Maybe you can tell them something about Joe Januschka."

"I ain't never seen Joe but twice in my life."

"How long have you been a wise guy, Nish?"

"I did my first kneecap when I was twelve."

"It's probable that sometime, somewhere, you've seen or done something the FBI would be interested in hearing about."

250

"When you call them, tell them I want to be one of those federal relocates."

"The U.S. Marshals run the Federal Relocation Program, Nish, not the FBI."

"Marshals?" Nish thought that over. "Does that mean I got to go be a cowboy?"

• • •

Brichter got Nish booked and put into protective isolation, then went up to Homicide and reported to Sweeney.

"So it's a cowboy he's thinkin' he'll be? Perhaps I should have a word with the wee lad."

• • •

Brichter went down to his squad room and dialed Philadelphia. This time he wouldn't let them take a message but stayed on the line until they located Martinson from Intelligence. Brichter hadn't gotten his first name, but fortunately there was only one of him. "Who is this?" said Martinson rudely, punching Brichter off hold.

"Detective Sergeant Brichter, that cop from East Overshore. You called me with a report on Tony Vigotti, remember?"

"Oh, yeah, I remember."

"You said at the time that a person who actually set fires for Fordero testified against him, then vanished into the Federal Relocation Program before you had a chance to talk to him."

"That's right."

"This disappearing witness: Had you ever actually seen him?"

"Hell, yes! I'm the one who busted him, but he squawked to the FBI and they took him away from me."

"Describe him to me," said Brichter.

"He was Angelo Gerald Coppalino, twenty-seven, five-ten, one seventy-five, curly black hair, brown eyes, big shoulders. Very typical guinea, even though he was born in Milwaukee

251

and didn't move out here till he was ten. Hey, you got him? Hang on to him; I'll be there on the next plane.''

"No, he's dead, I think. Someone matching that description was found murdered in the basement of a burned-out building.''

"Oh, Christ, the shithead!''

"Have you any reason to think he might have known Tony Vigotti?''

There was a sound on the other end as if Martinson were scrubbing his nose with the edge of his hand. "Lemme think. No. Vigotti left town ten years ago or thereabouts, and this guy's testimony four years ago was that he worked for Fordero three years, which makes seven years, so Vigotti was gone when Fordero hired Coppalino. Before that he was free-lancing his arson jobs, which is why I wanted to talk to him. I used to have a brother, a fireman, only he died in a fire that I think this bastard Coppalino set.''

"Was Coppalino married?''

"Yeah. His wife got pregnant during the trial. Name's Mary Irene, a very nice and pretty lady, but she won't tell you a thing.''

"She was spirited away right after we identified her husband, before I could ask her anything.''

"I bet. Her husband gets what's coming to him, so she dials a magic number and bing! she's gone. And will they tell you where they took her? No, sir. They won't even admit it was them helped her get away. It's a shame your honest citizen can't get that kind of service from the federal government.''

"No, it isn't,'' said Brichter. "The relocation program stinks. Their new identities fall apart when employers do any kind of check, so they have to go for the kind of job where no one checks—or take advantage of the new location to resume criminal activities. Sorry, I didn't mean to start on one of my

252

lectures. Have you got some pictures of both Mr. and Mrs. Coppalino, and could you send them to me by overnight mail?''

"Let me look in the files, but I'm sure we do. Tell me if it's him, will you? That way I can quit dreaming he'll come home and let me talk to him.''

Brichter hung up and sat a little while to savor the bright feeling that comes when a case suddenly breaks wide open.

The Federal Relocation Program began officially in the early 1970s with the passage of The Organized Crime Control Act, and has presented thousands of federal witnesses with new identities. Considerable sums are expended setting up new identities and moving the witnesses to new locations, sums that must be spent again if the witness gets into trouble. Yet the covers are flimsy, and it took the Social Security Administration, untrained in clandestine operations, some time to learn that it ought not to give sequential numbers to all members of relocated families, from the grandparents right down through the kids with after-school jobs. The Cleaveses' sequential social security numbers set off alarms in Brichter's head, but it took the conversation with Nish to set the right synapses sparking.

Brichter called Sweeney and the two went up to speak to Zak. "And here I was hoping to put handcuffs on the man who did it,'' mourned Zak when they finished.

"Why can't you?'' asked Brichter.

"Because he's dead, right? Jerry Cleaves is really Jerry Coppalino, who set fires for Vigotti's old boss in Philadelphia, right?''

"That's right,'' said Sweeney.

"He gets a new identity from the U.S. government and turns up in the same town Tony Vigotti lives in. So naturally he goes to Vigotti when he wants to get back in the business.''

"Wrong, Zak,'' said Brichter. "If you punched a violent

man in the nose and got away with it, would you later approach another member of his equally violent family and say, 'Hey, remember me?' "

Sweeney said, "The last person in town our friend Jerry would get near is Tony Vigotti."

"Ah," said Zak. "so that means it was Dave Wagner who hired him. And I have your report that you broke Wagner's alibi, for which I thank you. But I don't understand why Wagner felt he had to murder Gerald Cleaves/Coppalino."

Sweeney looked at Brichter. "You're the expert at making connections. Tell us."

"There's nothing complicated about it. Wagner was greedy. If he killed the man he hired to set his fire, he wouldn't have to pay him."

"Come on, there must be more to it than that," objected Sweeney. "He took an awful chance with that alibi."

"Okay, he didn't want someone walking around town who knew the truth about the fire. He was setting up Vigotti to take the fall, but the actual arsonist knew the truth. If Gerald got caught, he might talk—and for Wagner to be safe, Vigotti had to be put away behind bars." He smiled at Zak and Sweeney. "Make up your own reasons. Maybe Wagner thought we'd conclude it was an accidental fire. I mean, there's no history of successful fires in his background, so what does he know about lines of char and the melting temperature of brass? What he does know is that if they catch you burning your own place down, insurance companies don't pay."

"Yes, poor sod, he never figured on our Captain Kader." Sweeney put a brawny arm around Zak, who could only grin, too pleased to reply.

Brichter continued, "Then when you said arson and the ME said murder, he needed another story. And it occurred to him that here was a chance to both get out from under Vigotti and keep the money. Like I said, he's a greedy man."

254

"How do you know that?" asked Sweeney.

"Those screwy prices he charged in his store—did anyone ever notice that they were always a couple of dollars higher than the competition? And when he applied for welfare, he said, 'I got no pride where money's involved. I'll live on food stamps like the other welfare bums till I get what's coming to me.' "

"I saw that," nodded Zak. "It was on the news."

"The nerve of the guy!" said Sweeney. "On television and everything! Right, who's the best typist? I believe that's you, Obie. Let's go down to your place, grab a complaint form and hustle us up a warrant. We'll bag that brigand today!"

20

THEY put Zak in the back seat of the Porsche because his legs were shortest, and set off for Wagner's apartment. On the way, they discussed contingencies.

"There's no fire escape down the back of that building," said Zak. "The fire marshal ordered it replaced, and the old one was taken down, but the new one somehow hasn't arrived yet. Wagner's only way out is through the door we'll be standing at."

Sweeney grunted approval, and added, "He's just a little turd; if he puts up a fight, the three of us should be able to subdue him without drawing a weapon."

"What if he's got a visitor or visitors?" asked Brichter.

"Then we'll ask him to step out into the hall," said Sweeney. "Captain Kader, you reach around behind him and close the door, and don't let anyone open it again."

"Okay—but call me Zak, will you? Both of you. Who gets to tell him he's under arrest?"

"Me," said Sweeney. "You suspected him from the start, Obie came up with the proof, and since it's officially my case, I should get to do at least one thing. But since you wanted to so bad, Zak, you put the bracelets on him."

It took only a few minutes to get to the shabby apartment building Wagner lived in. It was a four-story red brick building, narrow, but as deep as it was high. The street was one-way, with parking only on the side opposite the apartment. Brichter found a double-length space near the end of the block, and pulled in. He reached for the microphone under the dash.

"Brichter," he said.

"Brichter," acknowledged Dispatch.

"We're going in at 320 Morgan."

"Copy. It's fifteen-nineteen."

They glanced automatically at their watches to confirm the time, almost twenty after three. Sweeney said, "Maybe we'll have this all wrapped up before quitting time." The trio got out and crossed the street.

The first floor was occupied by a store selling crafts made by the handicapped, and when they discovered the door leading upstairs was locked, they went into the store. A display of identification got them through another door that opened into the stairwell. Sweeney led the way, and a little later they stopped outside Wagner's door to regroup and catch their breath—he lived on the top floor back. Sweeney knocked.

No answer. "Mr. Wagner? It's Sergeant Sweeney, Charter Police. Open the door."

No answer. Sweeney knocked harder. "Police! Open up!"

No answer.

A door down the hall opened and a tiny woman with white

257

hair contained in a fine net leaned around her doorjamb to quaver, "He's not home."

"How do you know?" asked Brichter.

"He passed me on the stairs. I went down to get my mail and he was coming down as I was coming up. He said 'Hello' nice as you please and he went whistling out the door. I've been listening for him to come back, because I baked bread today and I wanted to give him a loaf for taking my garbage out all this month. But he's not back yet."

"Thank you, ma'm," said Sweeney, touching his forehead to her and she smiled and withdrew.

"What do you think?" asked Zak.

"I think we go back out and wait in the car for him," said Sweeney, already heading for the stairs.

He stayed ahead of the other two all the way down, back through the store and out to the sidewalk, so he was the one who spotted Wagner driving up the street. He stepped off the curb to flag him down and Wagner's parti-colored Mustang slowed, but then Wagner spotted Zak and Brichter hurrying out of the store and something in their wary eagerness made him lift his foot off the brake.

Sweeney shouted, "Hey! Wagner!" and moved farther out into the street, arms uplifted. Wagner tromped on the accelerator and headed right for him. Too late, Sweeney realized he was in danger and tried to leap out of the way. The car clipped him as it went by and Sweeney was somersaulted onto the sidewalk.

Brichter ran for him, stooping before he stopped. Sweeney rolled away from him, yelling, "I'm all right, I'm all right! Go get him! Go, go, go!"

Brichter and Zak ran across the street and piled into the Porsche, Zak reaching for the microphone as Brichter started the engine and roared away from the curb.

"Dispatch, this is Captain Kader with Sergeant Brichter,"

said Zak. "We're in pursuit of a green Ford Mustang with a blue door and black front fender on the passenger side." He gave the license number and said the lone driver was wanted for arson and murder. As they rounded a corner, he named the intersection and direction the Mustang was headed in.

"Seat belts!" ordered Brichter. He pulled his down, and Zak took the end and shoved it into the buckle before fastening his own.

Wagner accelerated and Brichter stayed right behind him. They were driving about fifty miles per hour, far too fast for conditions. The Mustang ran a red light, and Brichter, horn blaring, followed him. A jaywalking pedestrian escaped by making a gigantic bound forward. The Mustang ducked out, around, and back in front of a bus barely in time to avoid a collision with a car headed in the other direction. Brichter stood on his brakes to avoid rear-ending the bus, then jammed the accelerator down to get around once the way was clear. Zak, despite the belt, had to grab the door handle and brace his feet. "Can we get him, you think?" He was grinning through his mustache.

"Kader, go to channel two," said Dispatch.

"If he doesn't kill himself first," said Brichter. "You handle the radio."

Zak managed to switch channels on the radio set, glancing up in time to see Wagner run another red light, then increase his speed to make a green showing ahead. Wagner blew by another car. Its driver, startled, swerved and braked. Brichter, swearing, swerved harder and there was a whup-diddle-bam! as the Porsche momentarily ran onto the sidewalk.

"Kader, what is your location?" asked Dispatch.

"Lexington!" shouted Zak into the microphone, slamming against the locked inertia reel of the seat belt as Brichter yanked the Porsche out and around another car. "North! On Lexington, north! There's France, we're passing France Avenue!"

In another two blocks a squad car joined from behind, its siren a welcome warning of the chase in progress. A heedless driver pulled out from a left-hand side street, saw them, braked. To avoid him the Mustang went squealing hard around the corner. A rear hubcap popped off, collided instantly with the curb, flew up and over the Porsche. "We're turning—" said Zak to Dispatch as he reflexively ducked, and he looked back in time to see the hubcap smash into the windshield of the following squad. Wheels locked, the squad slid sideways across the street and into a telephone pole. "—And he crashed!" shouted Zak. "The squad car crashed; send an ambulance!"

"Kader, your location," requested Dispatch's cool woman's voice.

"Baron! Going east!" Zak returned his attention to the front. "Oh my God!"

There was a train blocking the street just ahead; Baron crossed a railroad track at the end of the block. Wagner did not look as if he were slowing, and Brichter appeared determined to follow him right to hell.

The tracks moved through the intersection at an angle that made a right turn impossible. There was a gas station on the corner, and Wagner whipped through it, sending a customer climbing up onto the roof of his car and another into a display of oil cans, one of which slammed into the side of the Porsche as they followed. A fine spatter of oil flew up onto Zak's window as the car made a controlled drift to the right and headed down the street parallel to the railroad tracks.

"Victoria, south on Victoria now," reported Zak. His voice sounded calmer, but that was only because he was beyond excitement, beyond even fear, into a state like dreaming, where shouting didn't help, and reality melted through your fingers like water. There was a big grain truck on the road ahead, and some oncoming cars made passing impossible. At what seemed the last instant the truck turned, and the two cars shot past.

Zak had been gripping the microphone so hard it hurt clear up to his shoulder. There did not seem to be enough air in the car to breathe. The pain in his shoulder became so severe he dropped the microphone to rub it.

The railroad ended at a cluster of granaries and just beyond them Wagner nearly lost it, making a turn onto Charter Road, raising a cloud of dust and small stones as he bounded onto the shoulder.

"Got you now!" said Brichter. Charter Road was four lanes wide and all roads leading into it were marked with stop signs.

Wagner tried; he kept the accelerator all the way down, he constantly changed lanes to block Brichter's attempts to pass. Twice he feinted a turn at an intersection. Then a moment's inattention brought Brichter alongside. Brichter grinned and began crowding him over, out of the left lane and into the pole-and-cable divider.

Brichter said, "Back me up, Zak; this is it!"

But Zak had lost interest in the chase. His head was against the side window, and he was staring unblinkingly through the oil-smeared glass. Brichter spared a glance and said, "Oh, shit!" He braked hard and put the Porsche into a controlled slide. Boxed as he was, Wagner had no choice but to brake himself. The cars came to a halt in a cloud of dust and smoke and a stench of burned rubber. Brichter hit his belt release, yanked his gun out, opened the car door and was trying to get out in the narrow space between his car and the Mustang when a sharp pain started with a bang in his middle. He looked over, through punctured windows, and there was Wagner, gun in hand, waiting for Brichter to fall—and ready to shoot again if he didn't. Brichter tried to fall back into his car, where the radio was, but instead fell down on the gravel between the cars. He rolled over and saw Wagner's legs as the man hopped the cable and started across the highway. "Halt, you bastard," he whispered, aimed carefully and shot Wagner in the foot,

261

which made him hop, stumble, and nearly fall. A tiny pickup truck, which had been swerving nicely to miss him, now struck him, tumbled him under its wheels and rolled him onto the shoulder on the other side.

Brichter watched the pickup stop a little beyond Wagner and back up, saw the driver, a young man, emerge, check Wagner, look over at the two cars on the other side and run back to his pickup.

"Hey, there's people hurt here!" he heard a voice say. Not his own, but someone else's, someone nearby. "Call the cops, call an ambulance!"

He wanted to tell them that Zak wasn't injured but having a heart attack, but was overtaken by a sudden darkness.

.   .   .

Kori was in what had once been the butler's pantry, a large room off the kitchen with a tiled fireplace and atrium door overlooking the kitchen garden. It was now her office, and her computer and filing cabinets lived there.

She was wondering if she was sounding a little too effusive in the personal comment she'd just typed—she was answering a letter from a new breeder inquiring about Copper Wind's stud schedule for next year. She had found it effective to mix boilerplate and individualized comments in answering letters, a process made easy by her word-processing program.

She took out the words "very" and "happily," then heard footsteps on the side porch. Danny opened the atrium door, his face scared. Behind him was McHugh, looking grave.

"What is it?" she said, standing. "Cris, what's wrong?"

"There's been a shooting," said McHugh.

She felt a stupid grin pull at her mouth as her insides turned to stone. "No!" she said. She turned her back to them, put a desperately calming hand on her belly. "No," she repeated.

"He's alive, he's alive!" said Danny, coming around her desk to take her by the elbow.

"How bad?" she asked, shaking off Danny's hand, still not looking at them.

"I don't know," said Cris. "All I know is, they took him to County General. I've come to bring you there."

She was climbing into Cris's car without any memory of leaving the house, and Danny was trying to stuff her long leather coat in after her. "He'll be all right, I know it," Danny shouted over the engine's roar.

She rolled the coat into a clumsy pillow and held it with both hands on her lap as McHugh drove down the lane and onto the road into town. She was wearing jeans and a white broadcloth shirt belted with a paisley scarf. One of his old shirts. Was that okay? Maybe she should have made Cris wait while she changed. But into what? What does one wear to go see if one's husband is dead?

"What happened?" she asked.

"A chase," he said. "He went with two guys to arrest Dave Wagner, and somehow it turned into a chase. He got Wagner stopped but the bastard shot him and almost got away, but a truck hit him. Hit Wagner."

"Is Wagner dead?"

"I don't know."

"What about the other two? Were they shot?"

"Sergeant Sweeney was run over by Wagner getting away at the start. We heard about that first; he's got a broken leg. I don't know about Captain Kader."

"Zak Kader? He and his wife are supposed to come to dinner on Sunday."

"No reason to cancel that."

"Except Peter's been shot."

"Hey, maybe it's just a scratch." He glanced at her. "I'm sorry I don't have more to tell you. They told me to come get you, and I left right away. Frank will know; he's meeting us at the hospital."

"Is Peter's car all right?"

He glanced at her, surprised, and she said, "If he lives, that's the first thing he'll ask."

.   .   .

He was alive, in surgery, and it wasn't a head wound, that's all Frank knew. They put her in a comfortable chair in a gently lit room next to a table with a phone and a box of Kleenex. She picked up the phone and called Dr. Ramsey at the college. "Gordon, Peter's hurt. We're at the hospital. Can you come?"

They began the wait. Frank Ryder took her hand and held it at such a clumsy angle that two of her fingers fell asleep, but she couldn't think of how to ask him to let go. Cris walked back and forth, back and forth, behind her chair until she wanted to scream at him to sit down. Her knee started to hurt for no reason at all.

The door to the room opened and Gordon was there. She wrenched free of Frank's grasp and ran to him, and he put his arms around her and held her close. Then she was able to cry.

He led her to a comfortable sofa and let her lean on his shoulder while he extracted from Captain Ryder and Sergeant McHugh the few facts: Sweeney was having a broken tibia set, Zak was in intensive care with severe cardiac complications, and Peter was in surgery. The two men who wrecked their squad car helping in the chase had only minor injuries. Oh, and Dave Wagner had a broken shoulder, fractured pelvis, and a bullet-shattered metatarsal arch.

"Pete must've shot him," said McHugh.

"Or he shot himself," said Ramsey. "Don't people frequently shoot themselves in the foot?"

A doctor stuck his head in the room and they stood. "Are you the Isaac Kader family?" he asked.

"No, I don't think they're here yet," said Ryder. "But I'm Captain Frank Ryder, Charter Police. One of my men was working with him on a case. Is there news?"

264

The doctor put on a professional face and spread his hands. "I'm sorry," he said.

"Oh, my," said Kori.

"We tried—and he tried—but there just wasn't enough heart muscle left," said the doctor. "I'll leave word at the reception desk, but if you see them, tell them I'll look in every ten minutes until we connect."

He left and the waiting began again. McHugh and Ryder stood in a corner talking and taking turns coming by to touch her on the shoulder.

Then another woman entered the room, an older woman with an eastern European face. She was weeping. A young man had one arm across her shoulders and the other under her elbow. "Oh, my Isaac, my Isaac," she mourned, and the young man patted her and murmured words of comfort.

A long-headed man with a hawk's nose and beautiful silver hair followed on their heels. Kori recognized him, he was the Fire Chief. He followed them to another couch, bent to include himself in their huddle and spoke quietly in a very deep voice.

Kori waited until he straightened, then went herself to stoop before the older woman. "I'm Mrs. Brichter," she said. "And I'm—"

The woman leaned forward and hissed, "You stay away from me! Your husband killed my husband!"

Kori, startled, reached out to touch Mrs. Kader lightly on her knee. "No, you don't understand. My husband is Sergeant Peter Brichter. He was working with your husband on this case."

The woman slapped Kori's hand away. "I know who he is! He is the man who kept right on driving while my Isaac died beside him! You should be ashamed to come near me, with such a husband as yours!" The woman began weeping loudly, and the young man put his arm around her, asking with grimaces that Kori go away.

265

As Kori rose she felt hands on her shoulders. It was Ryder. "Come on, leave her alone now," he said gently and led her away.

"What's she talking about?" asked Kori when they were out of earshot. "She says Peter let Zak die."

"She's upset."

"Where did she get that terrible idea?"

"Because Zak was riding with Peter; they found him in the car after the chase."

"Was it the chase that gave him the heart attack?"

Ryder hesitated. "Zak was talking on the radio, keeping Dispatch informed of the progress of the chase. He seemed fine, even enjoying himself, but stopped transmitting before the end, and we're not sure why. Peter didn't break off the chase, so I'm sure he didn't notice Zak was in trouble."

Kori groped for the sofa and sat down. "But surely he would have noticed, wouldn't he?" She glanced at the weeping Mrs. Kader. "Peter and Zak are friends!"

"Sure they are," said Ryder. "Don't go getting yourself all upset; we don't have all the facts yet." Ramsey came over to see what the problem was, but Ryder gave a brief shake of his head and he went away again.

.   .   .

Dave Wagner tried to feign sleep, but the pain in his foot and shoulder grew large enough to press a few groans out, and he opened his eyes to find the freckled redhead still planted in his wheelchair beside the bed. "Hello, me boyo!" said the redhead in a cruel and hearty voice. "You're under arrest for murder! You have a right to remain silent! If you give up your right to remain silent, you have a right to consult with a lawyer before I ask you any questions! Do you understand!"

"Don't shout, okay?"

"Do you understand?!"

"Yeah, yeah."

"Are you willing to answer my questions at this time?"

"Can I ask you one, first?"

"Absolutely!"

"Brichter: Is he dead?"

"Of course not!"

"Will you quit shouting? Where is he?"

"One floor down, in no pain at all! That's more than you can say about either of us, and one more answer than you asked for. May I ask you some questions now?"

"Yes, all right."

Sweeney's voice moderated in volume. "Did you know who Jerry Cleaves really was when you hired him?"

"No. But I knew something was screwy about him."

"What did you think it was?"

"I couldn't figure it out, at first. I'm from Milwaukee, a south-sider just like he said he was, and he knew that part of the city pretty well. You know, swimming at Kozi Park and fish fries on Friday nights. But he knew things kids know about Milwaukee, not things grown-ups know. The stampeding-buffalo diorama at the museum, and catching pigeons under the viaducts he knew; but not Safe House, where you have to know the password to get in and have a drink, or Riverside Theater. And that was wrong, because he said he came to Milwaukee as a teenager and left it when he was in his twenties. So I thought, why would he lie? Not that it mattered, but what if he's bullshitting about setting fires, too? My foot hurts, it really hurts. Can you get them to give me something?"

"In a little while. So what did you do about Jerry?"

"Well, I didn't want him to screw up my fire. So I asked him to tell me about one fire that I could check out, so I'd know he knew what he was doing. And he said no way, and I said then the deal's off. And he said could he get back to me, and I said no, he had to tell me about one right now. I didn't want him going out and digging up some fire and saying it was his, y'see.''

Sweeney nodded. "Smart move.''

"And he said, okay, there was this fire he set out east, a big old furniture warehouse, and he told me where and when—he wasn't sure of the date, but said it was a few days either side. So I checked it out, and sure enough, there was a big mother of a fire right about then in a furniture warehouse. Suspected arson, but nothing proved. So I knew then he was a torch, like he said.'' Wagner began to reach over his bad shoulder with his good arm. "Where's that little thing with the button on it? I *got* to ask them to give me something.''

"Here, let me.'' Sweeney picked up the call signal and put it down again. "There, okay? Someone will be here in a couple of minutes. How did you meet this Jerry Cleaves?''

"Just by chance. I was in a tavern I never been in before. Happy Daze, I think it was called. With a *z*. I'd been delivering a VCR to a customer, saving the cost of hiring someone and impressing the hell out of her, I hoped, so she'd tell her friends. Anyhow, I hadn't had lunch, so I stopped by this tavern with a sign that says it has the best burgers in town and I had a beer or two with one and another beer just for the hell of it, and pretty soon I'm bitching to the bartender about how shitty business is. And he leans on the bar and says his brother in Kankakee hired him a torch a year or two back and now he's doing better than ever. And I say that sounds like a wonderful idea, but how do I go about finding someone who will set my fire for me. And he laughs and says maybe I should go to Kankakee and ask his brother. So I laugh, too, and finish my beer, and I'm halfway to my car when this guy comes up behind me and says, 'Are you serious about having yourself a successful fire?' And I turn around and it's him. Jerry Cleaves. He was in there and overheard us talking and followed me out.''

"And then what happened?''

"Well, we met a few times here and there, never the same place twice and never his place or mine, talking when and how and how much. By then, like I said, I was suspicious, and he told me about this fire I could check out. But it was still weird, because the fire was out east and he moved down here a few years ago from Minneapolis. But I knew he must've spent some time out east, because he had some kind of Eastern accent. He said he was born in Maryland, which I don't know; maybe they have the same kind of accent. Where the hell's that nurse?"

"Why do you think they call us patients? Go on."

Wagner sighed. "Jerry kind of hinted one time that he used to know all kinds of tough guys, but he never outright said they were in the mob, or the Mafia or whatever. All the same, I started wondering. Then I read how Mafia bosses will what they call 'import talent' for special jobs, hit jobs and stuff. And I thought, oh Christ, maybe that's how he ended up starting that fire out east. And if he's in the Mafia, he knows Mr. Vigotti. So I told him the deal was off, and he said, 'Didn't the fire check out?' Real surprised. And I said, 'Yes, but I got a special kind of problem I don't think you want to get involved with.' He kept asking, 'What, what?' So I finally dropped Vigotti's name on him. And he said, 'Vigotti? I don't know him.' And I said, 'He's connected.' And he said, 'Are you thinking of screwing him somehow?' And I said, 'No, of course not. I owe him some money, and this is how I plan to raise it.' Which wasn't true; I planned from the start to blame Vigotti for my fire. I had to hire Jerry, because I had to have that fire soon. But after that I also knew I'd have to kill him, because the Mafia is like a brotherhood; once Vigotti got arrested, Jerry'd go tell on me. I didn't have any choice; killing Jerry Cleaves was self-defense."

"You could have let him set the fire and then paid Vigotti off, you know."

"No way! I was cleaned out; the only way to get back on my feet was to collect that insurance. I wasn't going to give a dime of it to Tony Vigotti."

.   .   .

A surgeon came into the family room and Kori, Ramsey, Ryder, and McHugh stood. There was a generous spatter of blood across his blue scrubs and Kori could not take her eyes off it.

"Yes, Doctor?" said Ramsey.

"Are you all waiting to hear about Sergeant Brichter?"

"Yes, yes," said Ryder impatiently. "How is he?"

"He's in the recovery room right now. We removed his spleen, which was opened by the bullet. We're replacing the blood he lost. We're monitoring him closely at present, but he's stable and won't need to go into intensive care."

"Is he awake?" asked Kori.

"Not yet," said the surgeon. "When he does wake up, there will be some discomfort, which you should be aware of when you go to see him."

"When can we see him?" asked McHugh.

"In a couple of hours," said the surgeon. "We'll move him into a semi-private room shortly, but it will be longer than that before he'll be able to appreciate visitors."

"You're sure he's going to be all right?" asked Kori.

The doctor smiled. "He won't be running any marathons for the next few weeks, but barring unforeseen complications, he should recover completely."

"Good. I want to go home," said Kori.

"Thank you, Doctor," said Ryder.

"What did you say, pet?" asked Ramsey.

"I want to go home."

"You'll barely more than get there when you'll have to come back," said Ryder.

"I'll come back in the morning, after chores," she said.

270

Ramsey took her by the shoulders. "You don't mean that."

"I do. He's not going to die and he'll be in pain, which makes him cross, so I want to go home."

She could not be moved from this decision, and the men raised their eyebrows at one another as they surrendered, thinking it an unusual stress reaction, probably brought on by her hormones. Ramsey said he'd drive her home and stay with her. Ryder and McHugh sat back down; they'd wait and see Brichter.

On their way out, Ramsey and Kori passed a little chapel, and she, seeing it, pulled free of his hand and went in. He followed, nonplussed. She went up to the second pew from the front and sat down. The altar was severely plain, spread with a white cloth on which sat a large, unornamented brass cross. She studied the cross, her expression unreadable, for a long minute. Then she stood and started out. At the door she looked back. "Thank you," she whispered, not to Ramsey, and went through the door.

21

"COME on in; since Peter won't be home, it shouldn't be any trouble to feed you."

"Pet . . ."

"We'll talk about it after dinner."

Danny and Mrs. Morales were assured of Brichter's undoubted survival and sent home. Then Kori and Ramsey sat down to an excellent late dinner of Chinese beef and pea pods, which she mostly ignored, becoming animated instead over Chinook's bizarre objection to her cooling sheet. "She acts as if it's out to kill her, and tries to rip it off. Yesterday she got it up over her head and genuinely panicked, and it took us quite a while to rescue her. Then, after we got her out of it, we had to let her trample it to death before she would settle down. She's a gorgeous creature, but difficult, not at all like her father."

Ramsey courteously pretended to be entertained by the story, and by another of Chinook's encounter with the farrier, until

272

the egg custard had been tasted and set aside, and they could retire to the living room.

. . .

"He was shot from almost in front," said the doctor, poking himself in the lower left midriff, "and it came out here." He poked himself in the back, not far from his spine. "The bullet unzipped his spleen and took a nice-size chunk of meat out of his back on its way out. But no other organs were hit and he's in good physical condition. As of now, we've no reason to think he won't recover fully."

With that good news to brace them, Ryder and McHugh went to stand by Brichter's bedside. They were pleased, of course, that he'd be all right, but concerned at how bad he looked at present, and so stood awhile in that embarrassed way men will, when they feel deeply but do not allow themselves to show it.

"Pete?" said McHugh at last.

"Yeah," muttered Brichter.

"It's Frank and Cris. How ya doin', buddy?"

"Okay." After a struggle, Brichter opened his eyes. "What time is it?"

"Little after ten in the evening. You were shot about six hours ago."

"No wonder it still hurts." The eyes closed again. "Where's Katherine?"

"Gone home. This hit her hard, Pete. I don't think she could manage seeing you like this."

"I see. How's Zak?"

"Well . . ." said McHugh, looking at Ryder; and they hesitated long enough over whether or not to lie that he guessed the truth.

"It wasn't the chase, Peter," said Ryder. "And there wasn't a damn thing you could have done to help him. The doc said Zak's heart was like tissue paper, it could have happened anytime, even in front of his wife at the supper table. This way, it

273

was in line of duty, so Mrs. Kader will get full benefits. Both she and Zak have known for months he could go at any time."

"Yeah."

"Your car's fine," continued Ryder. "I hear a fistfight broke out over who got to drive it from the scene."

Brichter didn't laugh, so McHugh did and said, "Your doctor says you'll be fine, too, in a few weeks."

"That's nice," murmured Brichter.

They didn't stay long—doctor's orders, and he kept drifting away.

But half an hour after they left, Sweeney wheeled his chair in. "Say, Obie, me lad!"

"Sweeney."

"I've been upstairs with Wagner. He told me all about everything." Sweeney leaned forward, a gleeful grin bringing a shine to his green eyes. "His game from the start was to blame the fire on Vigotti. But guess why he killed Jerry Cleaves or Coppalino or whatever his name is."

"I give up."

"Because he thought once Vigotti was arrested, Jerry would arrange for Wagner to take a Mafia-style hit." Sweeney sat back and waited.

The pale eyes opened. "Why did he think that?"

"Because he figured out all by himself Jerry was connected. He had about concluded the deal with Jerry to burn the building down when it came to him that Jerry's talk about his knowing a lot of right guys might mean something. He knows just enough about the Mafia to realize that using one right guy to cheat another could earn him a funeral. Since the deal was too far along for him to safely back out of it, Jerry had to go. QED."

"That's one explanation I didn't think of."

"You were right about the alibi, however. He set the fire up for the night he'd have to supply the beer, and went into Ogden's the day before, bought two six-packs and the cheese

274

whatevers, and mentioned the poker game as if he'd come away from it. He kept the beer in his trunk so it would be cold when he brought it up. Then on the Thursday he drove to his building, went down to the basement, and found Jerry just emptying the last gas can, right on schedule. He brained the poor fellow with a baseball bat, then left him and the bat to burn along with everything else. He even had a duplicate set of clothes in his car, so there was no blood or scent of gasoline about him when he returned to his game. It was just his bad luck one of his fellow players saw the fire before everything was burned up. He got the players to lie for him in order to delay our questioning of Ogden long enough for Ogden to become hazy about the day he was in. Very clever, but such forethought means this is first-degree murder—and, of course, since Jerry didn't care spit what happened to Vigotti, it's first-degree murder of a man he had no reason to fear. Shocking how wrong a clever man can be.''

"Shocking."

"Am I wearing you out? You sound tired."

"I'm mourning a friend I never quite claimed. Zak's dead."

Sweeney became sad. "Yes, I know. Too bad. But he had a bad heart; everyone knew that."

"Shouldna let him go on that chase with me."

Sweeney gestured at the big cast on his foot and shin. "Well, I wasn't exactly up to running across the street to hop in your car with you. Anyway, the two of you did one hell of a job stopping Wagner. Dispatch said Zak sounded as if he were keen on the chase right up to the point he stopped transmitting, and that he did a professional job of it. I'm putting the both of you in for a medal of valor."

"We'll pin his to his tombstone."

"Aw!" Sweeney rolled his chair back, then forward again. "Where's the pretty wifey?"

"Home. And I don't need any other visitors, so go away. I'm tired now."

275

"Brandy?" Kori asked.

"No, thank you, I'm driving."

"Won't you stay the night?"

"No, I don't have anything with me, and anyway, I want to go back to the hospital and see Peter."

With the name brought up again, she retreated to the couch, her face closing.

"Whatever is the matter?" Ramsey asked.

"He did something so terrible I don't know how I can deal with it."

"Peter did? What?"

"He killed Zak."

"Where on earth did you get such a notion as that?"

"From Mrs. Kader. Peter and Zak were in Peter's car, and Zak had a heart attack, but instead of stopping to help, Peter kept right on with the chase. With his paramedic background, he might have saved him, but he was so eager to catch Mr. Wagner, he let his friend die."

"You *believe* that?"

"Zak had the heart attack right in the seat next to Peter, and he did nothing."

Ramsey said, "When you're chasing someone up a city street at fifty miles an hour, trying not to be run over by a bus, your attention is not pulled from that task by a mere heart attack."

"*Mere*? This was a fatal heart attack! You'd notice! You couldn't help it!"

"Pet, what do you think a person having a heart attack does?"

She shook her head, exasperated. "Clutches at his chest, I suppose, struggles and groans awhile, then collapses."

"The only part of that I will grant you is the collapsing part. There may be no noise, no struggle, no groans. And when you're being held in place by a seat belt and shoulder strap, you don't collapse very far."

"What do you know about it?" she demanded.

"My great-uncle died of a heart attack while sleeping in the same bed with my great-aunt, and she didn't know it until the next morning when she woke and found him."

Her eyes widened, then dropped. "I'm sorry."

"It happened before I was born, and was told to me as a family story. Great-Great-Aunt Eloise had a servant get my grandfather on the telephone, then she took the receiver and said, with what I was told was typical economy of words, 'Clarence is gone.' "

"Are you saying that it's possible Peter didn't notice?"

"I believe absolutely he didn't notice. For heaven's sake, do you think he'd allow anyone, much less a friend, to die like that?"

"Well . . ." she said, and looked ashamed.

"You must have been greatly shocked by all this, more even than I thought, to have allowed Mrs. Kader's hysterics to affect you like this. I'm glad you had the sense to insist on coming home rather than confronting Peter with that in his present state. How could you seriously think such a thing of him?"

"I don't know." She drew her knees up and rested her chin on them. "I don't know," she repeated. "I'm so angry with him anyway."

"Do you mean you're still arguing with him over having a baby?"

"Not exactly. We made a bargain. He's talking more about his work, and in return I won't mention a baby for six months, unless he brings the topic up first. Which he will, in about fourteen weeks, when I go into maternity clothes. And then the trouble will really start. And what will I do? What can I say?" She draped her wrists across her ankles. "But suppose he'd died out there? What would I do with only a folded flag to hug? I'd haunt the cemetery where they put him; I'd never get over losing him, never!"

She had raised her head, fists clenched on her knees, as her

277

speech became more heated, but now she put her cheek down on her fists. "I know it's unhealthy to become that focused on one person. Before I married, a counselor told me that my restricted upbringing made it difficult for me to know how to love more than one person at a time. But that I needed to do that, to learn to share that focus, to love someone who will absorb it, need it, then begin to fight it, so I can learn to let go. I tried dating others, but they were all hollow, so I went ahead and married Peter. I suppose I could try adultery, but I'd rather have a baby. But suppose Peter comes to hate me for doing this to him? Suppose he thinks I did this to him on purpose?"

"Didn't you?"

"I told you how it happened; it was an accident!"

"A month or two before you conceived, did you bring up the subject to him?"

"Yes, but his reaction was so negative—" She was stopped by the smirk on his face. "Now don't go thinking such things!"

"What am I thinking?"

"Some sort of nonsense about my subconscious making its own decision!"

"Why do you think it nonsense? Remember long ago the nightmares, the attempts by your subconscious mind to tell the conscious mind what really happened the night your parents died? There is a powerful will within you, as in everyone else, and it must have its say. You say you've focused yourself on Peter. In your study of him, have you ever found any reason to believe there is anything in the world you could do to him that would make him hate you?"

"I don't know. I've tried never to hurt him. He's easily hurt, you know."

"That's true. Because he loves you. And you love him. How can loving each other produce a hateful thing? The baby was conceived in innocence, in love. She will bring with her the ability to stir love in both her parents."

"His parents. It's a boy."

Ramsey smiled. "You sound very sure."

"When I talk to him, he's a boy. I want to name him after you and his father. Gordon Peter, do you like it? And I want you to be his godfather."

He got up from his couch and went to lift a heavy drapery and look out an embrasured window. Her speaking of focus had reminded him of that earlier time, when he was her tutor and the focus had been on him. He remembered how he'd told himself he was relieved when the focus was shifted to Peter. But what a wrench it had been to walk her down the aisle to where Peter was waiting. Now she was giving part of herself back to him. "I am deeply honored." Without turning back, he continued, "Pet, you asked Peter to let you share his work, with all its terrors, fears, and horrors. And he agreed. What do you think he will feel when he learns Zak Kader is dead, and worse, you hold him responsible?"

He turned around. "You asked to share, and so now that's what you must do, not judge. He is his own judge, a harsher one than you could ever be. Your role as his wife is to temper his judgment with mercy. My advice is, let the other things go until he's well enough to deal with them. Then tell him and stand the uproar, which will end as soon as he sees how bravely you are standing it."

He came to lift her to her feet. "Meanwhile, come with me to the hospital and tell him how beautifully he handled himself today."

·　　·　　·

The nurse on duty said he was doing very well, but on the way up in the elevator Kori created in her mind an image of him lying in the prim white bed, pale and tired. There would be bandages, and one of those IV lines dripping colorless calories into an arm.

He was more gray than merely pale. There was a scabby

279

abrasion on his forehead near his left temple, made uglier by having been stained violet. A green-colored tube ran from a bottle of bubbling liquid across his upper lip, two little prongs poking into his nostrils. He was breathing unevenly, snorts and gasps punctuated with lengthy pauses. The bed was rumpled, as if he'd been thrashing around, though he was lying still now. There were two IVs, one colorless and the other purplish red, and the skin around the taped places where they entered his arms was lifted in a sore-looking way and was stained yellow-brown. A graduated plastic bag hung on a lower bed rail, and a tube leading into it dripped a vulgar yellow. His hair was damp and clinging, revealing how thin it was becoming. His eyes were sunken and his mouth was turned downward in a tight grimace. He looked old.

"Oh, my," she whispered, and her hand tightened over Ramsey's fingers.

Brichter's eyes opened. His gaze drifted to her, and he blinked slowly. *"Fy'n galon?"* he murmured.

"Yes, Peter, I'm here."

"They said you weren't coming."

"They were wrong."

His eyes closed again and he smiled faintly. "Come here please."

She came close enough to stroke his forehead with two fingers. "The doctor says you'll be fine."

"Yes, I know."

"You should have ducked."

"Funny thing about that. If I'd seen that gun, I would have ducked; and if I'd ducked, it would have put my face right in the way of that bullet."

"Oh, Peter!"

"Eddie told you I'm lucky."

"That's right, he did. Peter, I brought Gordon with me."

"H'lo, Gordon."

"I'm no end pleased that you are here to say that. But I think I'll leave you two alone for a while."

"So long as you're going, find out where they put my car? And see if you can get someone to wash that oil off it, will you? Before it damages the paint."

"Of course."

When the door closed, there was a resting silence, then Brichter said, "Until you came in I was wondering if I had in fact died and this was hell. Waiting forever for you to come and see me."

"Peter—"

"You see, I let Zak die right there beside me. He told me to call him Zak, and I was going to ask him to call me Peter, but I held off, because I was mad at him for even thinking I might be an arsonist. I wish Mrs. Kader would come and see me. I want to tell her I'm sorry I let her husband die."

"But you didn't. His heart chose that time to quit and nothing you could have done would have saved him. He was very ill, every day was a gift— a gift he enjoyed, partly because of you. You treated him like a real investigator."

"He was good, and he had the right instincts."

"Cris said the people listening in on the chase said it sounded as if he were laughing. Like he was enjoying the excitement. Like you get when you're driving too fast. Was he like that, someone who'd rather die of excitement than boredom?"

"Yes, I think so." He looked up at her. "I'm like that too, you know."

"Yes. And that's all right."

"I scared you, didn't I?"

"Yes."

"When you went home, you scared me. You know how you make promises when you're scared?" She nodded. "I promised that if you'd come back tonight, I'd let you have as many kids as you wanted."

281

"I won't hold you to that. Promises made under those circumstances are never any good."

"But one kid won't hurt us any, I suppose. I hope not. I'll try not to let it."

She poked him in the shoulder. "You know, don't you?"

"Yes. McHugh told me he thought you looked pregnant that night you served us the chili. I told him he was crazy, but Mrs. Morales got on my case a couple of days later, saying I'd better stop upsetting you in your condition. A fine thing, when the housekeeper has to tell the husband he's going to be a father."

"I didn't mean to get pregnant."

"I figured that. You aren't the sort to go behind my back, if one can go behind a man's back and still get pregnant. It's okay with me. I mean, it had better be, considering."

"You aren't going to suggest an abortion?"

"And have you hate me the rest of your life? No. Besides . . ." He grimaced, perhaps in pain. "It's there, now. It's alive. I know too much about killers to become one just because I'm not sure I can stand sharing you with someone."

"I understand it doesn't work that way: The love just grows to fit, however big the family. I want us to name him Gordon Peter."

"Then he'd better be a boy." He studied her face, and despite himself lapsed into the traditional male reaction to the news. "Are you all right? I mean, what did the doctor say?"

"The baby's due in July, and I'm fine. I love you."

"I love you, too."

She bent and kissed him very gently on the mouth. When she straightened there was a tear rolling down his cheek. "Am I crying?" he asked, surprised.

She laughed, wiped her own cheek. "No, that's mine."

"Good. Got to keep some kind of image here. Let's shake on the new deal, okay? Only don't let go."